GOOD DAYS AGO

by

Richard Cliff

Copyright © Richard Cliff (2025)

First Edition

ISBN: 979-8285893127

The author asserts the moral right under the Copyright, Designs and Patents Act 1988 to be identified as the author of this work.

All rights reserved. No part of this publication may be reproduced, stored in a retrieval system or transmitted, in any form or by any means without the prior consent of the author, nor be otherwise circulated in any form of binding or cover other than that which it is published and without a similar condition being imposed on the subsequent publisher.

Chapter 1

An almost moronic cheer erupted for nineteen-year-old Sonny Lopez when he walked into The Feathers public house with his shiny black sports bag at twelve o'clock one Friday lunchtime. The cry might well have been heard from one end to the other of that newly extended, one-through-road village of Cowton in North Yorkshire. That so many beaming others of similar age to him were gathered there was arguably down to Sonny himself because collectively they formed the football team belonging the village's only pub and had recently secured an unprecedented Amateur League Trophy – thanks in no small part to Sonny's season-long raft of goal scoring. Popularity was his. Their treat to themselves for the feat was to join with the pub's annual three-nights jolly-boys jaunt to Benidorm leaving The Feathers by coach for the thirty miles away airport that very afternoon.

'You all set for it then?' asked Trev the ex-rugby player landlord, himself going, as he handed Sonny a white-topped pint of lager that caught sunlight at the bar.

'What, this, or...?' Sonny happily goofed as he took it.

Trev's wife Wendy was the organizer of the trip; it was her who had booked it all online. It was joked that she regarded their annual absence as therapeutic for herself and the rest of the pub. The pair had taken charge of The Feathers seven years back when they were in their mid-thirties and had much welcomed the subsequent arrival of new houses in the village. Not everyone thought the same and futile, even vitriolic, objections had been the norm for a while. Previously the pub regulars had consisted mainly of rural types, some quietly well heeled. They were a sceptical fraternity, openly resentful of the influx of people who bought into the scattered cul-de-sacs of new houses that were to change the village demographic forever. That it was some of the more revered villagers among them who sold their land for development was never mentioned.

The village population had doubled – but the old and new entities never mixed, and segregation prevailed. As young families grew up, some of the village elders still thought of The Feathers football team as their paperboys which a couple had been – before they'd left school, got jobs and girlfriends, and generally left childhood behind in the space of half a dozen years; half a dozen years that had made no impact on those who still expected the local garage to source second-hand parts for their cars – and grumbled when they couldn't. It was said there was a lot of money in Cowton, but you never saw any of it change hands.

It was the first time any of the football team had put their names to the trip on the pinned-up A4 sheet of oft scrutinised paper behind the bar and there was a vocal element among The Feathers newer regulars who had misgivings about them joining their vaunted event at all. Previous runs had all been a great success, no nonsense – except their own, no tales told, nothing let slip. This time, with the prospect of newbies tagging along, a few negatives had been voiced: *We're not babysitting, As long as they behave themselves, They need to know that what happens in Benidorm,* had all been expressed.

The youngsters' tribal cheer for Sonny on the day of departure hadn't done them any favours, but the fact was they had won something in the pub's name. No one else had done that, there was not a darts or dominoes trophy to be seen. Thus, the football team could hardly be denied, they had earned their place.

Sonny was not of the village, or the county, or even the country. He was Brazilian, born into a favela shanty town in Rio de Janeiro. He had no ready recall of his father, a merchant seaman who seldom came home on leave, and whose absence eventually became permanent. A neighbour's boy said that Sonny's father had another family in Venezuela and had gone to live with them, none of which made any sense to Sonny, but nothing seemed to change on account of it. Sonny's mother died when he was nine years old. She had been sentenced to two years imprisonment for stealing food to feed her six children and within a year had died there of pneumonia. Sonny could, and did, remember her at will. His eleven-year-old brother Seve, the eldest child, did his best to hold together the family of three sisters and three brothers. Seve was shot and killed by police when he wielded a toy gun at tourists. Six months later Sonny's younger brother Paulo, dashing home to their tin shack with four stolen bananas, was knocked down and killed by a truck.

Events moved quickly after that. The three sisters, Sofia, Maria and Florence, aged seven, five, and four, were taken to a state-funded residential school for girls. Sonny was given refuge at La Esperanza, a charity assisted home where abandoned boys learned to carve wooden souvenirs which were sold at the cruise ship terminals. At night some of the boys would cry in the dormitory – no one came. Sonny's tears fell silently into his pillow, tears for his mother, for Seve who had stepped up in her stead, and for happy Paulo who tried so hard to emulate him. He just wanted them back, and for everything to be as it once was.

He missed his sisters, missed their big hope-filled eyes as they gazed into his, missed their utter belief in him, and them all being together. He determined that when he learned of their whereabouts he would sneak out of La Esperanza and go to them by whatever means, he would throw dirt stones at their window, they would look out as one and escape to their shack and be as before – and he would be provider. Such news, though, never came and he heard nothing of them. He felt despondent that he hadn't somehow kept everyone together, that he'd failed at the first hurdle and not tried hard enough for his family. The passing of each of their birthdays pained him greatly.

The working hours at La Esperanza were long, the regime strict and tasks carried out mostly in supervised quiet. At day's end, after the evening meal, Sonny, along with all the others, would file into a classroom where they were taught English language. It wasn't a fearful or an unkind place, no one went hungry or suffered harm, more that it was functional in its commendable purpose.

Total respite for the boys came once a week on Sundays, when they played football. On those days, any cares were put aside as teams hastily formed. They played the day's length, powered by both physical and emotional energies. Each boy soared. It took them to a much-needed different place, a place where friendships were made – and smiles were many.

Along with over thirty other boys, Sonny remained at La Esperanza for more than a year. During that time, he heard nothing of his sisters despite his repeated requests for news of them. By then he could carve wooden iguanas, snakes, statues and a host of symbolic objects almost without paying attention as he openly chatted with his new best friend Enrique.

When their end of residency came, it came quickly. Unannounced, La Esperanza closed, military personnel suddenly assumed control and the staff escorted away. The boys were all corralled into the dining hall, and work ceased. Sonny was then ten years old, as was Enrique. Between them the pair quickly hashed a plan to break free and get back to the streets of Rio where they felt they belonged and could resume their former lives and make good. It wasn't to be. Over the next two days rescue and charity workers wearing lanyards and armbands came amid obvious tensions.

During many hours there was much shouting and arm waving. The boys whose names were called were ushered outside and into waiting vehicles. Sonny and Enrique looked nervously at one another in the gradually emptying hall as they tried to decide if then was the time to make good their escape before they too were likewise dispatched. Choices, though, were not theirs. Sonny's name was called, and he was hastily guided away by aid workers. He twisted around and looked in alarm at Enrique. Equally alarmed and wide-eyed, Enrique stared back at him.

'Me and Enrique are together,' Sonny objected.
His words went unheeded as he was pulled along. In protest he struggled free whereupon Enrique shouted, 'Run, Sonny!'
Uniformed men rushed angrily forward; they seized hold of Sonny and one swiped Enrique to the floor with a wooden baton. Wailing, Sonny was dragged outside where he was pushed onto the backseat of a taxi. Two aid workers jumped in at either side of him and the taxi sped away on their urgent command.

Sonny was taken to Rio International Airport and handed over to other aid workers. No one really spoke to him, everything was done in murmured exchanges, secrecy, fear. Any questions he asked were waved aside with the shake of a head, as though only silence was permitted. He spent many hours in the airport halls, slept on their perforated metal benches until night and day had no meaning. The always watchful accompanying adults – their expressions betraying apprehension – stayed within touching distance of him throughout.

Numb with travel, Sonny was led off a plane in Manchester UK by thirty-something aid worker Gertrude who had singularly escorted him from Rio. Duly they were met by officials, and themselves led away from the regular disembarkation route and into a glass-walled interview room within the terminal where a badged immigration officer engaged at length with Gertrude. When the officer was satisfied that everything was in order, Sonny was handed over to a suited man and woman, she in skirt and jacket; the woman smiled kindly at Sonny and broke into Portuguese. Gertrude said goodbye to him, he stared at her in silence, shocked that she was leaving him – in his mind she was the only person who could get him back to Rio and she was about to return there without him. The man and woman both thanked her, and Gertrude left.

At Sonny's either side, the suited pair walked with him the short distance to an external multi-storey car park. Sonny knew from the feel and smell of such cold outside air that he was far from home; only the woman spoke to him as they made their way to a shiny white car, a car that he believed wrong handed, a car of officialdom because of its newness – and therefore menace. The man got in behind the wheel, the woman sat beside Sonny on the back seat, and they drove down the concrete exit ramps of the car park until they broke into daylight and joined the flow of heavy traffic beyond. They drove for two hours, passed barren expanses of moorland, where heavy grey clouds rolled not far above them, and then on through industrial areas, until they met with green fields that lay behind stone walls in a pleasant landscape. Sonny, though, was beyond understanding of what was happening anymore, what anything meant. He remained silent and unresponsive – lest hurtful men appear.

Sonny was taken to the North Yorkshire village of Cowton. There he was handed over to Mr and Mrs Johnson who welcomed him into their large, terraced house that was built of gnarled brick and had a long front garden. Mr Johnson was tall and thin, she bespectacled and homely, both were in their mid-forties. They were to be his foster parents, short-term, until a supposedly permanent placement could be found. There were no other occupants of the house, a house that Sonny thought gloomy – but not menacing. He was given his own thickly carpeted bedroom which overlooked an orchard-like back garden that had a tubular-framed swing at its far end. He soon learned that on every crest of the swing he could see over the hawthorn hedge to a field of cows – and would make cow-like noises if no one was around. Mr and Mrs Johnson invited him to call them Aunt Mo and Uncle Graham. Sonny was okay with that because such terms had no real meaning to him – other than as a precursor to the first name of an adult.

During the week Mr Johnson would go to work at the accountancy business he co-owned with a partner, Mrs Johnson would tend house and garden and make simple meals, highlighted at the weekend with a succulent roast dinner. Sonny liked the Johnson's; they never got angry or questioned him about his past. The only person he felt nervous in the company of was social worker Tina Duval. Tina had everyone call her T. She was in her early-thirties and would periodically come to the house, often with blonde strands of stray hair on her long black cardigan; Sonny distrusted the way she smiled at him as though his best friend who had endured all pain with him. She never arrived unexpectedly, and he always knew it was her who pulled up outside the house when he heard the sequential thud of car doors, one hers and one for the laptop computer that sat beside her.

At some timely point during her visit, he knew to present himself in the front room where she would ask him questions all of which, along with his replies, she typed into the computer. Mr and

Mrs Johnson never attempted to speak for him and through them he learned how best to deal with her, which basically was not to give her anything more than necessary. He would be politely dismissed at her invitation to carry-on with whatever he was doing, which was often playing with Ginger, next door's cat that would stray into the back garden; from the hallway he would sometimes then hear Tina ask if Sonny ever wet the bed, cried during the night, or other suchlike searching questions. On a few occasions he heard her say that she was making his case a priority. He didn't know what that meant and hoped he would be sent back home. Nothing ever seemed to come of it, though, so he ceased to care whatever she said and would seek out Ginger who readily answered his call to play.

Sonny had been with the Johnson's for a month when Tina's visits suddenly increased in regularity. One evening she eagerly put it to him that she had found a placement for him with a young couple who lived fifteen miles away in the 'very nice' village of Stanford Bridge. Sonny looked at Mr and Mrs Johnson for some level of approval – but their blank stares gave nothing away. The proposed couple had no children of their own and were keen to take him in, what enthused Tina most, though, was the fact that the lady of the house was Portuguese and could therefore speak Sonny's home language. Sonny wasn't overly asked his opinion on the matter and Tina pressed ahead with arrangements.

In the kitchen one afternoon, when alone with Mrs Johnson, Sonny told of his reluctance to make the move.

'They wouldn't put you anywhere that wasn't right, Sonny,' she said kindly. 'And I'm sure they're very nice people!'

'But what about Ginger?' he protested. 'Who's going to play with him, he won't know where I am, he'll be all confused with everything! I don't want to go, Aunt Mo! Why can't I just go back to Rio? Why is everyone doing this? I've done nothing wrong! I want my sisters back!' He burst into tears, and she hugged him.

'If you don't like it with them, you tell Tina and she'll bring you straight back here,' she said sternly.

'I know but everywhere I go is further away from home, Aunt Mo, suppose I never get back there, ever?'

'You will, Sonny, one day you will, and no one can say any different. Just go along with it for now and everything will come good, I promise.'

A week later, Sonny walked beside Mrs Johnson to the front gate. Behind them Mr Johnson carried a packed holdall for him and placed it on the back seat of Tina's white Audi. Again, Mrs Johnson reassured Sonny that everything would be alright; she briefly hugged him, and he sat on the front passenger seat. Tina got in behind the wheel, she reached over and fastened his seatbelt for him. Mrs Johnson closed his door and from the pavement she and Mr Johnson waved him goodbye; he waved back emptily and was driven away.

On their fifteen-mile journey, Tina spoke highly of both Stanford Bridge and of the couple thrilled to have him; through not being asked anything himself, Sonny remained silent. After her second incoming mobile phone call on the hands-free link, he ceased to listen and instead looked out at the passing terrain. At the village of Stanford Bridge, they turned from one cud-de-sac into another until they pulled up outside an open-fronted detached house that looked much like all the others around it. With bag in hand, he followed Tina up the stone-flagged garden path to the sentry-box like porch where she traded squeals of delight with the lady of the house who opened the front door.

'Rosetta, how are you?' Tina enthused. 'I apologise we're so late getting here; you must have been wondering where we were!'

'No, no you're not late,' Rosetta protested as her dark wavy hair bounced at her face. Her attention went to Sonny; she smiled broadly at him and palmed them both inside. In the immaculate lounge, Rosetta immediately broke into Portuguese to welcome him into his new home. Tina sat on the sofa and looked on approvingly. At some point Sonny was led upstairs by the two women and shown his bedroom, they left him there to 'get settled in' and went back down to the lounge where they talked at length, every word of which he could hear.

An hour later, Tina bid Sonny a cheery goodbye. Devoid of structured thought he sat at the round, kitchen table with Rosetta, she spoke kindly to him and made baked beans on toast for them both. She invited him to call her Rosie and explained that her partner Howard, a hospital services manager, was at work and would join them soon. She went on to say that she ran her own business from home as a Portuguese language tutor and that students would come to the house, sometimes during the evenings. Sonny thought her an openly pleasant, friendly person with a name that suited her. He felt at ease – ease that he deferred until Howard could likewise show himself.

As the pair talked, the thud of a car door in the driveway announced an arrival. The front door to the house opened then closed, followed by the sound of car keys thrown into an empty glass fruit bowl on the sideboard. A small man, red of face, came into the kitchen, despite his blue suit he looked dishevelled and flustered. He was thin – Sonny thought unnaturally so, and that he might be a person easily given to anger. He stared at Sonny as though in wait of introduction.

'Howard, this is Sonny,' Rosie said.

Howard continued to stare. 'Sonny,' he acknowledged awkwardly. 'Did we get that letter from the bank?' he asked Rosie.

'It's on the mantlepiece,' she said. Howard hastened away, and Rosie dissolved the moment with a compensating smile at Sonny.

'Howard always needs an hour or two after work to come back down to earth!' she said. 'He has a very stressful job!'

Over the course of that evening, Howard spent more time on his mobile phone than he did with Sonny. At no point did Sonny believe him to have *come back down to earth*.

On Sonny's first weekend in his new home, a succession of Rosie's friends came to the house, all keen to meet him. Her best friend Andrea brought along her own two boys, Adam and Sam, both similar in age to him, and the three went off to play football at the nearby recreation centre. He liked Adam and Sam; he thought they were good fun and the three happily kicked a football without rules or format. On the same field another group of boys, who the brothers knew, were also kicking around a ball. The two groups merged, and a slightly more structured game began. It was soon apparent to Sonny, though, that the game was not to be taken lightly by one of the other boys. His name, continually yelled by teammates, was Ross. Ross didn't like not being the scorer of goals – much less that Sonny, so effortlessly, did so. The brothers laughed gloriously after each occasion that Sonny triumphed, which further riled Ross until he could stand no more of it and stormed off the pitch with the shouted accusation: 'You're all just being stupid!'

    Back at Rosie's house the brothers could barely contain themselves as they relayed the exciting event to the adults, all of whom clearly knew of Ross. By the time Howard returned home from his day's golfing, the chattering group had left; he seemed to be in a lighter mood, which basically, as far as Sonny was concerned, meant that he wasn't in a bad mood. It wasn't long, though, before he chastised Rosie for speaking Portuguese to Sonny. Sonny went upstairs at Rosie's request.

    'He has to integrate!' Howard insisted. 'You won't be there when he starts school!'

    Sonny caught the remark from his bedroom, *starts school* wasn't something he'd considered; the question of why adults, all previously unknown to him, were compelled to acquire and control him was something which – increasingly – he had. That Sunday night, he looked out of his bedroom window, beyond which glowed LED streetlights, and knew there were no ramshackle alleys into which he could disappear, seek out his sisters, and be uncaringly happy beneath a warm dark sky.

    Weeks passed by in much the same manner; the brothers would come to the house and they and Sonny played football at the Recreation Centre, which everyone referred to as the Rec. On the occasions that Ross was also there he, along with a dozen others, was sometimes under the tutelage of Geoff, the village football coach. At Rosie's house the brothers would tell of Sonny's own flair for the game which had Rosie ask him if he would like to join the team, he nodded his wish to do so, and Rosie made enquiries. One Saturday morning Sonny went with her to the Rec and was introduced to Geoff. Keen to be selected, Sonny played determinedly and was soon noticed by those who looked on.

On his first proper match a week later, he majored in the game, and many shook their heads in wonder and knew they had witnessed something special. Even the opposition coach voiced praise of him. Three similar games further on, a petulant Ross complained to Geoff that Sonny didn't pass the ball, that he wasn't giving anyone else a chance, and that he himself could have scored two or three times had Sonny done so. Geoff calmly said to give him time to get used to English teamplay, which had Ross try to recruit similar complaints from others.

Rosie, often pitch-side whenever Sonny played, would applaud the efforts of the boys and of the only girl player Jocelyn. Ross's dad, similarly, pitch-side, was somewhat more selective in his booming-voice praise and was usually turned away when Sonny scored a goal. After a game, the brothers, who were not in the team, would hang around the Rec and join Sonny for another kickabout as Rosie wandered home. There, Howard showed no interest in Sonny's match exploits and urged that he instead join the golf club which ran a junior section; it seemed a source of frustration for him that it held no appeal for Sonny.

Sonny befriended the brothers, and his home life became settled. At one point a rumour raged throughout the village that he wasn't an orphan from overseas at all but was, in fact, a problem child from a wayward family in the northeast of England. This was said to be so by an undisclosed policeman who lived nearby and knew all about him. Rosie dealt with the rumour by ignoring it and as the stories became embellished so, too, did they become attributable to anyone who traded in them – until everyone denied that they had said anything lest they themselves be stigmatised as rumourmongers.

Any domestic normality changed for both Sonny and Rosie when Howard came home early from work one day in a state of fearsome anger. He had been suspended from the hospital he worked for after a complaint of bullying had been made against him by a female member of the domestic team. Seething, he sat in his armchair, breathing through bared teeth, and drank himself worse with vodka. Over the next few days, the situation further soured when he became volatile and unpredictable. Rosie would send Sonny to the shop for not-needed items, or to the brothers' house, to distance him from Howard – perhaps also that she herself wouldn't slip into Portuguese and stoke his anger.

A week later, Howard was called to state his case at a meeting with the hospital's HR department. He looked wild-eyed and sloppily shaven as he left the house to attend. When he returned home, he snarled that he didn't know the outcome and that they would let him know – he sat in his armchair and drank vodka.

Two days later he got a letter through the post to say that the complaint against him had been upheld. His employment was terminated with immediate effect. Already under the influence of drink, Howard stared at the letter in disbelief. Rosie told Sonny to go upstairs and then spoke softly to Howard. From the landing, Sonny listened to their conversation as he peered down.

'You'll soon get something else, Howard. You can move on and do better, you know you can!'

He glared at her. 'I'm just a laughingstock to everybody, aren't I! Runty little Howard... the going nowhere man! Well, I've had it with everything!' he raged and hurled away the letter; it closed back into its folded form and gently landed on the carpet beside him. He rushed out of the room and grabbed up the car keys from the fruit bowl.

'Howard, you can't go out in the car, you've already had far too much to drink!' she reasoned desperately.

'So bloody what!' he shouted. 'There's nothing here for me, you've got what you wanted, you've got someone far more important than I'll ever be!' He blustered out to the car and despite her trying to stop him he got in, reversed out and sped away.

From his crouched position on the stairway, Sonny immediately went to Rosie as she broke down in tears.

'Go back upstairs, Sonny,' she said intuitively.

'I'll make you a cup of tea,' Sonny said, himself startled by events.

'I'm just scared of what he'll do,' she said, distraught.

'Call the police, they'll stop him!' Sonny urged.

Rosie considered the suggestion in silence. Before any change of mind could manifest itself, she seized up the phone and rang them. An hour later a police car pulled up at the house. Visibly distressed, Rosie answered the door to a uniformed officer. The officer came in and they sat at the kitchen table. There he explained how Howard had crashed his car into another vehicle on a roundabout within a mile of the house. He'd been taken to hospital by ambulance with a head injury. The injury wasn't thought serious, but he would be kept in overnight. The suspicion that he was under the influence of alcohol meant that he was arrested, and charges may follow.

Police charges against Howard were formalised during his stay in hospital. The fact that Sonny was in a placement situation meant that the council's child-care department was informed of the arrest, and a social worker duly came to the house. It was decided that Sonny could no longer remain there. With his packed bag, he was led out to a waiting car. Rosie, beyond consolation, hugged him tightly at the roadside as her tears freely fell.

'Tell Howard I'm sorry,' he said to her, 'I really loved it here with you, Rosie, bye to Adam and Sam.' With that, he was driven away.

Sonny was welcomed back into Mr and Mrs Johnson's house where they continued to be his foster parents. Within a month of his return, he started school at the ten miles away Danby Town Academy. There, despite his initial reluctance to make friends, popularity came his way. His unique accent, tanned skin, his enthralling Brazilian origin – and his quickly-spotted footballing skills – all singled him out as a person of special interest. Girls thought him cute; jealous bullies targeted him with racial abuse, something which he'd never known.

When the bullying became an issue Mr Johnson enrolled him at a boxing club where Sonny learned its art. Sonny knew, though, he could never have fended off his main aggressor, a particularly unpleasant individual who went by the nickname Jazzer. Jazzer had the build of someone beyond his twelve years, even those in the year above kept clear of him. But it wasn't necessarily him that Sonny had to stand up to, and when one of Jazzer's entourage confidently stepped up to emulate his abuse, Sonny sent him away bloodied and crying. It wasn't long afterwards that Jazzer was expelled from the school when he attacked a teacher. The entourage dissolved.

As school terms passed, Sonny grew taller and his dark gazey eyes and limp black hair had girls fall madly in love with him. The boys wanted to be his friend, be in his company and be seen as such; they even wore similar clothes to his so that they might share his winning ways.

Sonny remained with the Johnson's and found comfort with his new life. He could smile again; deep within, though, lay an emptiness that new friends, football, boxing, or caring foster parents could never fill. He desperately wanted answers, answers about his sisters, about his friend Enrique – about when he could go home. Over time he accepted that he would have to wait until choices became his own, but one day he would go back and seek those answers – of that he was certain.

Sonny left the academy when he was sixteen. During the heady days of his final term, he met with an anomaly. His classmates had secured enrolment at either sixth form or onward colleges, some in formal training schemes, one unexpectedly in the Royal Navy, a few, though, seemed oddly non-committal with him about their choice. Sonny's girlfriend of nearly two years, dark-haired Janice, who was in the same class as him and herself going on to sixth form college, solved his mystery one lunchtime as they sprawled on the grass of the school sports field.

'They want to be you,' she said, eyes closed and head back – which profiled her round-tipped nose – 'you've shown them how, but they can't be you if you're there, can they?'

Sonny had no wish to remain in the education system but was legally obliged to do so. His solution was to apply for the job of trainee grounds-person, as posted on the advertisements board of the village newsagent. The job incorporated day release and evening education up to the age of eighteen at Danby College, which meant that he could potentially take up the role. He was subsequently interviewed for it by Gordon Levy, the facilities manager of Tan Hall, a country house estate five miles from Cowton.

His application was successful, and he began work one Monday morning in August. Tan Hall was set among a thousand acres of private land with golf course and fishing lake; it offered a full wedding service in the banquet hall and had woodland chalet-style holiday homes for sale or rental. His job was to cut grass, keep paths and trailways clear, empty rubbish bins, clear blocked gutters, learn how to use relevant machinery and tools and do whatever was asked to keep the estate functional. Each day he cycled to and from work along country lanes using an old mountain bike that a classmate had given him. He liked the job and was readily accepted by the other workers of the estate, which comprised three grounds operatives and a four-strong cleaning and replenishment team; the youngest of whom, raven-haired Samantha, was barely older than him, and who he thought stunningly beautiful.

Chapter 2

Sonny was still working at Tan Hall when his eighteenth birthday came around, by which time he was over six feet tall and of athletic build. He and Janice continued their relationship after they had left school and saw each other on a regular basis; she excelled at sixth form college and subsequently gained a place at Exeter University to study world famine. They hugged their goodbye's, foreheads touching, on a promise-filled July night.

Tan Hall found favour with him and allowed him to move into an outdated static caravan, sited near the machinery sheds; they set minimal rent on the basis that he be on call should the need arise. He was moved in by Mr and Mrs Johnson who had been his foster parents throughout the interim years. Mr Johnson shook his hand like a father leaving a son, Mrs Johnson hugged him tightly, as he did her. He watched them drive away along a stoney track and, after eight years of foundation-solid family life, again felt the pain of another parting. Samantha took an interest in him – which miffed skinny, tattooed Charlie, one of the grounds operatives – but Sonny wasn't much taken with her, mainly because of the knowing smile she would share with Janet her older colleague. Outside of work, he joined the newly formed football team at The Feathers public house in Cowton – started by the landlord to attract a younger element, and the new homes by then able to provide it.

Time slipped easily by for Sonny. He was aware, though, that by then he had spent almost as much of his life in Cowton as he had in Rio – where his heart still lay; even his thought words were in Portuguese. As though to remind himself of that place he would occasionally make wooden carvings just as he'd done at La Esperanza with Enrique at his side. The started-of items were laid about the caravan; he'd pick one up and further enhance it as the mood took him. He was aware, too, that at eighteen any choices were then his own and that somewhere he had three younger sisters whose big eyes might still seek his. But he didn't want to arrive back in his homeland without funds or prospects, put himself back there as a pauper in a place where paupers were many and thought criminal and worthless.

That he might learn something of his sisters' whereabouts Sonny rang the Brazilian Embassy in London, hopeful that they could provide information on state residential schools in Rio. They couldn't and gave nothing by way of contacts that might prove useful in his search. Nor did he get any worthwhile response to his emails to various government departments in Rio, sent from his own laptop computer on which he'd secured a wireless internet connection.

In the realisation that no help would be forthcoming from any quarter he formed his own plan with which to go forward. In all the time of his employment at Tan Hall he was yet to take any annual leave days, days which by then had accumulated and it was made clear to him that he either 'use them or lose them!' His plan was to go back to Rio on a visit and seek out his family. To better fund this he took a part-time job behind the bar at The Feathers. With earnings then on course and time off work guaranteed he felt elated that at last he would see home.

Two months before his then booked holiday, The Feathers took victory in an Amateur Football Trophy competition. Throughout the season Sonny was lead goal scorer for the team and his reputation and skills came to the attention of Danby Town Football Club. They approached him with the offer that he train part-time with them at the start of the next season on a voluntary trial basis. The opportunity had the potential for him to become a professional footballer, a skill possibly transferrable to Rio, and it greatly enthralled him.

Sonny had concerns when The Feathers team came up with the idea that they further celebrate their trophy win by joining with the pub's annual outing to Benidorm in a month's time. His focus was firmly on his own trip to Rio, and he didn't want any of his funds diverted elsewhere through frivolity. The team, though, were much enthused by the sudden idea and he didn't want to be dismissive of something which normally he would have welcomed.

When he learned that the cost of the all-inclusive break was quite low, thanks to Wendy's extensive research, he put aside any misgivings and went along with the scheme; soon a raft of fresh names was added to the list of those already going. He came to think of it as bringing closer his own visit to Rio – the outbound flight of which would depart Manchester a few weeks after they returned from Benidorm.

'It used to be twenty-one to get a passport!' old Justin said in derisory tone one evening as he stood and looked across the square horseshoe bar to where Sonny and pals were discussing the pub's trip.

'Changed to eighteen when colour television came out, Justin,' Trev mocked as he served him.

'Mm,' old Justin mumbled and went back to cohorts on the carpeted half of the open-plan pub.

'What's up with him?' ginger-haired Ferret, one of the team and long-standing friend of them all, said to Trev.

'Jealous!' Trev replied, 'And he thinks you lot are all too young for a real passport!' he added.

Ferret, mouth agape, stared across the void to where old Justin sat. 'I bet he didn't think our Al was too young to go to Afghanistan at eighteen and get his leg blown off, though, did he?' he eventually blurted with uncharacteristic venom.

In the rundown weeks to their trip, The Feathers mainstay regulars became animated, louder and more upbeat than usual as holiday mood set in. They even began to parley with the football team. One of their order, the aptly nicknamed, tall Giles, in usual commanding tone, tried to fool the youngsters with his comment that he hoped they liked fruit juice because in Spain the legal age to drink alcohol was a strictly enforced twenty-one. Ferret told him he'd got the numbers the wrong way round, Freddy said that it must have changed since he was there last year, Simmonds suggested he should worry more about any maximum age limit – no further attempts were made to ridicule the team.

Come the day of the Benidorm trip, Sonny pushed closed his caravan door and put the key in the nearby stanchion box of the water stop-cock as usual. With his holdall straddled by its straps tight across his back, he cycled to The Feathers waving to colleagues and residents as he went. There, he secured his bike in the walled back yard, went inside and was met by a raucous cheer; he responded with a pretend headed ball, grinned hugely and crossed the floor to where Trev had begun to draw off lager for him into a tilted glass.

Already gathered in their usual place at the bar was the trip-going mainstay crowd, all in high spirits – most dressed in cargo shorts and checked short-sleeved shirts – their designer holdalls beside them on the floor. The sports bags that belonged the football team sat variously on tables and chairs, and they themselves in trainers, pristine jeans and equally pristine logo-proud T shirts. The mood throughout was that of jocularity. It was too early in the day for the older ones to be in residence, their seats and tables lay unoccupied – the moment belonged to the Benidorm revellers.

Their day rolled on in sequential format. From The Feathers a private hire coach took them to the airport where the team followed seasoned hands through to neon lit bars in the departure terminal. Two hours later the party made their way onto the plane; they took their seats, fiddled with the overhead air blowers and grinned at one another over seatbacks. After a near three-hour flight, the party stepped into the fine bright air of an Alicante afternoon and boarded the airport service bus that fleeted them passed arid land to the high-rise resort of Benidorm. A one-hundred metre walk from the drop-off point had them arrive at the Hotel Cielo Grande where, on a gleaming marble floor, lead guest Kev checked everyone in, and handed over their collected and subsequently returned passports.

As the group stood back and waited, Sonny's focus went to a series of world clocks mounted high above reception, perhaps more noticed by him because one of them showed Rio time. With key cards then in hand, Sonny and Ferret went eagerly to the bank of lifts and sought out their four-digit room on the seventh floor where they chose a bed each, fathomed the light switches and tv, grinned into a stocked refrigerator and looked out from a balcony made private on both sides by full-height stucco walls. As they viewed the all-around blocks of flats and hotels, beyond which were distant mountains, Simmonds and Freddy appeared at the neighbouring balcony to the left as they too gazed over the rail. 'Hey, guys,' Simmonds called across, 'we're going poolside, you coming down?'

'We'll see you there,' Sonny enthusiastically agreed for them both. As he and Ferret turned to go back inside, Sonny caught sight of tall Giles and roommate Roy likewise standing on the right-side balcony; Sonny would have preferred teammates to have been in room occupancy there but nonetheless smiled as tall Giles glanced sideways at him – and believed that he doubtless had similar thought.

'So, what do you think to it, then?' tall Giles loudly asked him.

'Fabulous!' Sonny said, not caring that he would likely be laughed at.

'We had a full sea view last year!' Roy countered as he found a sight line around his much bigger friend.

Sonny had never quite warmed to Roy, due in the main to his inane grin and hair-trigger laugh which he thought both predictable and irritating. He decided, though, that Roy was a nervous type and didn't seek to criticise him. 'Mountains look well!' Sonny said as he nodded at the far distance, to which Roy made no comment.

For the remainder of that day the group laid by the hotel's outdoor pool, the sun trap area tropicalised with palms and parasols, where they indulged of drinks served through the outdoor hatch of the main bar. The evening buffet meal in an airy dining room gave them a needed break from sun and alcohol, after which they followed each other in a tour of the town's bars. By one-thirty in the morning they had all drifted wearily back to their rooms.

After an unhurried breakfast in the dining room on their first morning there, they all again sat about the pool to recover from the previous day's excesses. The older ones soon had before them drinks of vodka and orange – for the team it was more about bronzing oil and gazing skywards on sun loungers. In the afternoon, eager for whatever Benidorm had to offer, they went as one to the open-fronted music bars along the Levante beachfront where they joined with the carefree atmosphere. Sonny thought it a gloriously vibrant scene, so, too, did they all, as they sat in sunlight and let the day take care of itself.

On their second morning the team found distraction from early drinking when the hotel entertainments staff, who strolled the grounds with a clipboard, sought to enlist them in planned activities; a knockout competition of pool, followed by darts, archery, air rifle target shooting and basketball shots, all needed players, as did the afternoon game of seven-a-side football played against the neighbouring sister hotel. Sonny and teammates joined in with it all, the highlight of which was the keenly fought football match. Sonny provided two of their five goals, and they took the game five goals to three. For victories gained they were awarded signed hotel certificates and grinned hugely as they posed for the winners' photo shoots, the photos then posted on the hotel gallery wall and uploaded for all to see.

It was through participation in these events that the team met a hen party from Manchester – also staying at the Cielo Grande – who duly beat them in a highly vocal basketball shots competition, and then gamely formed a cheerleader group for them in the football match. The hens were on the last of a three-night stay and leaving for home early the next morning, content to remain within the hotel complex on their final night, already packed for departure, they sat at tables around the outdoor stage from where they waved the team over on sight, and pulled them onto the non-defined dancefloor throughout a format of a live artist, karaoke and disco which provided the evening's entertainment. Kev, tall Giles and entourage went on to their own favoured haunts.

When the hotel entertainment ceased at eleven o'clock the hens and team retreated inside to the lounge bar which traded as normal until midnight when drinks were then billed to rooms on a signed-for basis. At one o'clock the girls called it a night, as did most of the team who by then had no wish to trawl the town's bars – which included Ferret who had enthusiastically sampled the house speciality cocktails. Around that same time, Kev, tall Giles, Roy and the rest of The Feathers fraternity came back and made their way up to their rooms.

Sonny, Simmonds and Freddy decided it was too early for that, though, and went out to one of the entertainment bars at the end of the street for a few more beers. They returned an hour and a half later and turned in for the night. When Sonny let himself into his room Ferret's entry card sat in the electronic reader on the wall – the lights still on – but he wasn't there. Sonny remembered, though, that when Ferret had left them two hours earlier it coincided with one of the hens, who he'd been flirting with, likewise leaving the lounge bar, so that he didn't think too much of it and assumed the pair to be cosied up somewhere. He wedged a folded bar flyer against the door latch to prevent it from locking and got into bed.

Four hours later, Sonny's door was opened with an urgency that had him pivot upright in bed. Two uniformed police officers strode in followed by a suited man who wore a hotel lanyard. Sonny was told by one of the officers to remain seated on the bed, and they quickly checked over the room, to include the bathroom and balcony. Sonny noticed that Ferret's bed was still made, with no sign of Ferret. He asked the staff member what was going on. The man raised both hands in a halting manner and said nothing as the police went about their business. They paid great attention to the balcony where they took photographs of the handrail and tiled floor. In English, they asked Sonny questions: *What time did he go to bed, where was Ferret at that time, did they argue about something?*

At no point did they tell him what was behind it all, but Sonny grasped the obvious gravity of the situation and that bad news involving Ferret doubtless lay ahead. They were joined in the room by a swarthy middle-aged man in plain clothes who carried a black leather attaché case and had about him the trace smell of spent cigars; the man mumbled to Sonny that he was Dr Ochoa of the Benidorm Police Department. He examined Sonny's hands, arms, upper torso, scalp, wiped swabs beneath his fingernails, and separately sealed each sample into detail-labelled plastic packets which he placed in the attaché case. He then said something to the two officers and, with case in hand, left the room.

The officers told Sonny to get dressed; they led him down to the ground floor and across the strangely quiet foyer where he was shown into a meeting room and told to wait. A police presence was put in place outside the glass door. Two hours later Sonny was told by the same questioning officers that Ferret had gone over the room balcony – his and Ferret's room balcony – and that he'd landed in the service yard seven floors below. He was found by a kitchen porter at five o'clock that morning. Ferret was dead.

Sonny was shocked into silence at the news. He couldn't properly think and found himself staring without focus. Over the following hour he was asked for his recollections of the previous night, and several times was asked if he had been there at the time of the tragedy. His replies were written down and he was told to read the transcript and sign it. He was then allowed to go, with the instruction that he didn't leave the hotel or go up to the room until cleared to do so.

In the lobby area Sonny looked around for familiar faces but there were none to be found, likewise the grounds and poolside. A quiet stillness hung over the hotel, there was no hubbub, no one laughed, no one talked. Those that were there looked at him in distant silence. An hour later the team began to appear in the lobby, each with empty stare as they gathered around him to share their grief and hopefully learn further of what had happened. Simmonds, ashen faced, tightly hugged him, he said they had been confined to their rooms until interviewed by the police. They all knew of the tragedy but, like Sonny, not anything of how it had happened. The older ones, too, began to emerge and formed their own sullen group. Only Kev came over to the team to share with them their shock and sadness. Simmonds spoke for himself and others when he said despondently: 'I just want to get home, Kev!' The team agreed the sentiment – and allowed glistening tears to form.

Sonny was allowed access to his room later that day but was instructed by the police not to leave the hotel. He asked Simmonds and Freddy to go with him to pack. In the room the three of them looked around uneasily, and the question arose over what to do with Ferrets belongings.

'If we leave anything the hotel'll just bin it!' Simmonds said. 'We have to think what the family would want us to do – as though they're here telling us, and I don't want to get it wrong!'

'For all we know they might be on their way over!' Freddy almost willed.

'Do they even know about it, though?' Simmonds questioned.

Freddy looked agitated, 'Has Kev heard anything?' Sonny shook his head and said, 'I think we should just pack his stuff. He's only got a couple of shirts in the wardrobe. He was like me; he just shoved everything back in the bag when he'd done with it!'

Half an hour later with Ferrets bag packed they elected to put it in the luggage room beside reception. 'It feels like we've just left him in some mausoleum place – nothing said!' Simmonds anguished as they came out. He then offered that Sonny stay with them for that final night, Freddy also urged that he did so, and Sonny welcomed the suggestion. Obligingly, the hotel had a put-up bed brought into their room. That night, the team gathered there, they sat wherever they could and tried to put reason where none existed – together they made a heartfelt toast to Ferret with cans of lager. Hands that needed reassurance openly grasped those of others.

'Are we really to go back without him!' Simmonds said. 'On a plane home, and him not with us! Doesn't the hotel have a vicar person or someone, someone to say something. Where are all the embassy people… why is no one talking to us?'

There were no answers forthcoming and unashamed silent tears found their own path.

In the morning, none of the team wanted breakfast beyond coffee and orange juice. With their rooms vacated they hung about a corner of the foyer and awaited Kev's call for everyone to walk to the airport bus stop. The older ones grouped outside the hotel entrance and likewise waited. When Kev came over to the team to make sure everyone was ready to leave, Freddy urged that they 'go right now'. Kev nodded. 'Yeah, come on,' he agreed glumly.

As they hastily gathered up their bags, two uniformed police officers came into the foyer and crossed the floor to the reception desk. They spoke to a receptionist who pointed at the team. The officers went over and addressed themselves directly to Sonny, they told him to come with them. Sonny stared in shock and asked why. Without explanation they repeated that he come with them. In silence, he was escorted out of the hotel to the police car parked directly out front. An officer held open the rear passenger door, Sonny got in, and they drove away as The Feathers regulars stared on as one.

Chapter 3

Sonny was taken to Benidorm police station, a low-rise concrete building, where his escorting officers spoke to an expressionless man behind the front desk. Without looking at Sonny, the man referred to a computer screen. Sonny was told to place his luggage and all possessions, including wristwatch, wallet, loose change, mobile phone, any keys, onto the desktop where they were itemised, recorded and bagged. He was then led along a door-lined corridor, busied with staff, to a small, interview room and told to sit at a mid-positioned bare table. Nothing was said as a singular officer waited with him, standing next to the left-open door.

At length, a middle-aged man arrived dressed in a pressed, green shirt neat with the embroidery of high office, his mostly black curly hair grey at the temples, and his demeanour that of seniority. The standing officer remained in place as the man sat opposite Sonny, and in silence set down a faux leather, document folder which he opened flat so that both its halves exposed paperwork and a spine-retained pen. He then looked at Sonny.

Over the next hour the man, speaking English, suggested Sonny had been present when Ferret met his death, that perhaps they'd been behaving foolishly, much in drink, and Sonny had been unable to stop him from accidentally going over the balcony. Sonny refuted it all, and stuck to his truth that he wasn't there, and that others could confirm such on his behalf, his teammates, the hen party girls, perhaps even the bar staff, all could verify Ferret had left both him and the remaining group earlier in the evening, before himself along with Simmonds and Freddy went out to a bar – and he reiterated how Ferret wasn't in the room when he got back at the end of the night and that he never saw him after that. In response the man softened his voice. He said he understood how easily such misfortune could occur, particularly with holidaymakers because they weren't used to high-rise types of balconied accommodation, nor the generous alcohol measures and festival atmosphere. He said that drink was nearly always behind such tragedies, which sadly they saw year on year, and for the sake of closure for the bereaved family it would be best if Sonny: 'came clean!'

Sonny maintained his story, high in the hope that his innocence would prevail and that he could make his flight home. All such hope fell away when the man said they would continue the interview later that day. Sonny was escorted out of the room and put in a cell.

Alone in the cell Sonny's naivety fell away. He suddenly felt angry that he hadn't seen it coming, his innocence or otherwise was never the issue and any closure was not for the family – but for the police themselves. They wanted a conviction.

When later that day, his flight missed, he was led back into the interview room and the same man in green shirt came in and sat opposite him, Sonny asked that he have legal representation and that the British Embassy be made aware of his predicament. The man looked at him balefully and said it wasn't necessary because he hadn't yet been charged with anything, also the British Embassy was already aware of the situation because such was procedure in the event of a British national's death. Sonny asked if he could therefore leave, but the answer was no, he couldn't, not while enquiries were ongoing – and that a time extension for those enquiries might become necessary.

Sonny remained at the police station for two days and nights without any decision made. Meals were brought to his cell, hourly the door would be opened, and someone would look in briefly without speaking. He was interviewed in sporadic pattern by the same man in green shirt who tried persuasively, irritably, kindly, to get him to admit some measure of involvement in Ferret's death. He even suggested that with a signed, carefully worded statement, Sonny might be able to go home and face whatever action was deemed appropriate there. But Sonny steeled his resolve, he remained steadfast and stuck to his story throughout.

On his third day of incarceration, clinging desperately to self-belief, Sonny was again led from his cell to an interview room.

The man in green shirt came in and went through his usual setting out procedure. He then formally charged Sonny with causing the death of another; Sonny, numb, was returned to the cell.

When Sonny was next interviewed it was by a thirty-something man in a lightweight grey suit, white shirt and neat tie, who introduced himself as Sr Juan Philipo. He had been assigned as Sonny's state appointed defence solicitor – unless Sonny himself wished for private representation. Sonny told him that he needed whatever help was readily available. Over the following hour Sr Philipo gleaned everything he needed to know of that fateful night. In answer to Sonny's question of what was likely to happen, he said that if the current charge against him was proven then he could potentially be looking at five years' imprisonment. He also told Sonny that tolerance did not exist of overseas visitors charged with anything and that he might wish to consider some lesser charge if such could be negotiated.

'I'm not going to admit to something I had nothing at all to do with,' Sonny said in desperation.

Sonny began to lose track of days as he remained at the police station without further developments. Occasionally, an argumentative drunk would be put in another cell along the hall, doors would be wildly kicked, and abstract shouting would continue for hours. It was on those occasions that he felt all the worse for his predicament and glad when his own cell door remained closed.

Any questions Sonny asked about his case proved fruitless – everything was said to be either ongoing or pending further enquiries; definite answers were not forthcoming. His only opportunity to learn anything came through Sr Philipo, whose visits were unpredictable and lacked optimism. It was from Sr Philipo one morning that he became aware of the current date – that it was the day of his flight to Rio. He felt abandoned, that his footballing hopes, and possibly his entire future were shredded to satisfy some political mandate.

Laid in his cell looking up at a lime-green concrete ceiling, Sonny decided that when Sr Philipo next came, he would urge him to get the British Embassy further involved to assist a wrongly charged and wholly innocent British national and again tell him how he wouldn't be blindly walked into a conviction – should some behind-the-scenes waiting game be ongoing. Before he had opportunity to do so, it was mooted that Sonny be transferred to a correctional institute until the charge against him was put before a judicial hearing – which potentially could take months. He felt himself on the verge of despair and wondered where any help could come from.

With a near date set for his transfer to the institute, Sr Philipo brought him news. 'I think we've just made some rather significant progress,' he said, as though Sonny had been aware of his endeavours.

'Really?' Sonny said anxiously. 'In what way?'

'The case against you lay mainly in the fact that you were Sr Ferret's roommate, and the belief that you'd both been acting foolishly under the influence of drink. We needed to prove that you weren't in the room at the time of death. I think we've now managed to do that!'

Sonny, desperate to hear more, stared in expectation.

'Examination of both you and Sr Ferret showed no signs of struggle,' Sr Philipo went on. 'On that basis, any further tests are thought not in the best interests of State time and funds. The electronic door lock to your room recorded the occasions of entry card use and, on that night, the door was opened at one o'clock by Sr Ferret's card and again approximately two hours later by yours. This fits with your account of events. Also, you signed for drinks on time-stamped hotel receipts, they show two such transactions which place you in the bar just before and after one o'clock, and then, of course, the statements of Sr Mark Simmonds and Sr Frederick Logan who both had you with them the whole night until at least two thirty. The police believe that the time of death was one forty-five from Sr Ferret's broken wristwatch.'

Sonny looked bewildered. 'But that was always there for them to know... right from the beginning!' he reasoned blankly.

'Quite so, but only to those who looked!'

Sonny felt a surge of anger; anger that so easily he could be condemned by those in authority with their untroubled allocation of guilt. 'I am grateful to you, Sr Philipo,' he said calmly as he took everything in. 'Does this mean they're going to release me?'

'I have only just this morning presented our case; we shall have to wait and see what their intentions are!'

'Dare I hope?'

'Oh, there is always Esperanza for an innocent man!' Sr Philipo said with a smile.

The very word Esperanza had Sonny again stare at him.

An hour later, the cell door opened, and an officer told Sonny to follow him. Despite Sonny's expectation, they continued past the row of interview rooms and onto the front desk. There in the full light of day he was reunited with his possessions, which included passport. He confirmed all such with a signature and was told he could leave. He dragged his holdall off the desk, said nothing and went out into a sunlit afternoon where he breathed of warm air and thought it the gift of freedom into which he wanted to run.

Sonny made his way to Avenida de Europa where sat the airport bus stop and ticket office; such was his forced stride that his thigh muscles ached. He slackened pace to look more casual and not invite attention from any passing police vehicles should a mistake have been made over his release. It suddenly troubled him that perhaps his spontaneous plan wouldn't meet with approval from Sr Philipo, who might not know of events, or have advised that he wait until furnished with certain release papers in case any security blocks and checks at the airport hadn't yet been updated? Sonny considered all such, unsure of where logic belonged.

At the bus stop, he stood back among a myriad of sun-shaded commercial businesses where he bought an airport bus ticket, and waited tensely for it to arrive; he duly boarded and took an aisle seat among empty rows which had him less conspicuous from either the pavement or roadside. An hour later at the airport he booked a one-way flight to Leeds Bradford with the same company with whom – so long ago it seemed – he had joyously arrived, and which departed in three hours' time. Had there been an earlier flight to elsewhere in the UK he would have taken it, simply to get back on home ground but any flight necessitated clearance of Spanish security checks; he determined himself to appear untroubled and went airside without hindrance. At the departure gate he again presented his documents without issue and took his seat on the aircraft; the door was pulled closed and shut out sunlight that he no longer cared for. Only when clear of the Spanish mainland and over France did he begin to shed tension.

Three hours later, his flight touched down at Leeds Bradford Airport. He passed through its formalities and went out into the cold night air.

As he waited for the airport service bus that would take him to the city centre, he rang Simmonds and told him of his return. Simmonds expressed great relief at the news. Sounding hugely stressed, he told Sonny of how everything had changed because of the tragedy, of how blame, accusations and malicious gossip, had run rampant through the village. Ferret's brother Al had lurched into The Feathers, beyond control, and demanded to be told what had happened. Tall Giles tried to calm him down and said everyone was totally devastated by it but that no one really knew anything. Distraught, Al had said the truth will come out and if anyone was to blame blood would be spilled.

Simmonds also told Sonny that because he was the one arrested, he was being blamed the most. He went on to say that none of the team went into the pub anymore and of how different tales were coming out virtually every day. Even Kev was under fire for letting them go in the first place. Simmonds then suggested that he and Freddy come over to see him the next night so they could meet up in private and exchange what each had heard; meanwhile, he advised Sonny to keep his head down.

Sonny's journey back to Tan Hall had him take three buses, the final leg of which took him passed The Feathers. Through not wanting to talk about all that had happened, and himself greatly fatigued, he stayed on board until he arrived at the estate. There, he saw no one as he made his way along the bollard lit internal road.

He retrieved the key from the cavity of the stopcock stanchion, newly given to cobwebs, and let himself into his caravan – and its likewise newly acquired cloistered smell. He switched on the lights and, standing in the stilled air, felt that something was different; he decided it was himself.

The following morning, after a night riddled with punishing dreams of a concrete cell, Sonny strolled the grounds to visually announce his return – and restore some measure of normality. Among the greenery, he encountered Samantha and Janet as they bundled a cleaning trolley out of a holiday cabin, they both stared at him as though in shock. Perhaps determined to be the first to speak, Janet called out, 'Hi, Sonny!' He went over to them, and the pair expressed their deep sorrow at the sad news of Ferret.

'Does anyone know what actually happened?' Janet questioned.

Sonny shook his head. 'He fell... and that's all anybody knows!'

That evening, Simmonds and Freddy pulled up in Simmonds' car beside Sonny's caravan; he engaged their silent hugs, and they went inside. Over the following few hours, sitting on the wrap-around sofa, beer before them, they talked through every aspect of Ferrets demise, of how no one knew when the funeral might be, the ongoing aftermath, of Sonny's incarceration and thankful release and of how he'd missed both his flight home and to Rio. Simmonds told him they had begun a crowdfund for him in case he needed to meet legal fees – with him home free of any charges, Simmonds suggested that, with permission of those who gave, they hand the cash to the family to assist with funeral expenses. By the end of the evening Sonny felt a lot less alone.

The next day, Sonny rang Kev and told him of events, most of which he already knew. Kev said for him not to worry about covering his next round of bar shifts because eighteen-year-old Alice from the village would step in, and that 'for the time being at least' it might be best if he stayed away. He could collect his outstanding wages and bike at any time and 'as soon as things settled down' he could come back without hesitation. He also expressed relief that Sonny's ordeal was over. Sonny thanked him and said he would be there in a couple of hours.

As he set off to walk to The Feathers, Sonny was halted along the internal road by Gordon Levy who pulled up beside him on a golf buggy. Gordon welcomed him back without any reference to the tragedy and asked that he come to the office the following morning because there had been some developments within the company which he needed to discuss with him. He gave nothing away beyond that and Sonny sensed bad news about to come his way.

Late afternoon, Sonny walked into The Feathers. The only customers were old Justin and a few other retirees; all seated in their usual places. From behind the bar, Kev reached over and shook Sonny's hand. 'Glad you made it back okay, Sonny.' he said in even tone. 'It wasn't very nice having to leave you there.'

Sonny wanted to say it wasn't very nice being left there but knew they had little choice. 'It was a scary time, Kev, for sure,' he said instead, and looked around the empty bar room where only of recent times the team had gathered in abundant laughter.

'So, are you all in the clear now, then?' Kev asked.

'I am! They knew all along I had nothing to do with it!' Sonny asserted. 'They just didn't care. All they wanted was someone in a cell to take the blame.'

'So have they got anyone?'

'Not that I know of. I was told they singled me out because I was the roommate. Has anyone here been told anything?'

'Only that the family are still trying to get him home so they can give him a decent funeral. I don't know if he'd got any kind of travel insurance or not. It could be an expensive business otherwise! We had the brother in the other night. Best you avoid him.'

'Yeah, I heard,' Sonny murmured.

Together they looked over to where old Justin stood at the bar unashamedly listening to their conversation, the excuse of an empty glass before him; he returned Sonny's gaze with a brazen stare of disapproval. Kev went over and served him. When he came back, he handed Sonny his wages in the usual, pocket envelope.

'Best just for now, Sonny,' he said, 'if you give us a miss for a while. Things are a bit tense here!'

'Yeah, getting it!' Sonny accepted, dismally.

'And if I were you, as well,' Kev further advised, 'I'd be careful about who you say anything to, especially in this village! You wouldn't want to know half of what's been said already!'

That afternoon, Sonny sent an email to Sr Philipo in which he sincerely thanked him for his assistance and said that he was back home. Within the hour he had received Sr Philipo's personal reply, which read: *You are very welcome, Sr Lopez. I was most glad to be of useful service to you.* Sonny felt relieved at the reply, relieved to know that any shadow of suspicion was gone.

In the estate office of Tan Hall, Gordon Levy gave Sonny the news that an audit by the company accountant had identified areas of concern. Changes had been put forward. Among a list of recommendations, Sonny's job had to go. They would pay him for a ninety-day notice period and gave him a month in which to vacate the caravan. So that he could find another job they released him from duty with immediate effect.

On his way back to the caravan, devoid of meaningful thought, Sonny encountered Charlie in strimmer harness and hard hat with upturned ear defenders. Sonny thought he looked like a skinny moose and was tempted to say so, instead he told him he had just been made redundant. Charlie, though, seemed unperturbed by it, other than to say it might yet be all of them for the chop 'knowing this place!' Charlie then grumbled over who would do Sonny's job and wandered away.

Sprawled in the caravan Sonny tried to make sense of his now fragmented life. He pondered that only a short time ago Ferret was still alive, and that he himself had popularity and job security. At that point in time, he should have been down to his last few days in Rio, instead everything lay in tatters. On impulse he phoned Danby Town Football Club and was made an appointment to meet club manager and coach Danny Fisher the following afternoon. Sonny found himself inspired by the call.

Danny Fisher shook Sonny's hand as though to read a person by such brief contact; Sonny thought him a man given to his role of football manager, angular of jaw and with plentiful fair hair that could further enhance him if he chose to bother with it. It proved a fruitful meeting for Sonny, and he felt at one with the serious aura of the club and its bare, purposeful surroundings. Danny invited him to watch a section of that day's training and two hours later Sonny knew he wanted to be part of it all. It was agreed that he undergo a full medical examination through his own GP and given that the result was satisfactory, and the club in possession of the confirmation letter, he could begin training with the players, on an unpaid basis. The prospect lifted him enormously as he came away.

That evening, Sonny rang Simmonds and told him of the development – and to learn of any news concerning Ferret. Simmonds congratulated him on his achievement and predicted stardom to follow. He also said he wished it was himself getting away from Cowton – and that if Danby ever needed a mediocre striker, that Sonny put forward his name. As regards Ferret, he'd heard nothing, but it seemed the team were now being blamed for tall Giles' mobile phone going missing at the hotel, the loss of which they were unaware of – until then. Tall Giles himself had played it down and hadn't supposed blame of anyone, but assumptions were quickly made that somehow members of the team were involved, and embellishments made accordingly.

In a determined effort that his fitness would not be an issue for Danby Town FC, Sonny jogged for miles every day along the country roads that surrounded Tan Hall; it also served to focus his mind and not have him dwell on other matters. When his medical examination showed nothing untoward, he personally handed the confirmation letter to Danny Fisher who welcomed his enthusiasm.

As the football season closed in, Sonny began to train in earnest at the club's ground. He got to know the regime, the players, their aspirations and of their individual lacklustre performances in the previous season – it enabled him to better understand how his arrival harboured some concern among certain others; but he wasn't there to make friends – or to fail. He had to believe in his own footballing skills, skills which mustn't be allowed to desert him if he were to have any hope of income through it.

Sourcing accommodation became his next priority, and he enquired of whatever was available in the Danby area. He was pleasantly surprised when the best deal to be found was with a budget chain hotel two miles from the football ground. The only requirement to qualify for their cheapest room rate was that he paid for each full week in advance, non-refundable.

Less than two weeks before Sonny was due to move out of the caravan, he took a phone call from Simmonds. Simmonds told him that Ferret's body had been repatriated, and that the funeral was to be held at the village church the following week. The service would be private for family members only, and no flowers to be sent.

Sonny packed his belongings, including wooden carvings, into both his sports bag and a tool-branded holdall that he'd retrieved from a waste skip after grounds staff had frivolously discarded it. Come the day to move out, Simmonds pulled up in his car at the caravan to provide transport. As Sonny loaded the bags into the car Samantha came by and wished him all the best, for which he warmly thanked her. He closed the caravan door, put the key in its usual place as agreed, and they drove away. On the fifteen-minute journey, Simmonds told him that Kev had decided to miss a season with the pub's football team; all sorts of reasons were mooted but the general belief was that no one had the stomach for it.

Over the following few weeks, Sonny threw himself into his role of trainee footballer. He did the preparation work and, through observation, learned from those around him. He knew, though, it was only on the pitch where anything mattered.

Along with others on the substitutes bench, Sonny sat out the first game of the season. He knew it would be so and kept his attention on the gameplay before him. The gate was less than a hundred spectators, but their urgent shouts and woeful groans had the air charged with expectation. Danby lost the match two goals to nil. In the dressing room afterwards, everyone listened intently as Danny Fisher analysed the good points and failings of their efforts. Sonny's own belief was that players tried too hard to fulfil shouted instruction at the expense of imagination. He went back to the hotel believing his own contribution would bring much-needed drive and flair.

For the next match, on a rainy mid-week evening, Danny brought him onto the pitch late in the second half. Sonny was immediately shocked at the brutality of play which saw him frequently bundled off the ball. The referee looking or not, made no difference to the body-checking barges, the pushing and blatant grappling. He felt breathless and off-balance, and his discomfort showed until the final whistle blew. He'd impressed no one, except maybe Danny who told him afterwards that he'd stuck it well. Sonny, though, had learned something – professional football carried no passengers. Laid on his bed, beneath a wall-hung print of an orchid, he considered his own performance. He decided that getting involved in macho entanglements wouldn't serve him best, that he needed to find pitch space in which to weave his magic.

On Sonny's next appearance one Saturday afternoon, he was brought on in the first half of the game. Soon in possession of the ball, he backtracked away from body-knots, sidestepped into gaps, spun, outpaced many who couldn't match his speed and – through the narrowest of chased-down goalmouth angles – scored the only goal of the game. In that defining moment, he felt his presence justified as fans shouted approval. His team applauded, they had seen an unbridled talent – and everyone knew it.

'I was hoping you'd got something like that!' Danny said to him as the team ambled off the pitch, their breath evident in the cold air. 'I want you to build on what I saw today!'

Back at the hotel, Sonny rang Simmonds and told him that he'd scored his first goal.

'I know,' Simmonds said. 'Me and Freddy were there! It's a wonder you didn't hear us!'

Over the following weeks, Sonny saw further pitch time. He made the transition from overawed novice to that of revelling in the opportunity given him. His reward to the club was his undoubted ability to score goals. So far, though, he had funded everything himself from a dwindling bank account. His only payments had come by way of game attendance or goal-scorer bonus, but he knew he couldn't achieve that on every occasion, there could be injuries to endure, time spent on the bench when deemed prudent, even matches cancelled for whatever reason. He needed the club to pay him a wage.

His decided-upon tactic was to let each game speak for him as his momentum gathered. The club had no wish to lose him, and with his name increasingly on the scoresheet they made him an offer; he would be retained and paid as player employee. He was also allowed to move into the shared six-bedroomed terraced house owned by the club, which provided accommodation for apprenticed players and those transferred from elsewhere until they could make their own arrangements. He thought good fortune had turned his way.

Sonny moved into an anaglypta-papered bedroom, the last of the spare rooms, of a dormered post-war house along a terraced row close to Danby football ground. Except for one older player, the other team member residents were of similar age to himself, each hopeful for a continued placement with the club from which to launch their footballing career. Daily, they walked together to and from the ground where they trained and learned technical aspects of the game, to include diet and physio. He got to know his housemates well but recognised that a veil of self-belief lay between them and that they would never be longstanding friends; naked ambition permeated their lives and such ambition, he was aware, came with a sideways glance.

With a Saturday afternoon home game won, Sonny and housemates went for celebratory drinks in their nearby pub The

Woodman. As he stood at the bar a familiar female voice spoke up behind him.

'Do I get an autograph, then, or what?'

Sonny turned around to Samantha.

'Hey, Sam! How are you?' he said in surprise.

'Not as well as you, it seems. Footballer of the year I'm told!'

'No, I think you're actually mistaking me for someone else, there, Sam, cleanest boots maybe! How's things?'

'Good.'

'Are they all missing me?'

'No.'

'Well, I hope you're keeping my van clean; I might need it back if things go badly.'

'Well, you can't... it's gone.'

Sonny huffed affrontery. 'Gone! making sure a bit, there, aren't they?'

'The riding stables down the road wanted it; took us two days to de louse it!'

'Oh, it would. So have you been to the game just to see me, then?'

'No. I'm out on the lash with him,' she said, indicating a morose-looking individual who looked back at them across the floor. 'So, what did they tell you at the Hall?'

Sonny shrugged. 'That there'd been an audit and... hey-ho, me to go!' He shrugged again, as though the rhyme was deliberate.

'You know that was all bollocks, though, don't you!' she said. 'There was no audit. When they heard about what happened to Ferret, and then you arrested for it, they panicked. They were scared it would give the place a bad name. Stupid Charlie hadn't helped. While you were away, he'd been looking through your windows and then went round asking everyone if they felt okay because you'd got voodoo dolls all lined up in there!'

'Voodoo dolls!' Sonny said in disbelief.

'That's Charlie! He'd have said anything to get you into trouble, it was like it ever since you came, and they all said I fancied you. He's been trying to get into my pants for years. He never will!' She turned in the direction of her glum boyfriend. 'He won't either! Anyway, I'd best get back before he throws his teddy out. I'm glad you're okay. I'll see you around.' With that, she went over to the glum boyfriend.

'Seems like a nice girl!' Mickey, one of the housemates, gently said to him, unsure of the background story.

'You know what! I actually think she is.' Sonny replied.

Over the coming months, Sonny kept himself focussed on successive games of football and continual training; he began to make a difference to the club's standing in the league. One routine day, well into the playing season, as he sat next to Danny Fisher on a pitch-side bench, Danny casually asked him, 'So, where do you see yourself next year, then?'

The question took Sonny by surprise; he felt it weighted with a known. 'How do you mean, Danny?' he said.

'There's been one or two clubs looking at you. A few scouts on the terrace!'

'You're not wanting me out, are you?'

'No. Absolutely not. But every club needs a goal scorer – and you're on that list!'

'I'm okay where I am,' Sonny confirmed. 'There's an ambition, but not that sort. I've got family in Rio I want to look up... I thought maybe at the end of the season – now that I'm earning some decent coin!'

'I'm going to tell you something, Sonny. Coin is what it's all about. If you keep on like you are doing, the glory clubs'll be knocking on the door waving it about until you can smell it from the pitch!'

Sonny pretended to sniff the air. 'Nothing yet,' he said humorously.

'What was Danny saying to you on the bench?' Mickey brazenly asked of Sonny that evening as they all sprawled about the living room.

Sonny noisily blew out air as he considered an answer. 'Just asking how everything was going, really,' he said. Ensuing silence harboured disbelief.

As the football season progressed, Sonny's score sheet and reputation grew. He glowingly featured in post-match analysis in the town's newspaper and his name was often heard during local radio coverage of games. It coincided with rising gate numbers and increased interest in sponsorship for the club. As predicted by Danny, offers came in from other clubs looking to lure him for the following season. Within the confines of his office one day, Danny again broached the subject with him.

'I'm going to lay the cards on the table, Sonny,' he said. 'We don't want to lose you, but you need to be aware of how things are. I'd be failing if I kept you outside the loop!'

'Is it a loop or a noose?' Sonny joked.

Danny re-oriented three A4 sheets of corporate-headed paper that were side by side on the desktop and slid them forward to Sonny, each a formal transfer offer for him from higher league clubs. 'Look at the numbers,' he invited.

Sonny glanced over the sheets without touching them. 'Big boy's numbers,' he said at length.

'You'd get a signing-on bonus, plus uphill wages. Wages that we couldn't afford to pay you here!'

'So, what do you want me to do?' Sonny asked.

'For now, nothing. But I'm not going to hold you back. Talent like yours could take you right to the very top. Don't miss the boat, Sonny, a footballer has a very short sell by date. And then it's over, believe you me... it's over! My advice – grab it. If you were my son, I'd say get the big bucks while you can. Think about it for a week or so, I'll find out what salary you'd be on, with them – and us, and you can give me an answer then.'

As though to preserve any offers that had been made Sonny lifted his game still further. His name was on the town's tongue. By the end of the playing season, he had made his choice. He would move on to the twenty-mile away, two divisions higher, Leeds club Northern Star.

A week after his final game with Danby Town, Sonny idled on his bed early one evening and got a phone call from Simmonds.
'Hey, Mark,' Sonny welcomed. 'How's it going?'
'Yeah, good, Sonny, how's it with you?'
'All good – as far as I know! We're going to mosey down the pub shortly. They've got a lager pump with my name on!'
'Top man! We're in the Feathers – and I've got someone next to me who wants to say hello!'
'Hi, Sonny!' Janice shrilled from Simmonds' side.
'Janice!' Sonny said loudly as he pivoted to his feet. 'How are you?'
'I'm good! Congrats on the footy thing,' – her voice closer as though in sole possession of the phone.
'Thank you. How's uni?'
'Final year coming up!'
'Wow! Where's that nearly gone? When did you get back?'
'About two hours ago! Then all these giddy girls came round and used me as an excuse for a cheeky mid-weeker!'
'You just don't need it, Janice! How long' you home for?'
'Four days, I'm back Monday.'
'Want to meet up?'
'I'd love to, I didn't know how you'd be fixed?'
'Always ready to be in a fix with you, Janice,' to which she giggled joyously. 'How about Friday?' he suggested.
'Yes! Let's do early doors and then we can have a big catch-up?'
'Too right! Five-ish – under the clock, if that suits? – you call it!'
'No, that's good. I'll be there!'
'Okay, then, Janice, look forward to seeing you.'
'Me too you, see ya Friday, Sonny.'
'Well, that's a hot date you owe me now!' Simmonds said, reunited with his phone.

44

Sonny laughed, happy for the call. 'Anyway, how come you're in the pub so early... and it's only Wednesday!'

'Glad you asked, celebrating, actually.'

'Oh, yes?'

'I passed my accountancy exams.'

'Right! well done, Mark, yeah, that's great. Does that mean you're fully accountable now?'

'Tax deductible!'

'Good for you! Who's in then, apart from Janice and co?'

'Well, a minute ago it was just me and Freddy – then that lot showed up, nothing to do with us, so it got pretty noisy all of a quick!'

'Anymore been said about Gilesy's phone, and all that?'

'Not that we've heard. We actually stopped coming in, but like Freddy said, why should we keep out, just because of them and their stupid gossip!'

'Good for Freddy! Easy for me to say, I know, but he's bang right. And well done with the exams, Mark!'

'Cheers, Sonny.'

Sonny found himself in good spirits at the prospect of seeing Janice again; he went downstairs to join the others, and they went as one to The Woodman.

The following day, Sonny went to a Turkish barber shop and came out with a neatly razored haircut; the barber, obviously delighted to work on a well-known Danby Town footballer, and on such hair, asked to photograph the finished result to advertise his business. Sonny readily agreed, and the barber waived the charge of the haircut.

Mid-afternoon on Friday, Sonny looked over his minimal wardrobe and lifted out a blue and white checked shirt that he matched to a casual jacket – black and lightweight with pointless brass studs and straps. He wondered what Janice might expect him to look like and then recognised that he had a heightened awareness about meeting her again. He'd been on a few dates since their parting, all pleasant and meaningless – but this was Janice. He left off the aftershave in case she thought him newly fickle.

Sonny arrived early at their chosen meeting place and sat on a bench along a gardened embankment made bright with geraniums beneath the Victorian townhall of Danby, its dominance enhanced with a four-sided clock tower. It was a place they had often sat throughout the years, usually on a Saturday when they were drawn to the bright lights, which for them meant one of two cinemas and a neon-lit coffee house, previously a bank. As he waited a group of joggers passed by, some of whom recognised him and offered a greeting without breaking stride. He considered how it might have been in his favour had Janice seen how those of the town approved of him.

Brief minutes later Janice came into view; she fixed her smiling gaze upon him, and he got to his feet. Standing before him she upwardly and silently pressed a deep kiss into his cheek, he embraced her, kissed her forehead and looked into hazel eyes that shone with exuberance.

'Janice, it's just so good to see you,' he said.

'And you too, Sonny, and how did you get up there?' she mock queried as she looked up at him."

They both vented happy laughter and reached for each other's hands.

'Let's go somewhere where we can talk,' he said.

'How about the pub at the railway station? I was in there the other night, it's quite nice – and quiet. You fancy it?'

'Sounds perfect!' he agreed. 'Let's be off and beat the rush!'

In The Railway Station pub, they sat across a timber-inlaid iron table and talked of their time apart.

'That was a real shock with Ferret,' she said. 'It should never have been him. It shouldn't have been anyone!'

'No, it was just so... rotten cruel. He ought to be in the Feathers tonight singing himself daft. I don't think we'll ever know what happened. The Spanish police tried to involve me; they knew I had nothing to do with it, but they didn't care a jot about that.'

Over the following few hours, the pair chatted and ate a Yorkshire pudding dinner as heavy rain slewed noisily against big sash windows beside them; neither asked the other if they'd met anyone else. Sonny was intrigued when she said of her job interest with a foreign aid relief agency and that it was something she could see herself doing once she got her degree. She was quite enthralled at the prospect of it and felt both time and university fees would be justified if it came about; in turn, Sonny's own plans that he would soon go to Rio, albeit briefly, to seek out his sisters had her equally enthralled. She knew his background and that over many years he had spoken in heartfelt terms of his intention to return there.

'I hope you find them, Sonny. It would be so special if you could. It might be best to do some serious spadework first, though, before you go jetting off, you know, online stuff. It could be a time-consuming mission. Especially if it comes down to kept records. It's a long time ago, and without at least some leads... place names, or whatever! You don't want to just turn up and say, *Where are they?* It could save you an awful lot of shoe leather... and air fares!'

'Yeah, I know. I tried. I got zipidy! We were not favoured people.'

'It would help if you knew where they'd gone, they might even still be there now!'

'I was never told, Janice. They wouldn't have been told where I was. No one told us anything! I'm starting to wonder if I just dreamt it all up. I'm nearly twenty and I've lived two different lives! Which one do I belong to, which one's mine? I remember when I first got here as a kid and I thought, yeah, one day I'll be eighteen, and then I'll go home and sort everything out. Now I'm scared I'll go back and not recognise anything, not belong there anymore. You go somewhere you haven't been since you were kid and there's no way you'll just step back into it, and it still be like you thought!'

'Sounds to me, Sonny, like the sooner you get on a plane and get some answers, the better. You've waited long enough.'

'You know something else, Janice, I don't even think in Portuguese anymore. I just want to be who I was meant to be, right now I don't know whether I'm an English footballer or a Brazilian immigrant! I want to see and feel that place again, I want to find my mother's grave, tell her I've always loved her, that I haven't forgotten her and that I'm looking for my sisters. That's when my life finally becomes my own and I can move on from there!'

'I suppose deep down we all think we belong where we came from. And like you say, nothing's ever as you thought if you go back. But you're going to have to go to find out!'

At the end of their evening, they took a taxi the few miles to her parents' house in Tanlow, an old and upmarket borough of Danby. The taxi waited for him as together they went through the stepped gateway into darkness between tall bushes of the lengthy front garden. There they held each other in a stilled embrace, his mouth went to hers, welcomed by arms that drew him in.

'Good luck in Rio!' she said. 'Whatever you find there, Sonny, don't let it change who you are!'

'No. I hope you get your degree, Janice.'

She swiftly kissed his cheek, he – her temple.

'Keep safe,' she said.

She walked up the rain-greyed pathway; he made his way back to the taxi and wondered when next they might meet.

Chapter 4

Using his laptop computer Sonny made a flight booking to Rio, due to depart Manchester in three days' time, and then pre-booked himself into an airport hotel for the night before. With that in place he set about choosing an hotel for his two-week stay. He decided on the four-star Hotel Cristal in the beachfront neighbourhood of Botafogo – his interest inspired in the main by a traveller report which revealed the hotel to be wholly owned by a Sra Alves Marques Ferreira, a director of Boca FC one of the premier football teams of Rio. He thought it an inspirational choice. He cleared his room in the house, packed his two bags and, with Danny's okay, put the larger one in the under-stair's cupboard for collection at some later date.

Before Sonny's own day of departure, four of the housemates disbanded for the summer break, they shook his hand and wished him well, which left only himself and Mally in the house. Of them all it was Mally who he best got along with. At thirty-two years of age Mally was the oldest player on the team and unlikely to be poached by a major club; he himself, though, seemed untroubled by the fact and had just secured another season with Danby Town, this time as player cum assistant coach. Mally was further pleased when the club allowed him to stay on at the house in some overseer role and felt his future to be secured.

On the Friday morning of Sonny's upcoming departure weekend Mally answered the front doorbell and then led a uniformed policewoman into the kitchen where Sonny idled at the table with his phone and scrolled almost mesmerically over his flight details.

'Police lady to see you, Sonny,' Mally said, as though a little unsure of how to announce a woman police officer. He left them and closed the kitchen door after him.

'Sonny Lopez?' the officer enquired pleasantly.

'Yes,' Sonny said as he stared up at her.

'I won't keep you long,' she said. 'Basically, we're just following up on a report sent to us by the Benidorm police.'

Sonny felt his skin cool. 'Oh, right,' he murmured. He proffered her an opposite chair at the table. 'Have a seat,' he invited.

She smiled and sat down.

'I understand the police there interviewed you after the sad death of Mr John Ferret, a member of your party?' she said.

'Yes, they did,' Sonny replied, and felt himself slip into defence mode. 'But to be clear, it wasn't my party, it was a pub trip from Cowton!'

'Oh, I meant no inference! There's no suggestion of anything untoward here – Benidorm have raised a query, and they've passed it onto us. To be fair, I think it's more a desk clearing exercise on their part, than anything else!'

'Can I just ask,' Sonny broke in, 'should I have some legal representation before we go any further?'

'Well, there's really no need. I mean, obviously you can if you wish! But this is purely formality, nothing at all sinister I can assure you.'

'Okay,' Sonny said, awareness triggered.

'It seems the hotel where the tragedy occurred have found a mobile phone near to where John was discovered,' she went on. 'The screen was smashed, as though perhaps it fell from height, and the Benidorm police have questioned if it's in any way connected to the death? They're not pursuing it themselves, but they thought that perhaps we might care to!'

Sonny stared at her, at a receptive expression, and tried to decide how cautious he should be with any answer he gave.

'I don't understand how they've only just found it?' he said. 'It was... a year ago now!'

'Apparently, it fell through the cage of an air conditioning unit and got stuck inside the casing. The maintenance men found it only recently.'

'Have they not been able to interrogate it?' Sonny reasoned. 'Get the owner number out of it, or anything else?'

'Apparently, it's pin-coded, and they couldn't open it! My question is, could it possibly be your phone?'
Sonny slid forward his phone already laid on the table.
'That's my phone,' he said. 'It's the only one I have, and I've had it for two years. So no, there's no possibility of it being mine. None whatsoever.'
The policewoman nodded deeply. 'That's fine,' she said, as though satisfied. 'If I can just ask as well, if you know of anyone who did lose a phone at that same time?'
Sonny considered recent Feathers gossip told to him by Simmonds. 'I believe there was,' he said. 'But I can't be certain.'
'And who was that?'
'Well, I heard it was one of the older guys with us, but it's best if you ask at The Feathers in Cowton, they'll know more about it!'
The officer wrote down details in a notepad. Satisfied, she thanked him for his time. As he walked her to the front door, she thanked him again and went out to the patrol car parked at the roadside. Back in the kitchen, Sonny rang Simmonds. 'Wait till you hear this, Mark!' he said.
Sonny felt a degree of unease at the police visit. It mirrored too closely his questioning in Benidorm; the fact that he had an upcoming flight made it more so. Early that evening, Simmonds rang him back and said the police had been to The Feathers and Kev confirmed how one of their party had, indeed, claimed to have lost his phone in Benidorm. Kev gave them tall Giles' full name, and they were later seen parked at the house. That was all anyone knew, Simmonds' furthered, because tall Giles hadn't been to The Feathers since their visit, which was in-keeping with his routine. Roy was in as usual but knew nothing of it and had become irate when pressed by anyone for information. *"This village and rumours!"* Simmonds mimicked of him, 'Like, yeah, Roy, we know, have some! The trouble is, though, Sonny, everything's going to get dragged up all over again!'

'Yeah,' Sonny agreed wearily. 'Don't you just know it! Keep me informed of anything, Mark. I'll give you a ring on Sunday, yes?'

'Yeah, do that, Sonny. I wish I was flying out with you!'

Sonny was troubled that his return to Rio could again be jeopardised by a resurgence of the tragedy. The following day, with his room fastidiously cleaned, he mooched about the house and repeatedly checked his phone for missed calls or messages. Such was his irrationality that Mally could stand no more of it and insisted they go to The Woodman earlier than said in order that Sonny might calm down.

The following morning, Mally, driving his dated Audi A4, took Sonny to Danby bus station. At the roadside they shook hands and wished each other well. After a then thirty-minute bus journey Sonny made his way through Leeds city centre to the railway station and boarded a Manchester Airport train. Two further hours later he walked into an airport hotel, and a spacious room that he thought welcomingly cool and silent.

Early that evening, sitting in the segmented lobby bar, Sonny again reminded himself that the following morning he would fly to Rio. He pondered why he supressed triumph over his return and realised that the closeness of his childhood dream brought with it overwhelming emotion. He let go of tangled thought and rang Simmonds.

'Hiya, Sonny,' Simmonds answered. 'How's it going?'

'I can nearly smell the coffee, Mark.'

'Good for you. got an update for ya!'

'Go on.'

'That phone business and Gilesey! He was in the Feathers this afternoon yawping about it. He said it's not his phone that they found over there, he's never used a pin code so it couldn't be his! He reckoned there's probably any number of phones gone over those balconies, and towels and pairs of knickers and goodness knows what else – and none of those were his, either!'

'So, it's a nothing, then!' Sonny conjectured.

'Seems so. 'Course, it was all too much for old Justin. As soon as he heard that you and Ferret were in the next room to Gilesey he had the case solved, didn't he! Kev threatened to bar him if he didn't shut up making accusations in his pub!'

'So, how's old Justin got it figured?'

'Oh, apparently, we're all plankton for not seeing it straight away! It's so terribly obvious, you see! Ferret tried to thieve Gilesey's phone from across the balcony and he went over with it! He's got you down as holding onto him, the pair of you off your heads in drink, and it all went wrong!'

'Jeepers,' Sonny muttered. 'What right has he got to say something like that! He's blackening Ferret's name, and mine! That man needs to zip it!'

'Oh, there's more! And I've got to hold my hand up here, Sonny, I should have kept mouth shut, but I said Sonny'll not be best pleased when he gets back from Rio and hears that dumb comment. In comes Justin, *"What! He's gone to Rio, and they let him go! Well, that's the last anyone's seen of him!"* I'm glad Freddy was there because he proper blew up. He told Justin straight that he shouldn't be saying anything about it, that he's blaming and slandering people and he knows nothing. It was getting like that. Wendy had it right, though. She said if that's what happened then that phone would have been Gilesey's, wouldn't it? Old Justin didn't have an answer for that, and Wendy said she didn't want it mentioned again for the sake of Ferret's family.'

Sonny moaned. 'Where do people like him come from! And so, was that it, then?'

'Yeah, pretty much. It was a flare-up that's been waiting to happen, really, and this phone thing's just set it off.'

'Text me if there's any more comes up.'

'Yeah, I will. Sorry to put a dampener on your getaway.'

'No... I want to hear it, Mark, whatever!'

'Have a good holiday, Sonny.'

'Cheers, Mark.'

Chapter 5

Sonny's flight to Rio took off at nine o'clock the next morning. The plane seats were sparsely taken, and he had a three-seater window row to himself. As they ascended through the grey cloud tiers and sunlight flooded the cabin, he let go of that which he'd left behind. He knew a very different world lay ahead – that at last he was going back – and no man's hand could stop him.

Twelve hours later the background hush of cabin air changed as the plane lowered itself through a series of weightless descents. Between streaming cloud bands in the lessening light, Sonny caught sight of Sugarloaf Mountain and felt a surge of euphoria – frustration too, that his birth-right had for so long been denied him. At the bumping of aircraft tyres on the runway he believed himself finally home.

Sonny struggled to slow his stride as he made his way along the enveloping airbridge and into the Arrivals Hall. His urge was to break into a run, to look around for his sisters, as though there by chance, and shout, *I made it!* When eventually clear of the building, a process made longer because he didn't hold a Brazilian passport, he breathed of warm and humid air, air that he believed familiar, as was the all-around spoken language of his childhood – he hadn't forgotten. A thirty-minute taxi ride took him from the airport to the Hotel Cristal; a journey which fleeted him along concrete highways until they entered the palm-lined avenues of Botafogo, lively with its many bars, restaurants and hotels.

The Hotel Cristal was a substantial and modern high-rise hotel that stepped directly onto the street – its white façade much lit through occupancy. His check-in was made easy by a pleasant receptionist who allocated him a room on the tenth floor and directed him across the foyer to a bank of lifts. In the room Sonny inserted the door card into its reader which initiated various lights – and then dropped his bag onto the bed. Keen for whatever the view, he tugged on the wall-anchored drawstring that opened curtains from across the balcony and stepped out to where he gazed over a near-and-far spread of buildings, their rooflines lost to a darkening sky as far beneath traffic trailed its lights and gave frequent vent to horns.

So that he fully immersed himself in his day of arrival, he showered and went back down onto the streets. A hundred metres from the hotel he came across a small café bar that looked onto a cluster of twisted trees among bare earth where families were sitting on public benches, some on their own folding chairs. He got a beer from the bar and sat outside at one of its cane tables on ground made uneven by tree roots. There, at ease in the warm night air, he looked upon the distant, lit statue of Christ the Redeemer, dominant city-wide on its overlooking hilltop. He sipped of beer and accepted that he no longer knew what to feel.

On his first morning there, after a buffet breakfast in the hotel's expansive dining room that was adorned with children's artwork, Sonny made his way along busy streets to the seafront and an empty, white sand beach, its calm water's edge tide-lined with dried seaweed. He reminded himself that he wasn't simply there to indulge of sightseeing but had a mission to fulfil; he was on a countdown to departure and needed to find answers. At some point along his way back to the hotel he sat over a strong-bean coffee in a workaday café and had to refrain from asking those around him if they'd ever heard of La Esperanza. He considered that in his ten years of absence a lot of things may have changed but remembered that strangers who asked questions were always regarded with suspicion. He asked nothing.

When he passed a line of idle taxis along a rank, he was tempted to take a ride and seek out his old favela in the North Zone of the city. He decided, though, such a plan was flawed. Favelas had no street names – the homemade shacks no recognised status – and he accepted the possibility that his might no longer exist because it wasn't unknown for problem favelas to be razed by government forces. Nor would it be a safe visit because he knew the North Zone endured a bad reputation – and the fare even be refused. He carried on walking, and considered, too, how he may not regard himself as a tourist but doubtless to everyone else – he was.

Back at the hotel, he used one of the computer stations in the guest business suite to gather details of government departments which he then contacted by phone. Two hours later an appointment had been made for him to meet with education advisor Sr Alvarez, the following morning.

Generously furnished with directions, Metro names and street map given him by similar-age-to-himself hotel receptionist Amelia, whose badged name found his eye, Sonny sought out the Municipal Chambers that overlooked a tree-backed terrazzo square in the Centro Zone of Rio. The symmetrical, stone building, old and immaculate, stood grandly next to lesser others, its importance self-announced; he went up the full-width steps and into a cool interior where uniformed, armed personnel stood at their positions under a vaulted ceiling in an air of controlled calm.

There, he announced himself to a white-shirted man sitting behind a free-standing enquiries desk. The man made a desktop phone call on his behalf and asked that he take a seat at one of the bare-wood benches against a far wall. Fifteen minutes later a mid-forties thin man wearing a dark blue suit strode up to the desk and then came over to Sonny, who got to his feet. The man introduced himself as Sr Alvarez, and they shook hands. Alvarez proffered him toward a small table that lay openly in mid space and invited him to take one of four chairs neatly in place around it, he himself sat opposite.

'How may I be of assistance to you, Sr Lopez?' he asked.

'First of all, thank you for seeing me at such short notice,' Sonny said politely.

Alvarez nodded.

'It's a fairly long story, actually,' Sonny began, anxious not to lose focus. 'I was born in Rio. When I was a child, my mother died in prison here.'

Alvarez displayed no emotion.

'I was put in a place called La Esperanza.'

Again, no outward register of thought.

'I have three younger sisters who I believe were sent to a residential state school,' Sonny went on. 'I'm not really sure which one. I was taken to England and brought up by foster parents. I'm still a resident there. I'm now twenty, and I would very much like to find my sisters.' He paused to allow some feedback – to be sure that he was in the right place and talking to the right person. Alvarez looked at him as though to analyse what he'd just heard.

'You are twenty now, and how old were you then?' he asked.

'I was ten.'

'And how old were your sisters?'

'I was ten... so they would have been eight, six, and five!'

'And where did you live?'

'We lived in a favela in the North Zone.'

Alvarez nodded deeply. 'There would have been no records kept,' he said. 'Ten years is not so very long ago, but those from the favelas were rarely kept on file. The belief was that if something wasn't recorded then it didn't exist! However, that doesn't mean there is no hope of you finding your sisters. I was involved myself with the North Zone possibly around that time, though I have no personal knowledge of individual families. Historically, it was common practice for orphaned girls to take up residence at convent schools, they would stay there until of leaving age when, hopefully, they would be educated enough to gain employment. But it became a problem! The convents couldn't keep on taking the growing number of girls who were in need. The government was faced with two choices, either leave them on the streets to become part of a bigger problem or make alternative arrangements. One was unthinkable, the other costly. But around that same time other factors came along. Namely tourism, and the eyes of the world which had Brazil centre stage on a few issues, including that of child poverty! A solution was found. It was called project twenty-thirteen! which all sounds very dated now, of course, but back then it was the cutting-edge political phrase of the day. Basically, construction companies were invited to participate in building a new residential school, solely for the purpose of housing potentially hundreds of displaced girls. It was a sizeable project, and willing companies were recompensed with other contracts. It was an effective way to get all such girls off the streets, break the misery cycle and have them garner prosperity to the benefit of all. The school was named The School of the New World, it was built and opened around ten years ago, it is possible that your sisters were taken there, and given their ages, that they might actually still be there!'

Sonny stared at him, shocked that he knew so much. 'I've obviously come to the right man,' he said.

'There is no certainty, of course,' Alvarez qualified. 'You will need to contact the school direct and ask your question. But... it's a reasonable place to start. So, was there anything else?'

'I'd like to find my mother's grave,' Sonny said on impulse. 'I'd value any suggestions you might have, there?'

'You say she died in prison!'

'Yes.'

'Do you know which one?'

'No, I don't. I just remember she went out one day and didn't come back. Neighbours told us she had been arrested for stealing food and that she could be gone for a while. We never saw her again. It broke us, and we never recovered. I went to La Esperanza and the girls... somewhere! I remember it like it was yesterday, but we never knew where she went!' He fell silent as his recall of events had its impact.

Alvarez slid out a blue slimline phone from an inside pocket of his jacket and made a call. A woman soon answered, and he asked that she send to the front desk a print-out of details for both the school and the Women's Correctional Facility in Rio.

'You have quite some ground to cover,' Alvarez said when he'd closed down the call. 'Is there anything more you'd like to ask?'

'I'd like to know about La Esperanza!' Sonny said, keen to garner all that he could from the meeting.

'La Esperanza was set up with much the same purpose in mind as the New World School!' Alvarez resumed. 'But there were crucial differences. Firstly, the number of students was far less, all boys, and funding for it was absolutely at a minimum. Children, by law, cannot be put to work and schooling is a legal requirement. La Esperanza taught them carpentry skills and gave them classroom teaching to comply with that law. As such, it performed its function well. But unfortunately, it had an inherent failing. Its location! It commanded a large plot on prime level ground, a highly desirable feature for any prestigious building project, and that included the proposed new Conference Centre! La Esperanza was seconded to make way for it, and they bulldozed the site. Architects' plans were like something from a space-age cartoon, certainly the building costs went into orbit! Then came the labour troubles, backhander accusations, unaccountable monies, the list went on, as did the arrests for government corruption! I don't recommend that you go there. La Esperanza no longer exists, and a lawless element have since moved onto the abandoned site.'

'Abandoned?'

'Yes. The plans never came to fruition. The court cases are still ongoing, and there is no longer any appetite for the project – there simply never was any government funding for it. A white elephant I believe is the phrase!'

'What happened to all the kids that were there? There were dozens of us!'

'I really don't know. I can only assume, that like you, they were relocated. Where to, I have no idea.'

Sonny nodded acceptance and asked nothing further.

Alvarez stood up and smiled kindly at him. 'The desk will call you over when your contact details come through. You have my best wishes, Sr Lopez.'

Sonny likewise stood and firmly shook the offered hand. 'Thank you, Sr Alvarez, you have given me every hope, thank you, very much indeed!'

Sonny felt a measure of urgency as he came away from the Municipal Chamber with the provided contact details neatly folded in his shirt pocket. Back in his hotel room he carefully palmed flat the singular A4 sheet and rang The School of the New World.

It proved a lengthy phone call during which he twice stated his case in full. He was asked to phone back in an hour. He made that call and was transferred to Sra da Silva, the diretora of the school.

'Good afternoon, Sr Lopez,' Sra da Silva said, her voice that of easy calm. 'I understand you wish to meet with members of your family who may be resident here?'

Sonny felt a rush of elation that his sisters might, indeed, be there. 'Thank you, for taking my call, Sra da Silva. Yes, I'm trying to contact my three sisters. We've not seen one another for ten years since we were separated as children. I'm very keen to meet up with them again.' He was tempted to further explain how he'd never known where they were but didn't want to introduce any questionable distance.

'Well, what I need to do here, Sr Lopez, is ask that you send a cover letter and some form of photocopied ID to the school, preferably a photo type document, a passport would be ideal, if you wish to scan items and forward them to us then that would be perfectly acceptable. I'm afraid we can't confirm our resident girls or allow contact until these measures are in place. Should a meeting then be arranged we would require that you show the original documentation at the time of visit. It is school policy for security purposes, as I'm sure you will fully understand!'

'Most certainly,' Sonny agreed. He went on to explain that he lived in the UK and was staying at the Hotel Cristal until he flew back in two weeks' time. Sra da Silva asked that he provide whatever documentation he had with him, to include return flight ticket, and that they would proceed from there – the school would then contact him as soon as practicable.

Within half an hour of Sra da Silva's call, Sonny forwarded his documentation and cover letter to the school from his mobile phone. For the remainder of the day, he remained within the hotel complex and standing on the first-floor sundeck, considered how quickly things had moved forward. He felt reason for optimism that he might soon meet with his sisters – optimism because

Alvarez had taken his requests seriously, and the school hadn't rejected his approach.

Sonny's room phone rang the following morning shortly after he'd got back from breakfast in the dining room, he'd not known it ring before and assumed it to be a hotel query of some sort as he picked it up. The caller was Sra da Silva.

'Good morning, Sr Lopez, I hope I haven't caught you at a bad time?' she said.

'Good morning, Sra da Silva,' he replied, greatly surprised. 'No, not at all, thank you for calling!'

'That's quite alright. I just wanted to let you know that we've received your documents. Obviously, you are on a tight timeline but be assured we are dealing with your request. I expect to be back in touch with you at some point later today. We have your mobile number, so you needn't be concerned about missing our call. This is purely to update you on progress!'

'Thank you, Sra da Silva, I'm very grateful. Can I ask... is there any chance that my sisters are there?'

'As a rule, Sr Lopez, we never raise expectations on either side until checks are complete, but under the circumstances I can tell you we do have a name match, though please do not take that as confirmation, and we will ring you as soon as we know further.'

'Thank you, Sra da Silva,' he repeated, a little stunned.

'You are very welcome, Sr Lopez.'

As he awaited news from the school, Sonny kept himself to the hotel and marginal grounds – during that pensive time it occurred to him how the earlier phone call to his room had perhaps been part of their security checks. At one o'clock in the afternoon he answered his mobile phone to Sra da Silva.

'Good afternoon, Sra da Silva,' he said in modulated tone.

'Good afternoon, Sr Lopez, I have some news for you!'

'Oh, yes!'

'I've just spoken with your sister Maria Lopez, so I can confirm that she is here with us at the school. I explained that you have asked for a meeting, and she was thrilled at the prospect, we just need to arrange a time of visit. I must stress, however, that our rules for visitors are strict. Only the agreed persons can attend, you must report on arrival to the school reception and any type of baggage items and mobile phones will have to be deposited there until departure. We do not allow any packages to be exchanged, and throughout your meeting a member of staff will be present. They will not be intrusive and will sit some distance away; they are there for security purposes only and as such carry personal alarms. We also ask that you sign in and out at reception and that the allocated time slot be strictly adhered to. Is that all acceptable to you, Sr Lopez?'

'Absolutely!' he agreed blindly.

'Did you have any particular day in mind for your visit?'

'No, as soon as it's convenient for you, really.'

'In that case how about tomorrow afternoon at one-thirty?'

'That would be excellent!' he said – relieved that she didn't say *come now,* and him not be mentally prepared.

'On arrival, you'll be shown to my office, there's something that I need to talk through with you first, and then in keeping with guidelines you may have a one-hour meeting. So, I shall see you tomorrow at one-thirty, Sr Lopez.'

'Yes. Thank you! I'll see you tomorrow, Sra da Silva. Bye.' Sonny lowered the phone to his side – awed that he was about to bridge ten years of separation, anguish and uncertainty which went all the way back to his childhood.

He pondered that his sisters might expect him to look as before, possibly not even recognise him, or think him somehow different. Sra da Silva's comment about needing to first talk through something also caused him slight unease but he thought perhaps the school may seek some financial recompense for the girls' years of boarding and dismissed any concern in the light of such a positive outcome. He felt tempted to then further test his seam of good luck and contact the Women's Correctional Institute but decided against it until after his visit to the school. Such a call might easily generate high personal emotion, and he needed full happy focus for the next day. It was also possible that the girls knew something of it.

Tiredness swept over him at that point. He attempted to shower it away, and went down to the foyer, in need of distraction. Receptionist Amelia glanced up at him and he went over to her, bolstered by achievement and scented, hotel soap.

'Thank you, for that earlier,' he said. 'I found where I needed to be, no bother at all!'

She smiled and he gazed into her dark eyes, at her teardrop shaped face and naturally tanned, flawless skin – he thought her beauty mesmeric, beauty nakedly exposed by a neon blue scrunch band that held back her straight, black hair in a ponytail.

'Good,' she said. 'Glad I could help.'

'I hate to be a pain, but I've got another one for you!'

'Go on.'

'I need to be at The School of the New World tomorrow at one-thirty. I was wondering if maybe you knew of it and had any suggestions about how best to get there?'

'The School of the New World is about twenty minutes away by taxi, and that would be your best way to go. If you like I can make you a booking?'

'Yes, if you would,' he agreed.

'And you need to be there for one-thirty so I would recommend a booking for one o'clock, is that okay?'

'That's perfect. I'm not actually sure how long I'll be there for, it might be a couple of hours, so is it best if I just call them when I'm done, do you think?'

'I would say it's best that they wait! They'll do that for a fixed price per hour, and it'll be better than calling them later when it gets busy. The school is a little up in the hills! Would you like me to include that?'

'Yes, please.'

'And in what name?'

'Sonny Lopez.'

With that, she picked up the phone and made the booking as he pretended not to look at her.

'That's all done for you,' she said when concluded. 'You just need to be out front at one o'clock. It will be a yellow taxi!'

'Thank you.'

'That's quite alright. Is there anything else I can help you with today?'

'No, I think that's everything, thanks. I've troubled you enough,' he said with a broad smile. He would have liked to talk further with her but didn't want to appear the creepy guest and so moved away.

At the far end of the foyer, a wall-mounted sign with blue lettering and angled-down arrow indicated the Gymnasium and Indoor Pool, he went to seek it out. The gym, situated in the basement area, was near the separate spa and pool – the chlorine smell of which practically led him there. His room card released the gym door, and he was surprised, that given the comprehensive equipment within, one was there.

The gym rules of use, though, meant he had to wear sportswear, he went up to his room and changed – the gym was still empty when he returned. He switched on the electrical socket for the plugged-in radio and began a workout routine that took him an hour to complete. It was a welcome spell of time which allowed him to burn away gathered anxiety and prepare for what he knew would be an emotional reunion the following day. His hope was that there was enough left of cheeky little Sonny for his sisters to recognise.

Sonny walked through the hotel foyer ten minutes before his taxi was due. Amelia was on duty behind reception and flicked him a glance as he crossed the floor. He felt too nervous about the afternoon ahead to stop and chat with her and went through the automatic sliding glass doors to then stand outside on the pavement. Brief minutes later his taxi pulled up and they joined with the day's traffic.

The School of the New World was situated beyond the city fringes on cut-out ground in a scrub hillside. At first glance its identical collection of four centre-faced buildings looked colonial in style. A nearer view showed a utility build in cream stucco that sat behind wire mesh perimeter fencing with separate, tubular gates for vehicular and pedestrian access. The taxi nosed to a halt at the roadside entrance and from a small gatehouse a uniformed security guard appeared and blankly looked at them across the diamond mesh. Sonny got out and announced himself, without a word the guard unhurriedly pushed back the linear gate; the taxi drove partway through, and the guard directed him to park on nearby red gravel that already held several cars – he then pointed Sonny along a single-flagged pathway that led to the school's reception office.

    As Sonny walked its fifty-metre length the thought came to him: *This is where they came – all those years ago!* He felt a bridge back to that time and considered that perhaps three girls stared out from one of the many windows as he approached, and excitedly said: *He's here, it's Sonny!*

    He followed neat signage to the building which housed the reception office and there presented himself at a small, open window in a vestibule where hung the faint tar smell of linoleum floor tiles. The receptionist went through visiting procedures with him, she checked his documents as ID, laboured through the mobile phone and packages policy and got him to sign the Visitors Book. With that done, he was escorted by another staff member along an empty corridor to a closed door that was sign designated Diretora Sra da Silva, the escort knocked and led him inside without pause.

    Within, a slight woman got up nimbly from behind a darkwood office desk, she came over to them, offered her hand to Sonny, and introduced herself as Sra da Silva. She was small, her slender face deeply lined, and tanned by ancestry, at her wrists were bare wooden beads – a turquoise ribbon her only indulgence of bright colour tied at the end of long, carefully braided grey hair which hung to one side and kept her face free of its nuisance. Dressed in a light-dragging brown skirt and navy-blue cardigan over an elaborate white blouse, Sonny thought her difficult to age. She thanked his escort, Paloma, who left them. Sra da Silva then invited him to sit guest-side at her desk, whereupon she retook her own swivel chair.

    'I can see the family resemblance,' she said analytically as she gazed at him.

Ill at ease, Sonny smiled politely and waited – for what, he didn't yet know.

'I remember your three sisters coming here,' she said. 'We have forty-seven girls' resident with us at the moment. I remember each of them coming!' She paused as though in reflection. 'Unfortunately, I have some sad news for you, Sr Lopez. Your youngest sister Florence had contracted cholera before she got here. There was nothing we or the City Hospital could do to save her. She passed away shortly afterwards. I am so sorry.'
Sonny exhaled breath and groaned involuntarily.

'And I dearly wish that that was the only bad news I have to impart,' Sra da Silva went on. 'The eldest sister Sofia came of age to leave us two years ago. Sadly, she died of an overdose six months later. You have my deepest condolences, Sr Lopez.'

Sonny stared at her; his mind blighted with shock. 'Two years ago!... I could have been here! I could have... done something,' he said emptily. 'Where's Maria?'

'She's here – and she's beyond thrilled that you've come. I understand if you would like to postpone for a day or so to take in what I've so unfortunately had to tell you?'

'No! we've both waited long enough. How is she?' he said, his voice dry, as tears formed.

'Maria is an absolute delight. She's very bright and very caring. She works one day each week at the City Hospital on a work experience plan. She wants to be a nurse. She is a rare and beautiful person.'

'Can I see her?'

'Of course.'

Sra da Silva got up and went to the door, she swung it fully open and quietly spoke to someone nearby.

'If you are ready, Sr Lopez,' she then invited.

'We've put you in an empty classroom,' she said as Sonny stood beside her at the doorway. 'If we can agree the one-hour maximum duration. And can I ask that you call by here before you leave. This is Sr Belo,' she introduced of the short heavy-set man in the corridor who clutched a pink, document wallet at his chest, 'he will accompany you.' Sr Belo politely nodded, and said, 'Good afternoon, senhor.'

'Good afternoon, Sr Belo. I feel a bit nervous!' Sonny confessed to Sra da Silva.

'Oh, I think under the circumstances you can expect all such,' she assured him.

'If you'll follow me,' Sr Belo said, and led the way into a vacant ground floor classroom that was neatly set out with over twenty desks, each with a closely pulled-up chair. He spun one of the chairs around to face another across a desk near the door and invited Sonny to be seated there. He went to the far end of the room and engaged with his own work taken from the document folder.

Five minutes later a tall girl stood in the open doorway. Sonny's stare immediately went behind her, but there was no one else there. He looked into the face of the girl, at her gleaming eyes, and saw that it was Maria.

'Sonny?' she said.

'Yes!... Maria?'

They came together in a tight hug. Sonny pressed a kiss to her temple, she to his cheek; he leaned back and gazed at her as their tears freely flowed and they clutched each other's hands.

'Look at you!' he said incredulous, through waves of joy and shared laughter.

'We always knew you'd find us!' Maria said. 'We never stopped looking out for you! I just wish the others were here right now!'

Sonny closed his eyes, but the tears would not be held back.

Over the next hour, the pair sat on the two facing chairs, hands often clasped across the desktop, and talked through every facet that they could recall of their childhood years – and of those apart. Maria broke down when they spoke of their brothers Seve and Paulo and their sisters Florence and Sofia, Sofia whose memory was so recent and raw, and of their mother about whom she knew so little. She asked Sonny to describe her, to reinforce her own younger-age memory of what she looked like, and nodded deeply, eyes frequently closed, as he did so.

She recalled her own recent agonisingly painful loss of Sofia. 'We came here as three,' she said. 'Then we were two. We had side-by-side beds. When I used to cry in the early years, Sofia would say *Don't cry, Maria, everything will come good, you'll see.* She was so excited about getting to eighteen, she did work experience as a hairdresser, it was what she wanted to do. When she left, she said she would sort out accommodation for us both so that when I left, we would live together. I only saw her a few more times after that. It all went terribly wrong for her out there; she told me to stay here for as long as ever possible.' She turned her head to a side, 'Oh, Sofia,' she sobbed as tears fell between the closed fingers of both hands at her face. 'I'm so sorry, Sonny, what a horrible, horrible welcome for you!'

'There's nothing horrible about this welcome, Maria, and don't you even think such a thing! I can't begin to tell you how much it means for me to be here! We're going to go forward in their name, you and me, there'll be no more sadness for us, Maria, we've had more than our share – no more, not for us, I absolutely promise! I should have been here years back and I hate it that I wasn't! It's me who should be saying sorry, Maria, not you!'

When Sr Belo put his papers back into the document wallet and stood up, they both felt that only brief time had elapsed.

'I'll come and see you as many times as I can before I go back, Maria, I'll clear it with Sra da Silva, we've got a lot more to talk about and we're going to proper work everything out. I want to get into a football team here, and I'm not going to disappear for years again, not this time. I'm coming home.'

'Promise?'

'I Promise.'

Sonny was led back into Sra da Silva's office by Sr Belo who then left them. Sra da Silva invited Sonny to resume his earlier seat. 'So how was Maria?' she asked.

For half an hour Sonny and Sra da Silva talked through their hopes and wishes for Maria.

'I'll support her in whatever way I can,' he asserted.

'Good! She will need it. She has only one more year left with us and then she's hoping to become a student nurse. She's certainly bright enough and caring enough for the role, and hopefully her exam results will make her a good candidate. But she would need funding for accommodation and other expenses, and it is a significant outlay. The fact is, family support will be vital once she leaves here in whatever role she undertakes, and we will not be able to assist her beyond that time. It's the point when all our girls have to engage with the real world and let go of us!'

'Yes, It'll be a difficult time for her,' Sonny acknowledged. 'After so many years, she's been here longer than at home – there were six of us there once! And then to leave by herself! But she won't because I'll be here on the day! I'd like to see her as many times as I can before I go back to the UK. I don't want to interfere with lessons, and I can come at any time.'

'Oh, I'm sure we can work around lessons, so long as it's what Maria wants. We encourage all such family support for our girls. I'll look at her timetable for the coming week and discuss it with her. If you ring tomorrow afternoon, we'll arrange visits.'

'Thank you, Sra da Silva,' he said, his words ripe with gratitude.

Sonny got into the waiting taxi and went back to the hotel – his thoughts wholly detached from passing surroundings throughout the journey.

As he then crossed the empty foyer Amelia looked up at him from behind reception.

'Did the taxi work out alright?' she called over, which he liked to think wasn't what she really meant, and he went to chat with her.

'Perfect!' he said. 'And like you said, it was better that they waited!'

'Good! I'm pleased it went well.'

'I went to see my sister, actually!' he volunteered. 'We haven't seen each other for ten years!'

'My goodness!... Is she staff... or –'

'No, student!... she leaves next year.'

'She must have been absolutely thrilled!... she knew you were coming?'

'Yes, but she only found out this week, I had to find her first, hence the thing with the Municipal Chambers, long story really. But yes, it was fabulous seeing her again. She's sixteen now, the last time I saw her she was six!'

Amelia's locked expression signalled that she wanted to hear more.

'There were two other younger sisters as well, actually, but... sadly they passed away...'

'I'm so sorry to hear that.'

'Yeah, I didn't know until I got there, I'm still taking it in. It's a bit of a toughie, really!'

'Are you alright?'

'Oh, yes, at least I think I am. Big boys don't cry, do they – and that's a lie on stilts if ever I heard one! But yes, thank you for asking, I'm holding up. More importantly, Maria's holding up, she wants to be a nurse!'

'Good for her!'

'Yes! And I'm not in the least surprised. That's her through and through! She would always be the one to cry when something bad happened to you.' He reminded himself that Amelia was the hotel receptionist and smiled at her as though in conclusion. She responded with a smile of her own.

Later that afternoon, laid on his bed, he let the shock news of Florence and Sofia blur his vision. He tormented himself with the question, *what good to be good at anything when he hadn't defeated the suffering of his younger sisters, where was he – the big brother – when again he was needed?*

He didn't have any appetite for food or for a workout in the gym and instead went down and sat with a beer on the streetside terrace of the hotel bar. As he looked over the low wall of the terrace, a cream-coloured motor scooter emerged up the concrete ramp of the underground car park at the end of the building, and sped past him along the street. He could see that the rider, despite integral helmet, was Amelia, she gave him a quick wave but before he could respond she was gone. He felt lifted by the gesture and gingerly made a sideways check for any other potential recipients of her attention; there were none.

The next day was Sonny's fourth in Rio, and he was aware of how quickly his remaining time there would diminish. For two hours he worked out in the hotel gym, which took him up to lunchtime – at one o'clock he rang The School of the New World from his room and was put through to Sra da Silva. She welcomed the call, and they arranged a meeting between himself and Maria for the next day at eleven o'clock.

With that in place, he went down to reception, Amelia was on duty, and he asked if she would again book him a taxi for a wait visit to the school. In what was a quiet time at the desk he also asked if she had any knowledge or opinion of banks in the city that were adept at money transfers from overseas bank accounts; he thought it a reasonable question given the international nature of the hotel. She had familiarity of the subject and advised that he personally approach one of the major banks in the Centro Region while he was in Rio, because to do so remotely from the UK might prove difficult and time consuming.

Sonny found his bank in the Centro Region of the city later that same afternoon. For him to open an account, however, proved less than straightforward. He had assumed that being Brazilian born would automatically deem him a Brazilian national, such was not the case; he was deemed a foreign national. There were procedures to be gone through, procedures that required a residency permit, a police form to be filled in, and as much personal ID as he could muster. The bank, though, welcomed him as a new customer and began the process of setting up his account.

Sonny's next meeting with Maria saw them occupy the same empty classroom, again accompanied by Sr Belo with document wallet. Maria wanted to talk at length about their family shack and carefree lives of that time – and took on a contented stare as they recalled it. 'Rain never sounded so good as when we were all huddled together under our tin roof with mama!' was one of her fond memories.

'We were so happy back then,' she said. 'You and Seve and Paulo would be out playing in the dirt with all the other kids, throwing stones at the wild pigs. There was always something going on and some exciting tale to be told when you got back. Us girls would be playing house with our dolls. Why couldn't they have just left us alone, Sonny? We weren't harming anybody. They dragged mama off to jail over a loaf of bread or something that she only took to feed us. That horrible place killed her. In truth, it killed Seve and Paulo, then Florence and Sofia, all because of a lousy cents-worth of food!' She shook her head in utter sadness. 'Is our shack still there, do you think?'

'I'm not sure, the whole favela might be gone.'

'What about all our stuff? Mama's dresses, pots and pans... everything?'

'I don't know, probably the neighbours took it. They would have known we wouldn't be coming back.'

'I've got nothing of mama's,' she said emptily. 'No photographs of her, not even her hairbrush or bits of jewellery. They shouldn't have done that to us, Sonny, should they?'

'No. No they shouldn't,' he agreed solemnly.

'And I know I've got my dream of becoming a nurse, but do you know what troubles me deep down, and I've told this to no one else... but in a year's time will I be too scared to want to leave here? This place is all I've known since we came in as three frightened little kids. I'm the only one of us left, I still have their things, their dolls, Clarissa and Molly! This school is my link to our family. Sofia's name is still scratched on the wall outside!' She sobbed uncontrollably. Sonny got up and hugged her.

'We're done with sadness, Maria,' he said. 'We're going to live happy lives for their sakes! and they're going to look down and smile and be happy for us! You just pass every exam that anyone puts in front of you, do it for them, and I'm going to help with everything as much as I can, and I'll never stop!'

Sra da Silva, in Sonny's subsequent meeting with her in her office, stressed how academic success by students at the school could prove vital for future funding, and that she herself would reinforce any application Maria made to the hospital's recruitment panel should the time come. She had also put together a suggested schedule of visits for his remaining time in Rio.

Sonny went back to the hotel, changed into sportswear, and went to the gym. On that occasion others were also there. They hadn't switched on the radio, and he didn't know whether they were unfamiliar with user practice to do so, perhaps didn't want it on – or if, indeed, they'd switched it off. He didn't seek to ask and began his workout in a quietness punctuated by the end-stop thud of cable-pulled weights and the pounding of feet on treadmills. Twenty minutes later the others were gone, he switched on the radio and began his workout over again.

After the gym session, he didn't care to be in his room for longer than it took to shower and change, after which he made his way down to the hotel bar; Amelia wasn't on duty, so he carried straight on without breaking stride. Over the bar, the young barman asked if he intended, 'watching the game?' Botafogo football club Boca FC would be playing that evening, the match to be featured live on tv and shown on the big screen in the hotel bar.

'Yes, I think I will!' Sonny decided, quite taken with the idea.

That Sonny watched the match served him dual purpose. It took care of his evening and gave him chance to view and analyse the way the game was played in Brazil. He believed himself equal to it.

Amelia was back on duty the following morning and offered up a smile as Sonny stood before her at reception.

'I'm glad I asked you about that bank business,' he said. 'I thought I was Brazilian until I got in there! I am! But it seems I'm not. Spooky really!'

'Did you get sorted?'

'Pretty much, they're on the case for me. I've got to sign one or two things yet, but it's looking good, so, thanks for that!'

'That's okay. Did you go see your sister again?'

'I did! She got a bit upset, talking about family and our old home, me too to be fair! But we talked through some happy memories... she soon picked up again!'

'Good.'

'So, where were you yesterday, then? Absent from parade, I noticed!'

'Day off, actually.'

'And well earned, too! I hope you enjoyed it. I sat in the bar and watched the footy. That was good.'

'Yes, I know it was. I was at the game!'

'You were?' he said surprised.

'Yes, me and a bunch of others. You probably heard us; we got quite loud!'

Sonny associated Amelia only with the hotel and knew nothing else of her – and yet she knew so much about him. He was intrigued by her and asked, 'Are you a Boca fan, then?'

'Oh yes, most of my friends are,' she said. 'We don't make all the games, but if it falls right, we go. Shout and scream, make a night of it It's good fun! How about you, are you a footy man?'

'It's what I do for a living in the UK!'

'Really! What team do you play for?'

'I've just signed up with Northern Star for the new season. You maybe haven't heard of them; they're a Leeds team.'

'I've heard of them,' she said, her expression somewhat fixed at his wrong assumption. 'Well, why don't you get yourself a transfer to Boca and then we could scream and shout at you!'

'Now, that would be good! I like that idea, all I need is a decent enough scoresheet, and then maybe! Hold those screams! I can wear orange and white!' he clowned.

The pair broke into easy laughter.

'This hotel is owned by one of the Boca directors, actually,' she said.

'Yes, I read that somewhere!' he replied vaguely, so as not to admit he'd done traveller research before he arrived.

'They hold their end of season and Christmas party nights here.'

'I bet they're good nights?'

'Oh yes!'

Again, easy laughter was theirs.

That next week, Sonny had three scheduled visits at the school. He knew his commitment to Maria would be paramount for her future and reasserted his promised support at every opportunity; for her part, she understood why he had to return to the UK and that much depended on his ongoing success there on a football pitch. Mid-week, they both felt the approach of his final visit to be held on the Friday afternoon – his departure flight set for the following Monday.

Whenever Amelia was on duty, Sonny spoke to her at some quiet point during her shift. He had no real way of knowing how she perceived him, whether she was the seemingly interested receptionist – or merely indulged him, perhaps tolerated him because he would shortly be gone, or if she saw something other in him. With four days left of his stay he felt the need to know. He could have wrapped up his approach to her along the lines of gratitude but didn't want any blurring of the edges.

'I was wondering, Amelia,' he began, at his chosen moment over the reception desk, 'if we could maybe have dinner out somewhere, or a walk on the beachfront, maybe lunch if you're on day off, I apologise if I'm being forward, I don't want to step on any toes... and obviously only if you're totally comfortable with the idea?'

Her face briefly held its pose as though quick thought was needed. He believed rejection to be in the making. She took her gaze to his – he looked down at the desk to make it easier for her.

'Yes, I'd like that,' she said. 'I'm day off tomorrow, actually... a stroll on the beachfront sounds nice. Perhaps we could do that?'

'Absolutely!'

'How about one o'clock at the Cesta café,' she suggested, 'it's that little place next to the yellow supermarket on the beachfront, we could meet there? They do a neat coffee!'

'I've passed it! I think we should, and it would be rude not to try that sort of coffee!'

'Oh, it would!'

'Right, then, let's do that,' he said with a confirming nod. 'I'll leave you in peace now before you change your mind – let you get some work done!' He came away from the desk and tried to unfix a silly grin as he went.

He filled the remainder of his day in instalments, he went to the gym, the indoor pool for the first time because no one else was in there and he could plough up and down or freely back-float, even sunbathing on the roof terrace, that had its own outdoor pool, both of which he'd previously been unaware of.

For his rendezvous with Amelia, Sonny put on the last of his unworn buttoned shirts, last because it was dull black – with marginally too-tight short sleeves. He noticed Amelia's older colleague Morena look up at him with rather more interest than usual as he passed by reception. He felt sure it wasn't because of his shirt.

The Cesta café sat along a broad seafront esplanade; a broadness enhanced by palm-planted centre-islands. He was fifteen minutes earlier than arranged and glanced into the small café where a half dozen marble-topped tables lay mostly unoccupied – Amelia not yet there. He preferred them to go in together and so waited for her on a pavement bench, which gave an easy view in all directions. Single minutes later Amelia walked toward him. Dressed in a loose, grey silk blouse complimented with a white string shoulder bag and tight blue jeans, he thought she looked stunning. She was quite tall, which hadn't previously occurred to him because he'd only seen her across the hotel reception desk – which might have had a slightly raised floor behind it. He got to his feet and unnecessarily hoisted a hand. She smiled, came up to him and they met with a near touch of cheeks.

'Hi', she said.

'Hi, Amelia, how are you?'

'I'm good, thank you. How are you?'

'I'm good too,' he replied and boosted the moment with a broad smile.

They went into the café and ordered coffee from the otherwise unoccupied waitress who came over to their window table as they settled themselves.

'I apologise if I'm keeping you from anything, Amelia,' he said. 'I know how valuable time off work is!'

'Nothing that won't still be there later,' she assured him.

Over coffee their light conversation allowed each to learn about the other. It surprised him that Amelia wasn't a hotel receptionist by work choice but there to fund a university degree course in commerce that she was undertaking remotely; she was at the end of her first year and on the verge of an intermediate exam.

She told him how she shared a flat in the Botafogo suburbs with her sister Juanita, who was a single mother, and that on certain evenings when Juanita went to her part-time job in a supermarket, she herself would babysit 'Cassia and Christiano, two of the most gorgeous infants!' In turn, Amelia was enthralled at his background, in her own words he was the only person she had ever known who came from a favela. She was quite open about the fact, and it held no stigma for her. When they left the café, they strolled the beachfront chatting – mid-afternoon they shared a seafood platter at a café which Amelia knew, along a side street.

In that relaxed manner, their afternoon passed. At five o'clock, in the throes of a rush hour, they queued for a public service bus, its weight-laden tyres pungent with heat as it pulled up beside them. He remained on the pavement and watched her board, the bus pulled away and she smilingly gave him a fingertip wave standing in the centre aisle – all seats taken; he thought it signalled her approval of their time together and walked back to the hotel. There, Morena fixed him with a stare as he crossed the foyer to the lifts; he attempted a look that gave nothing away – and accepted that he probably failed.

That next morning, Sonny, with great resolve, addressed a subject which, thus far, he had ducked. From a drawer in his room, he brought out the A4 sheet of paper given him at the Municipal Chamber and rang the Women's Correctional Facility. It proved a laborious call and twice he was transferred to another office. He was eventually told that no information would be given over the phone and that he had to make an appointment to attend the facility and bring along personal ID in order to learn anything about a past or present inmate. The term *inmate* immediately caused him discomfort. He was made a tomorrow morning appointment for eleven o'clock.

Sonny stepped out of a wait taxi at the Women's Correctional Facility, a twenty-minute drive from the hotel. The expansive block sat behind graffiti-laden walls in a part-industrial, part low-key residential area. He hated the thought that his mama had spent her final days in such a depressing place and closed his mind to the torment she would have endured at being incarcerated there, knowing that her children were at the mercy of the State and that she could spend years apart from them – his only solace, that he followed her footsteps into that same place.

In a room given purely to functionality it was eventually confirmed to him by a uniformed member of staff, who along with a guard wore the trappings of self-protection, that his mother had, indeed, been sent there and subsequently transferred to the City Hospital where she died. Any personal items she may have possessed would have long ago been discarded, and they themselves had no record of where she was buried. As he came away from the facility, he determined never to speak to Maria of what he felt a descent into a hope-denied place. Though greatly dispirited he pressed ahead in his mission and, back at the hotel, rang the City Hospital. He was duly put through to the Medical Records Department who said for him to present himself there and bring along as much information as possible.

At the hospital, Sonny was directed from Main Reception down a floor-polished corridor to the Medical Records

Department. There he pressed a buzzer at a counter in an empty waiting area and a smiling young woman came through a staff-side door; she took his details, invited him to take a seat, and went back. Ten minutes later a middle-aged woman came through the same door, document folder in hand, she asked him for proof of identity and when satisfied, opened the folder across the countertop. From her, he learned how his mother had died ten years ago from pneumonia and was interred at the Sao Francisco Xavier Public Cemetery, in what would be a pauper's grave. The woman kindly furnished him with contact details of the cemetery; he thanked her and left.

Sonny rang the cemetery from his room. The call was answered by an elderly-sounding man who had the most automaton tone he had ever heard. The man asked for all details and told him to phone back in an hour. Sonny went down to the gym – did little – and then made the call. A recorded message told him that the cemetery office was closed for the day.

In the morning, he again rang the cemetery and spoke to the same automaton person. The man, though dour, had something to offer; the grave of Sonny's mother bore no name and was marked with a five-digit number on a wooden cross. The man quoted the number, briefly paused, and put down the phone.

Suddenly in need of happy company, Sonny went down to reception in the hope that Amelia would be on duty and free to chat with him. She was.

'So, have you any last-minute plans for the weekend?' she asked.

'No! I've got my final meeting at the school with Maria coming up, and after that it'll just be a wander-about, a slow pack and a long countdown. How about you?'

'Want to come to the footy with us lot on Saturday afternoon? Boca are at home to Rio Sangue. Bring Maria along, I'd like to meet her!'

The unexpected invite had him momentarily silent as he considered the prospect. 'I think she would love that,' he said. 'So would I!'

'Well, that's Saturday sorted out for both of you, then!'
Their combined grin turned into laughter.

Sonny greatly welcomed Amelia's invitation, more so because it was her idea, but it contained elements that slightly nagged him, the day would have its facets, he would have to share Amelia with her friends, whom he'd never met, Maria potentially present and the distraction of a major football match might prove a tough juggle, but he'd given his answer and a positive approach was needed; it also had the appeal that his and Maria's then extra day together would take the sting out of their final, tomorrow meeting at the school.

Sitting across from Sra da Silva in her office on Friday morning, Sonny apologised for the short notice and asked if Maria might be allowed to go with him the next day to the football match, if she so wished.

'Oh, she will be thrilled with the idea,' Sra da Silva said. 'She's a very sporty person; she's been captain of the netball team for a few years now. The girls often watch a football game on tv... they get quite vocal! I would just need to go over a few day-release conditions with you first.'

With all agreements in place for Maria's day-release, Sonny was again led into an empty classroom by Sr Belo who typically retreated to the far end of the room and occupied himself with paperwork. Sonny sat at a desk near the door and waited. Moments later Maria came in; she radiated him a smile and they greeted. Both then sitting across the desk, he relayed Amelia's invite to the match – which Maria excitedly welcomed. It surprised him that she knew Boca would be playing, and of the team colours, she even had an opinion of Rio Sangue and described them as a 'bad lot!'

She seemed amused he'd so quickly made the acquaintance of Amelia, and that she had invited them to the match and be among her friends. He assured her that everything would be fine and that she needn't be concerned about any of it, which was really a footnote to himself. He was glad that Maria wanted to go, it would give him chance to spend time with her in a non-school environment. To him, she would always be the little sister whose big fun-loving eyes should never have seen the emotional pain to which she had been exposed. If she changed her mind about the game, then so would he and then devote their day to doing anything she wished.

Sonny leaned down on the hotel reception desk and unfurled a pleased-with-himself expression. Amelia looked up from a computer screen and asked him what Maria's response had been to attending the game.
    'Oh, that's nice,'' she said when he told how thrilled she was. They then had a discussion, frequently interrupted by a ringing desk phone, about how they should all meet up.
    In his room, Sonny looked over his meagre luggage and reassured himself that he could be ready in an instant for his homebound flight on the Monday morning. The prospect, though, made him anxious; he disliked travelling alone, disliked a crumpled bag on a hotel room luggage rack and not know exactly when to pack and questioned why he was leaving when he had finally reconnected with family and Rio – even though he knew the answers. Other considerations, too, apart from pre-flight jitters, manifested themselves; despite their exciting day ahead, he was yet to say goodbye to Maria.

Sonny arrived at the school, midday Saturday to find Maria already standing by the reception office where she broke into a huge grin as he came in. In shiny orange jogging bottoms, white trainers and a white T shirt beneath a thin, silvery jacket, she had dressed in a determined nod to Boca FC. Sonny signed the mandatory legal form readied for him at the reception window and the pair made their way to the waiting taxi; along the path she turned to one of the buildings and waved at a group of girls who hung out of windows and had begun a chant for Boca, it made her laugh.
    Sitting in the back of the taxi the pair then set off to meet Amelia and her friends at the Zuma café bar near the club training ground and official accessories shop. Already gathered there when

they arrived was a sizeable crowd of supporters, nearly all in team colours in some form or other. Sonny, familiar with a noisy sporting event, hoped Maria could cope with such a vocally charged atmosphere, but knew that she worked in the City Hospital one day each week and hopefully was accustomed to the emotions and clamours of excitable and at times irrational people. Amelia immediately came over to them as they got out of the taxi – which he was glad for. He introduced her to Maria, and she and Amelia touched cheeks.

'Thank you, ever so much for inviting me,' Maria said. 'I'm just so excited!'

'Oh, I really hope you enjoy it, Maria,' Amelia replied. 'Come on, I'll introduce you both to everyone.'

They went over to a small, mixed group of people who looked on expectantly as they approached. Introductions were made all round and Sonny tried to lock-in as many of their names as he could. They were a happy bunch, all similar in age to Amelia, and he thought them perhaps her ongoing school friends of old.

Everyone soon then boarded one of the matchday coaches which took them to the Estadio Olimpico Nilton Santos, a giant all-seater oval stadium that held tens of thousands of supporters, its multi-levels suspended by external steel wishbones. The match was deemed important to both teams – and the gate number correspondingly high. The game was hard fought, and back-to-back groans, vitriolic appeals and chants erupted up to the final whistle. Boca won, two goals to one. Maria was enthralled with it all, she integrated confidently into their little group and they in turn readily accepted both her and Sonny.

On their return taxi journey to the school, Maria said how she thought Amelia the loveliest person, and her friends, too, had been great fun. As they neared the school, though, she quietened, knowing that their present time together was over. They walked into reception in silence, he signed her back in, and they stood to one side to say their goodbyes.

'Thanks for coming back, Sonny, please don't let it be another ten years!' she said as tears formed.

'I won't! Stay strong, Maria, stay right! I just need to get to the other side of a football season and then I'll be back. Maybe even sooner if I can snatch a week... I'll write you! Whatever happens, work hard on those exams, do it for you – do it for the family.'

They hugged tightly, her face shiny and wet. At the door he turned and gave a little wave as she looked on emptily, she offered a silent wave of her own, and he left.

His onward journey to the hotel held none of the day's triumphs. He didn't want to be in his room, nor did he want to go to the pool or the gym – he felt his visit was over.

Sunday was Sonny's last full day there, Amelia wasn't on duty, and he spent the afternoon strolling the beachfront – followed with beer at the bare-ground bar near the hotel, his thoughts random and self-analysing throughout. That evening, bag packed, he sat in the hotel bar and purposefully had a late night.

On Monday morning, he went down to the dining room, he felt too light in the stomach to eat anything much and settled for cereal, fruit juice and coffee. He made a final check of his room and slid a banknote partway under the desk lamp for the maid; bag in hand, he said, 'Thank you, room' and came out. Over the following hour he sat about a quiet outdoor area of the hotel where he drank further coffees and waited for Amelia to arrive for work at eleven o'clock. She came in early and helped to check-out guests, which might have included him had he not already done so.

With the lobby then clear he went over and stood before her. 'Morning,' he said.

'Morning. How was Maria when you left her?' she asked.

'She got a bit upset, but she was okay. She absolutely loved the whole day, and the game! we both did – I thank you for that, it was a bit special – good of you – good of your friends, as well!'

'That's okay, I'm glad it worked out for you both. It must have been a mind-numbing couple of weeks for her!'

'I know! me turning up's been a lot for her to take in. But she understands how things are with my job and everything. I promised her I'll be back at the end of the footy season, if not sooner for another visit, and then forever if I can swing a contract with a club here! Can I email you, Amelia... text you, or write? Sorry, I'm rushing, the brain fog's setting in!'

She slid out a letterheaded, blank A4 sheet of paper from a plastic tray beside her and wrote out her personal details.

'Ta,' he said as she handed it to him, he folded it and zipped it into an empty end pocket of his bag. 'Good luck with that exam!' he added.

'Thank you. Do you want me to book you a taxi?'

'No, I'm just going to go now and walk to the rank, a touch early, but... I might as well get out to the airport – job done. I'm glad I chose here, Amelia!'

'Good! So am I.'

'Bye for now, then.'

'Bye, Sonny, have a safe journey.'

At the airport, Sonny variously wandered and sat about the departure terminal for five hours. There the thought came to him that ten years earlier he had been forced to make the same journey which he was about to undertake voluntarily. He brushed aside the uncomfortable memory and immersed himself in the self-certainty that he would again return to Rio, funded through the gift of his own sporting prowess; a gift which burgeoned in the very place they had sent him and which he determined would secure his and Maria's futures. In that way they would be partway reimbursed – if ever such were possible.

The closing of the aircraft doors quelled the demons that tormented him over his departure. He sat back and let the next twelve hours take care of themselves.

Chapter 6

At Manchester Airport, Sonny made his way along an enclosed window-galleried skywalk and went down an escalator to the rail platforms. His train journey to Leeds proved slow, slower than that of the outgoing leg – which he felt much longer ago than its actual two weeks. Along the way he did a search on his phone for hotels in the direction of his new football club, and from Leeds railway station took a taxi to The Dormer Hotel. There he checked-in for a three-night stay. That evening in the hotel restaurant he ate a steak dinner beneath giant-sized retro lightshades, and then in a totally dark and silent room slept a series of nonsensical dreams.

Expected to begin pre-season training with Northern Star within two weeks of his arrival back in the UK, Sonny didn't want the inconvenience of excessive travel to and from the club ground. He began seeking accommodation in that immediate area and found what he wanted in one of the free newspapers that laid around the hotel foyer. From the lettings section of its pages, he rang property landlord Alan Bostock and agreed a viewing with him for a one-bedroom self-contained flat.

On what was a damp Wednesday morning, Sonny walked to the let address at the far end of a broad, tree-lined cul-de-sac that had Georgian detached houses to both its sides, some of which were music or language schools. His own viewing interest, though, amidst a short, terraced row, appeared much less grand with gnarled brickwork, old timber gutters and sash windows. As he waited on the pavement an open-backed utility truck pulled up beside him and a thirty-something man in black body-warmer and white T-shirt got out from behind the wheel; unhurriedly the man lifted a wooden toolbox clear of the tailgate, 'Morning, Sonny, is it?' he said.

'Morning, yes,' Sonny replied.

'Alan Bostock!' the man introduced and offered a hand without breaking stride. Sonny engaged the hand on the fly and followed him along a stone-flagged path that centrally divided a short garden between shoulder-high brick walls.

'There's one or two jobs I need to do,' Bostock said, 'so... while I'm here... And what do you, then, Sonny?' he asked as they stood at the matt black front door.

'I'm a footballer.'

'Ah, who with?'

'I start with Northern Star in two weeks.'

'You see, straight away I'm thinking parties. And the last thing I want is any complaints!'

'Well, there won't be any, parties... or complaints.' Sonny defended. 'I don't know anyone... And I'm not a party person!' Bostock said nothing to that and let them in using his own latch key. The entrance hall, laid with the original black and white floor tiles, much age-crazed and faded, lay gloomy and silent before them – on the right-hand wall a square bank of four mailboxes each had a token-padlocked door, individualised with chromed metal numbers. Bostock explained how the postman only used the front door letterbox and that it was the residents themselves who boxed mail to suit.

He showed Sonny around the furnished first-floor flat, where permeated the not unpleasant smell of old but good quality fabrics. The tenants of the other three lets, he explained, were all quiet professional people, whom he might only seldom see or hear as they came and went. Sonny liked the flat, it suited his no-frills mentality of the moment. He agreed the terms and conditions and, on a monthly basis, took it on.

Two days later, Sonny dropped his bag on an ungiving three-seater sofa at his new address which had him as moved in. He bought stationery and, sitting at the lounge dining table, wrote a letter to Maria – he went straight out and posted it. From his phone he sent a buoyant text message to Amelia and then rang Mally, who sent over his stored bag by taxi. During that time, he received Amelia's texted reply which offered pleasantries of her own.

Sonny began pre-season training with Northern Star at their thirty-thousand-seater ground. It was a daunting experience for him to join such a highly ranked club, some of whose players were nationally known and would arrive driving high-end vehicles. He felt almost invisible as he joined the large squad in training and had to remind himself why he'd been chosen, and that their first team players had once similarly begun. He kept his head down and did the work.

When the playing season commenced, Sonny spent game time on the benches to observe and learn. He knew it would be so and wasn't bothered by it – his time would come. He got his chance one rainy mid-week evening in a meagrely attended match when their main strikers were strategically substituted, and Northern Star majored against a dispirited Westborough Town FC. At half-time, Northern Star were four goals to the good and Westborough yet to score. Sonny was brought onto the pitch along with two other new hopefuls – the youngest of whom was seventeen – that they garner gametime experience and allow management to view their acquisitions in action, risk free. Sonny supressed any urge to panic as the ball fell to him, instead he flicked-on his skill switch, as he himself believed it, and weaved into the penalty area from where he freely scored; the goal itself was a placid tap-in at an open goalmouth – the way that he commanded the ball passed several opposition players, though, to place himself there and then feign the goalkeeper had management open-faced as they looked at one another.

Sonny wasn't encouraged to overly believe in himself, and the regular playing format resumed, but he'd opened his account and set a new club record for the quickest debut goal. On every occasion of play he justified his presence on the field – if not with goals, then in his assist of others and always that he never gave up however late in the game he was brought on.

He wrote regularly to Maria, unable to bear the thought of her in disappointment if he didn't. To Sra da Silva he sent an email asking that should she have concerns about her at any point, then to please contact him by email, phone, text, or letter. His bank in Rio emailed him electronic forms to fill in and then confirmed that his account was set up and simply required incoming funds for it to become active. He made a money transfer from his UK bank and saw remotely that it had landed. In due course, Amelia emailed him to say that she had passed her intermediate exam and congratulated him on his: *fruitful start* with Northern Star – that she had followed his progress both pleased him and gave added focus. It all helped him settle into his again-new life.

Sonny's scoresheet with the club began to rise noticeably and as the season progressed, he featured ever more in matches. Supporters wouldn't tolerate for long him not being on the pitch in a losing game and would break out in a chant of: 'Bring on Sonny Lopez!' He became a player that the club wasn't about to let go of and his wages were re-negotiated by manager Lou Gomero so that he wasn't tempted away by other clubs who showed interest in him. Sonny's bank account began to reflect his newfound status.

In an evening match on the rundown to Christmas, Sonny scored an audacious goal which secured an important game; as he came off the pitch, palming the hands of dejected opponents, Northern Star coach Alex said to him, 'Are you in love or something!' Sonny thought it perhaps not a bad analysis.

On Christmas Day, Sonny stayed alone in the flat, it didn't trouble him, and he spoke at length on the phone with Amelia. The pair exchanged news, best wishes and caught up on each other's lives. On his mantlepiece sat a row of Season's Greeting's cards, centred among them one from her, and one from Maria.

At home one mid-week evening in January, Sonny answered his phone to Simmonds.

'Hiya, Mark, how are you?' he said brightly.

'Yeah, I'm good, Sonny. No need to ask how you're doing! I thought you might have changed your number or something by now, you know, gone ex planetary!'

'Well, when you're desperate for calls, you know!... Good to hear from you, Mark, how're you keeping?'

'Keeping tidy! Things don't change much. The guys in the Feathers still can't believe it when you come up on the telly after a match, *Hey, it's Sonny! Tell him he still owes me that fiver*, all that stuff. Anyhow, that's not what I'm ringing for. I don't suppose you've heard about Gilesy?'

'No! what's he done?'

'Right! I thought maybe you wouldn't have heard. You remember that mobile phone nonsense, the one they found in the hotel yard, the one that wasn't his because he didn't use a keypad code?'

'Yes.'

'Well, it turns out it was his, wasn't it!'

'Was it, now!' Sonny muttered darkly.

'Yes. And he knew it too. He lied!'

'Go on.'

'The police over there regarded that phone as potentially crime scene related. Ours thought it more a case of lost and found, they went through the motions and that was all. Well, Benidorm managed to unlock it, didn't they... and it seems there's a video on it of Ferret in the hotel room that night, they reckon it shows him lunging at the phone and going over the balcony with it in his hand. That's what they're saying happened! It's all coming out now! Apparently, the police have been back to Gilesy's and questioned him about it, he admitted the phone was his and that he had it on a selfie stick filming the night lights from his balcony, he turned around because Roy said something to him, and someone grabbed it off him from your side. He said he had no idea who it was or that they'd fallen! He claims he banged on your door to get his phone back, but no one answered so he decided to leave it until you'd both sobered up! He heard no more until the next morning when it came out about Ferret. This has all come from Roy, because the police then went round to his and put it to him!... he went proper crackers and said he knew nothing of it, that he was in bed as soon as they got back in that night. Next thing, Roy's in the Feathers shouting about what Gilesy's now claiming!'

Sonny groaned.

'So now Benidorm are even more convinced there's a case to answer,' Simmonds went on, 'they've handed it over to our lot and the press have got hold of it!'

'Can it get any worse!' Sonny muttered. 'So why didn't Gilesy say all this back then, instead of keeping schtum and letting me take all the blame?'

'He reckons that when he heard of the tragedy the next morning, he just felt sick and numb and didn't know what to do, he thought you were in with it, especially when the police carted you off... and when you got back home, no charges made, he said he kept quiet because there was nothing to be gained by blaming Ferret!'

'When I got back home!' Sonny scoffed. 'I could have been years in that place. What football career would I have had then? What good would I have been to my family in Rio when I had no prospects of anything? He would have let me rot in some Spanish jail and said nothing – watched footy in the pub without a care! That's the truth of it, and we've all of us shared the blame ever since. And how much time has he had now to polish up a story – maybe even taken legal advice?'

'For sure!' Simmonds agreed. 'And how does anyone know if he's telling the truth now? Like someone said, why did he lie about it being his phone in the first place after they found it?'

'I don't think he knows what truth is! So, what's happening, then?'

'I don't know, everyone's just hanging on for whatever comes out next. I'll keep you informed!'

'Please do, Mark.'

During the winter months, Sonny got an email from Maria, sent via her school hub, which said that she had begun her final exams; an email from Amelia told that after much consideration she had decided to go full-time as a student at Rio University and would continue to work at the Cristal in a part-time role. The change would allow her to sit the degree exam fully three years sooner than would otherwise have been the case.

Late one Sunday afternoon as Sonny loafed about at home, he answered his phone to Simmonds.

'Yo, Sonny!' Simmonds greeted.

'Ayup, Mark, how're you doing?'

'Good! Have I caught you at a good time?'

'Hang on, let me check... yes, yes, they've all gone now!'

'Gilesy!'

'Go on.'

'The police have been back to his again and he's sticking to his story that someone grabbed his phone, and that it must have strayed over the divide when he turned around to talk to Roy – who he now says must have been talking in his sleep! Roy's told him straight to leave him out of it, he's not having anything to do with it. Gylesy's keeping low! Carole, his missus, knows he's been seeing another woman from work, which one or two others in the village knew about, and she's had enough of everything! In fact, word is it was her who sent that phone unlock code to Benidorm to see if it was his! Roy's now come out and said what he thinks happened. He has it that Gylesy was filming around the balcony because he thought Ferret was making out with one of the girls from that hen party and Ferret clocked it!... And he hasn't got that out of thin air!'

Sonny moaned an exhale of breath. 'And it was supposed to be us that were lacking!' he said. 'So, all along Gylesy didn't tell the truth because he didn't want to own up to his own grubby involvement – better it be me that gets sent down – lives ruined! And all he had to do was keep quiet!'

'Yeah, well, he's come unglued, Sonny. And everyone knows it now. Anyway, there's more!'

Sonny moaned again.

'No, this is a bit nicer, not much, but at least it's in our favour. It's coming up two years since then.'

'Two years!' Sonny said, incredulous.

'Yeah, I know! Two years next month. We weren't allowed to the funeral, of course, but things have changed now. The family have been asked if we can lay flowers on the grave, they said they would totally welcome it and for us to go right ahead and do it! We're all meeting in the Feathers at two o'clock three weeks this Sunday, on the tenth. We're going to put on the team shirts, take a bunch of flowers apiece and walk through the village to the churchyard, heads held high. We're going to show Cowton what decency looks like!'

'Brilliant!' Sonny exclaimed. 'Just brilliant! Count me in.'

'I was hoping you'd say that. The plan is that none of us has a drink until we get back to the Feathers, then we make a toast to Ferret and let rip from there!'

'So, who's put all this together, then?'

'Kev. I think when he heard what's come out, he just wanted to do something and he ran it by Al. Wendy's putting on a spread, and it's going to be a day to remember!'

'But there's only us doing the church walk, though?' Sonny questioned.

'Only the team, led by Kev. Ferret's footy shirt'll be over a chair in the pub with a pint of lager in front of it! Keep a dry eye if you can! I know I'll struggle, and I won't give a toss!'

'You and me both!'

'It's going to be a biggie, Sonny, and we're going to say a proper goodbye to him!'

'I'll be there, Mark. Feathers, two o'clock on the tenth, yes?'

'Yes. And don't so much as look at me until it's over... or I'll totally go to bits before we even start! See you there, Sonny.'

The following week, the football season almost at a close, Sonny made an email approach to Boca FC and expressed his wish to join the team. Around that same time, he got a text message from Maria to say that she had sat her first exam and felt: *comfortable* with the way it had gone.

Chapter 7

On the appointed day of respect for Ferret, Sonny walked into The Feathers and was greeted with earnest handshakes and hugs from ex-teammates of the pub's football team. Kev poured him a glass of lemonade from a willing soda gun – everyone likewise with glass in hand, and all glad that Sonny was there to add further gravitas to the day. Football talk lessened the tension, and light banter broke out until Wendy came through carrying a large cardboard box. She placed it on the pool table and pulled open the interlocked flaps; inside were the team shirts, neatly folded and pressed. She took them out individually and laid them around the table.

'Okay, lads,' she said. 'There you go. You can put them on in the kitchen and leave your stuff in there.'

Each with shirt in hand, the team made their way to the pub's unused kitchen and any jocularity fell away. On their way back, all then in blue shirts, old Justin, newly arrived, was sitting at his usual wall-side table in the otherwise empty lounge and watched them file passed. When he caught sight of Sonny he half rose from his seat and waved him over with some urgency. Sonny blindly obliged and old Justin brought up a folded-over carrier bag from beneath the bench seat. 'Grandson's a keen Northern supporter,' he said intensely. 'I told him you'd be coming in and he asked if you'd sign his shirt for him!' From the bag old Justin pulled out a Northern Star shirt along with a black marker pen, he spread the shirt on the table and thrust the pen, minus cap, at Sonny. Sonny stared at him – into eyes that registered no understanding of the day – and numbly signed the shirt. Old Justin folded it back into the carrier bag and said, 'Keep the young'uns happy, that's what it's all about!' He secreted the bag beneath the bench seat and sat down as Sonny re-joined the team.

'What did he want?' Freddy asked him.

'He wanted me to sign a shirt for his grandson.'

'He never!' Freddy gasped... Him! The old…! I hope you told him where to go?'

'Probably should have,' Sonny considered, 'but then I'd be as sour as him, wouldn't I?'

'That's all he's come for,' Freddy railed. 'That and a gawp. He's never in at this time!'

Everyone was then drawn to silence as Wendy and Alice filed in with bunches of flowers which they carefully set down on bar-room tables. As the pair silently carried out the task, the vicar of Cowton, middle-aged Rev Allister Morrison of St Hilda's church, came in from the street, complete with collar of office, and stood in the doorway. 'Beautiful flowers,' he said in timely admiration.

'Rev Morrison has kindly agreed to lead the procession,' Kev revealed as he handed him a glass of lemonade. 'And I for one would like to say a thank you to him. It's very much appreciated, Allister!'

Rev Morrison graciously nodded, and the team murmured their own gratitude. Sonny sensed a ramped increase of tension at the man's very presence – and recalled how they had willed such a presence two years ago in Benidorm.

'Right then, guys,' Kev said, 'grab yourselves a bunch of flowers, they've all got cards attached. There's pens here, put your names on, a few words if you want. Then we'll make our way.'

Everyone selected their flowers and empty stares told of messages being considered. Eventually all pens were laid back down.

'All done, guys?' Kev asked. Silence had it that everyone was. 'Right, then,' he said. 'Let's do the walk!'

Led by Rev Morrison they made their way silently along the main street pavement, each cradling a bunch of flowers. Many of the villagers who had looked out for them came to their front doors, some to their garden gates, and spontaneously broke into continued applause as the group passed by. At Ferret's house his parents and brother similarly came to the gate. His mother wept as they too applauded. In the church graveyard the team laid their flowers on Ferret's grave and momentarily paused in respectful silence. For each of them, it graphically laid bare what had happened to their friend. Deeply moved they made their way back to The Feathers, further accompanied by Rev Morrison.

In their absence Wendy had laid Ferret's football shirt over a chairback and put before it a freshly pulled pint of lager; along the bar she had set down a long line of shot glasses filled with gin. As everyone looked on, Kev picked up an end-of-line glass and in the watchful silence said, 'Pick up your shots, lads, and we're going to make a toast because we never forget our friends.' With the team readied, Kev held aloft his own glass and loudly proclaimed, 'To Ferret!'

'To Ferret,' the room echoed in unison.
'Hip hip!' Kev prompted.
'Hooray!' came the response.
'Hip hip!'
'Hooray!'
'Hip hip!'
'Hooray!'

Kev swiftly drained his glass, put it back down on the bar, and everyone followed suit.

'Allister will now say a few words and then begin a minute's silence for private reflection,' he said.
All eyes went to Rev Morrison.

'Thank you, Kev. I'm sure I am not alone in my wish to say a heartfelt thank you, to both you and Wendy for bringing everyone together for this memorable occasion,' Rev Morrison said. 'I think perhaps a show of appreciation might be in order!' The room broke into spontaneous applause. 'Top man, Kev!' someone called out. Silence fell. 'You know, I watched John grow up in this village,' Rev Morrison resumed. 'I saw him go from being a small boy who believed in Father Christmas, into a fine, sporting young man. I'm pretty sure it was John who taught me how to swear, actually,' he said detachedly – which rippled the room with mirth. 'He enriched everyone's life who knew him,' he went on. 'When John laughed, the world wanted to hug him. I look around me now and I see those same fine qualities; that's John's forever legacy to each of us. No, we won't forget our dear friend, we never will. Let us go forward and be glad that he chose us to know him. Through our coming years may we apportion happy thoughts to his memory, carry him high in our hearts and in that manner, he will live on. A minute's silence for John now please.' The minute's silence began.

'Thank you,' Kev said at the end of the minute, timed by himself from a wall clock. 'And thank you, Allister, for your wise words of comfort. The family have asked me to express their gratitude to you all. Now let's have the drink Ferret would want us to have! Who's ready for a pint?' He made his way behind the bar to Wendy and Alice and commenced pulling pints to the shouted-out orders.

Once unshackled from its sorrow the occasion became a happier one; Ferret's drink remained in front of his shirt throughout, and some said they could sense his very presence. Everyone was keen to hear of Sonny's new footballing life, and he was happy to catch up on their news, one had got married, most were in relationships – two had offspring. It all confirmed to him how time moved on regardless of anything. No one mentioned tall Giles and none of his immediate cohorts came in. Some of the blameless outer fringe turned up later, they nodded without focus on anyone specific and quietly blended into their usual places. A surprise for Sonny came as he stood next to Simmonds – and Samantha came in, she went straight to Simmonds' side, clamped his arm with hers, then leaned over and swiftly kissed Sonny on the cheek.

'Hiya, Sonny,' she said. 'So, where's the Lambo, then?'

'It's on the bar next to the beefo!' Sonny joked, to which they all laughed.

'How's he been?' she asked him, with a side-nod at Simmonds.

'Spot on!' Sonny said, he knew the reason behind the question, much less that it was Samantha who had asked it.

'He's been panicking for weeks about this, scared he'd break down! you know what he's like!' she said.

'He wasn't on his own, Sam, I can assure you. Anyway, it's good to see you! how's things?'

'Things is good, I even know a famous person now.'

Rev Morrison stayed for over an hour, in what became a party atmosphere; he chatted with anyone who cared to engage with him and shook many appreciative hands as he left. Throughout the afternoon and into the evening, few left the pub. Old Justin overshot his usual home time, Sonny knew why, though, when someone pointed out that he never came away from the bar without something on a plate – or a glance across to their side to gauge the mood and see who was there.

At some point, Ferret's brother Al came in and shook the hands of the entire football team; their mother, he openly said, had drawn tremendous comfort from the day's events. He fell silent when he caught sight of Ferret's shirt with a pint of lager set before it; he took a photo of it on his mobile phone and turned away as his shoulders tremored. Samantha went to him which had him break down. He quickly recovered in good grace, and the party rolled on in his brother's name.

At ten o'clock that night Sonny engaged with sincere hugs and handshakes and went home in a taxi, after what many felt had been a highly emotional day.

Fresh in from training that next evening, Sonny snap-unscrewed the cap of an energy drink bottle from his fridge; drink in hand, he sank heavily into the sofa and rang Simmonds.

'Well, I think we can say we did Ferret proud there, Mark,' he said.

'No question!' Simmonds agreed emphatically. 'It was the best, and I've got to say – let 'em suck it up!'

'Absolutely. I liked the way the vicar took it on, that really gave it some clout.'

'Oh, for sure it did, that man was a star! It wasn't just us stepping up, he proper rubber-stamped it. There won't be a wrong word said about us now!'

'And you didn't tell me you and Sam were together?'

'No, well, we've been going out for a while now, I just got used to everyone knowing, really.'

'You've done well; she's a cracking lass!' Sonny complimented in earnest.

'Yeah, we get along. How about you, anything doing there?'

'Mm, nothing this side. I'm cosy with a little lady in Rio, but if I don't manage to conjure up a team over there to play for then that might struggle!'

'Well, they're going to want you, aren't they – the women and the clubs!'

'Not so far, they're not, not the club I've applied to anyway. I'm still waiting to hear! If I don't get anything back soon, I'll try with some of the others.'

'But meanwhile you're okay at Northern?'

'Oh yes.' Sonny confirmed. 'How could I not be! And I don't want to get my head in a mess and throw it all away! It's a bit like what you Yorkshire lot taught me; know which side your bread is buttered!'

'The way you score goals, Sonny, the bread'll take care of itself!'

'Any word on the odious one?'

'No, no one's seen him for a while now. She's about but he's not.'

'I just can't believe what he did – I could still be there in a cell! How could anyone do that? Northern were supposed to be playing a charity match in Madrid, I thought there's no way I'm stepping back on Spanish soil, anything could happen. Luckily it was cancelled, but I wouldn't have gone!'

'The truth came out, Sonny.'

'Yeah, by the skin of its teeth, but yes... thank goodness.'

'Anyway, everyone was glad you could make it yesterday,' Simmonds rallied, 'it was a full contingent and we nailed it!'

'I was glad to be there, Mark. Keep me informed of stuff!'

'You're my prestigious go-to person, Sonny! I'll definitely keep you informed!... *Oh, it's that Sonny Lopez again, wants to know stuff, such a pest!*'

'And say Hi to Sam, for me.'

'Hi, Sam!' Simmonds shouted, turned away from the phone. Samantha's reply came back loud enough not to need repeat: 'Hi back to whatisboots!'

Chapter 8

The close of the football season saw Sonny's name prominent on Northern Star's goal ladder. During the week of their last game, he received a letter from Maria which told that she had passed her penultimate year exams. He responded with a letter of congratulation and said that he would soon again be in Rio, albeit for another short visit. With a then several-week gap in commitments, he booked himself on a flight, and emailed Amelia his update. She immediately replied and said she was looking forward to seeing him and to let her know if he wanted a reservation at the hotel; he confirmed that he did. He also sent an email to Sra da Silva with his dates of stay and asked if he could visit the school, in reply she assured him that he was more than welcome to do so.

Sonny stepped onto his early morning Thursday flight to depart Manchester and was unexpectedly offered a free upgrade to business class. It was his first taste of privilege. He decided not to ask why he'd been selected in case a mistake had been made.

Twelve hours later, he delighted in his own return to Rio, as though in celebration and proof that he could do so at any time. On what was a humid night, he took a taxi from the airport to The Hotel Cristal and was checked in by Morena who made no comment to the fact that his reservation was in the system or that he was a repeat guest.

In the morning, from his room, he arranged by phone with Sra da Silva to take Maria out for the next day, Saturday. He then reacquainted himself at length with the seafront and hotel gym.

At five o'clock that afternoon, Amelia came on duty. Sonny waited until the foyer had quietened then beamed a grin at her over the reception desk.

'Welcome back, stranger!' she said, and broke into her own welcoming smile. 'It's nice to see you again.'

'Nice to see you too, Amelia, how are you?'

'I'm good, thank you, you're looking well.'

'Not half as well as you,' he said eagerly. 'How's uni?'

'I'm loving it! It's all a bit frantic jobwise and at home with two toddlers tearing about, but I wouldn't have it any different!'

'Glad to hear it.'

'Have you seen Maria yet?'

'Tomorrow!'

He told of how he had arranged to take Maria out the next day, and that they were going shopping or whatever else took her fancy.

'Oh, she'll love that,' she said.

'And I was wondering if maybe we could get out together again at some point?'.

'I'm sure we could! We could do Sunday midday if you like?'

'Sunday's perfect!' he agreed.

On Saturday morning at Maria's school Sonny got out of a wait taxi, booked by Amelia, and made his way across silent grounds to the reception office. Maria was already there and grinned hugely when she saw him. They hugged, he signed the requisite form over the desk, and the pair strode eagerly away.

'So, how's it gone since I left?' he asked as they careered down a winding hillside into Botafogo.

'Good! We've got the first lot of exams behind us now, and everyone's totally chilled!'

'Ready for the real thing next year?'

'Yes.'

They got out at Rio Sul Shopping Mall, which Maria knew of but was yet to visit. There, they wandered shop-lit marbled floors throughout the multi-level building and had coffee and lunch at its franchise eateries. As they sat on curled plywood furniture and ate southern fried chicken with their fingers, Maria said, 'I'm not as scared now as I was about leaving New World! Things seem a lot clearer now, somehow. I don't feel like a kid anymore.'

'Good! You did well with the exams.'

'Yes. We all study pretty hard anyway, everyone knows the deal out there!'

'Yeah, it's a tough place to start out!'
'How's Amelia?'
'She's good. We're meeting up tomorrow.'
'It's obvious she loves you, you know – you can see it! But do you love her, that's the thing?'
'I don't know... maybe.'
'Well, that could be you sorted!'
'And what makes you so all knowing about this stuff?'
'Favela!'
He laughed.
'It hurt you too, didn't it?' she said, '– what happened to us back then. Maybe more so because you were older, and you remember it better.'
'Maria, I can still taste the bare earth that we played on!'
'I wonder what happened to Christa and her family,' she said. 'Angelina, and Jose, you remember them?'
'Yes, I remember them. And Seve and Christiano Sarmiento, and their dog Putch! But I have no idea where any of them are now – apart from Putch, he was an old dog then!'
He told her that he had traced their mama's burial place.
'Have you been?' she asked emptily.
'No. I thought we'd go together, maybe when we're both a bit more settled with things!'
She nodded in agreement. Sonny went on to say how he was yet to find a football club in Rio to take him on, and that he needed to play another season in the UK and nail his game in order to be of appeal.
'You nail your football game, and I'll nail my exams!' she told him.
As they further wandered the mall, he said, 'I've decided to buy you something for your seventeenth!'
'Oh, yes?'
'Yep, a mobile phone! you don't have one, and it's time you did, so let's go find!'
At a mobile phone shop within the mall, Maria chose a smartphone in white that she liked the look and feel of; Sonny

bought it and set up a connectivity contract paid through his bank account.

By the end of their day, the pair were laden with multiple carry bags hooked onto either hand. They laughed in unison when she objected to him buying her anything further – on the grounds that neither could carry any more.

On Sunday morning, Sonny walked the few hundred metres from the hotel to a pavement kiosk and waited there for Amelia, as they had arranged. Within ten minutes of him, Amelia, in loose-fitting giraffe print bottoms and sleeveless white bouse, a beach bag looped over a shoulder, strolled up and they greeted with a happy grin and the barest touch of cheeks. At the adjacent bus stop they boarded a public service bus that took them to Copacabana beach, a ten-minute ride away.

The beach, bright under a full sun, was busy its entire length with leisure seekers. Sonny and Amelia got down to swimwear – she then in peach bikini, he in legged, black trunks – and settled themselves on rental sun loungers. As fancy took them, they went to the water's edge, plunged warm waves, rinsed away seawater at a push-button shower station and variously collected fried shrimp, chilled melon segments and coffee from a beach café. At some point as they lay, her arm rested lazily across him, her cold wet hair then welcomed against his sun-warmed chest, they kissed, as the all-around drone of the beach went on undecipherable and non-intrusive.

Late in the afternoon, they caught a bus back to Botafogo, their fellow passengers mostly Sunday beachgoers who likewise returned to the suburbs. A few stops before his, Amelia got off, they waved and smiled at one another through the windows as the bus pulled away; in the remaining minutes to his own stop, Sonny indulged of the thought that everything seemed brighter when he was in Rio.

On Monday morning, Sonny rang Boca FC. The team, though, had an away game the next night and there was no one available to meet with him. During that same week, he twice visited Maria at the school. At the end of his second visit, the pair hugged their goodbyes and to ease the moment, of what effectively was his departure back to the UK, he said his next return would hopefully be 'on a one-way ticket'. Sra da Silva, in Sonny's subsequent meeting with her, told how Maria had passed her exams with exemplary grades, that she was highly regarded at both the school and City Hospital where she continued to do work experience and there was every justification for her to apply for student nurse training in the coming year when she would leave.

    On Thursday, he again contacted Boca FC and again was told there was no one available to meet with him – and that he needed to send a full cv to club manager Alberto Ferreira.

    Sonny and Amelia arranged to meet on her next free day off. The weather on the day was squally and they happily settled for a seafront walk and lunch behind closed bi-fold doors in a street café. There he expressed disappointment at his lack of result with Boca. She said for him to keep on trying, to send his cv, to approach other clubs in Rio – and not to lose hope.

    Sonny checked out of the hotel at ten o'clock in the morning and took a telephoned taxi to the airport. Five hours later, airborne, he involuntarily flexed his toes as though in sand and wished himself laid next to Amelia on a sunlit beach. The words in his head said: *wrong way again.*

On what was a rain-soaked Tuesday, Sonny stood along Manchester Airport rail platform. As he waited, the unfriendly voice of a total stranger rang out to him across the tracks, 'Oi, Lopez, get back over them Pennines where you belong!' Sonny consoled himself that it was a measure of his own pitch success.

    Too travel weary to bother with the overstuffed mailbox in the cold hallway, Sonny let himself into his flat and set about restoring its normality. He sent Maria a phone text message to say that he was back, which proved the communication link. Fatigued, he then slept through the afternoon; early that evening he read Maria's texted happy reply – and rang Simmonds.

    'Hiya, Sonny,' Simmonds answered. 'How was Rio? 'Cos I wouldn't know!'

'Hiya, Mark. Yeah, it was great! Thought I'd give you a ring, see if there's any news on things?'

'Only that no one's seen Gilesy! You see her about, but not him. There's still no charges been brought and the belief is there won't be either! Roy won't even discuss it. He just goes off in a huff if anyone so much as mentions it.'

'Anything been said about Ferret's day?'

'Oh, there's one or two said all the right things, as though we were never in doubt! And a lot that say nothing because it's not what they want to believe, but that's Cowton for you!'

'And how's Sam?'

'She's absolutely fine, still sticking it to me! What about you, you fending them off with sharp sticks?'

'No, I'm thinking of advertising, actually.'

'Now, why do I have to doubt that! So, are you still good to go with Northern?'

'I am! Pre-season starts next week,' Sonny confirmed.

'Good! Nothing doing over there yet, then?'

'I just can't seem to raise any interest!'

'Their loss, Sonny, and we don't want to lose you.'

'Well, we'll see how it goes, give my regards to Sam, and I'll catch you later, Mark.'

'For sure, keep netting 'em, Sonny.'

'Cheers, Mark.'

The pre-season football training soon became that of in-season play. On the pitch, Sonny was determined to further prove himself. He played to his skills and let nothing distract him from his singular purpose. His name was repeatedly on the scoresheet, on occasions he seemed unstoppable, and the fans loved him for it. He would sometimes be asked in post-match interviews where he found such incredible drive and passion for the game; he would answer that he saw it as the only way to win. Privately he was scared it might all be taken away from him overnight, as almost it had been in Benidorm, or perhaps through injury or loss of form. He sent his cv to Boca FC, and researched email addresses of other

Rio clubs – full in the knowledge that he possessed no other skills with which to secure a life there. Boca replied and said that his application was under consideration.

Sonny was invited to model Zastro sports clothing, an upcoming sports brand in Leeds. Soon he could be seen in magazine advertisements and on bus shelter illuminated signboards across the city.

One Sunday evening, Sonny took a call at home from Simmonds.

'Ayup, Sonny, I hope you're wearing all that jazzy Zastro gear!' Simmonds said.

'Never out of it, Mark, they've got spies everywhere! How 'you doing?'

'Doing great! You never sound any different, I love it!... Oh, hang on... Sam says she starting to worry about you – your phone's never engaged!'

'Tell her to ring me now!'

'Got some bits and bobs of news for you,' Simmonds went on buoyantly.

'Oh, yes.'

'Yep, no charges are to be brought against Gilesy, and he's buggered off to live in Canada with his fancy piece.'

'Should have been Benidorm!'

'Fat chance. And Carole's moved down to Devon.'

'Okay.'

'And me and Sam are getting married.'

'Whoa, that was a bit in reverse order, Mark! Congratulations! I'm in shock!'

'Yeah, me too!'

'So, she's the one?'

'No... I am!' Simmonds clowned.

'Well, I'm pleased for you both.'

'We're getting married at Cowton church, and Freddy's best man! Sam's running riot with the guest list, but you're definitely on there! Be good if you could make it, Sonny!'

'Hey, what's this if business, I'll be there, Mark! Cowton church, I think that's great! Where better?'

'That's what we thought. Sam's thinking of trying for a reception deal at the Hall, but she's not sure about that yet. We might take Kev up on his offer with the Feathers.'

'Oh, that'd be brilliant, Mark... in there!'

'It would actually. Kev says he'd give us the kitchen and the bar room all night! I thought Sam would flip over the idea, but no, she's up for it. It'd be a good night!'

'Too right! and all in Cowton,' Sonny rationalised. 'Sounds like a winner to me.'

'Yeah, that's what I reckon. The girls are all off on some spa day thing for the hen do, and me and Freddy have come up with our own version.'

'Oh, no, spare me, I'll go on the girly thing!' Sonny said, his tone ripe with self-preservation.

'No, honestly, we've come up with a cracker! Everyone's onboard with it!'

'Fools... All of them!'

'Jars in the Feathers!' Simmonds revealed. 'That's all I want. How simple is that!'

'A sensible plan! So, when's all this happening?'

'Not sure yet. We're still fixing the dates, but the Feathers can be anytime when everyone can make it. I'll let you know.'

'Well, I suppose I could be dragged into it,' Sonny laboured.

'Good man. Oh, and Janice is on the guest list, and she's coming!'

'Good.'

'I'll give you a call a bit closer up!'

'Okay, Mark. Pleased for you both. My commiserations to Sam!'

At that point in the football calendar, Sonny had become a player highly sought after by other clubs. Still awaiting offer from Boca, though, he had no desire to commit long term to Northern Star, or any other UK club – and neither did Northern Star have any desire to lose him. In frustration he applied to Fluminense, another of the clubs in Rio. The late timing of that application, however, saw him sign up for another season with Northern Star.

Sonny's occupancy of the flat became irksome for other residents of the terraced row when it became generally known where he lived, and fans habitually trailed passed the address hoping to catch sight of him. Previously, he would walk to the football ground but his standing at the club, along with televised post-match analysis, and slick advertising by Zastro which showcased his good looks, changed all that as adoring teenaged girls routinely gathered along the cul-de-sac and openly screamed whenever he appeared.

When complaints of noise and invasion of peace and privacy became prevalent, Sonny knew it was time to move on. His solution was to rent a luxury flat within a gated complex two miles from the football ground, the discreet location, next to open hillside fields, gave freedom from intrusion for himself and fellow residents. On match days he took a taxi to the ground, and for regular weekday training he either walked or caught a bus – none of which troubled him.

One wintry Saturday, late afternoon, Sonny wandered into The Feathers for Simmonds' stag night and joined with the gathering. The expected friends were there, and easy jocularity was given its head. For the first time, Sonny noticed how they had all moved on from looking like youngsters.

For Simmonds' and Samantha's wedding, Sonny bought himself a grey linen suit which he matched to a white shirt and tan shoes. The reception held at The Feathers meant that everyone could walk there from the church – which included Rev Morrison. The only disappointment on the day for Sonny was that Janice couldn't make it; she had sent her apologies, along with her love and best wishes to the happy couple but was unable to be there because she was: *entrenched in Somalia.* Toasts and speeches were made; drinks were bought with abandon and kisses and hugs flowed ever freely as guests made merry until late to music played by the hired DJ.

    A few weeks on from the wedding, Sonny got a text message from Maria to say that she had passed all her exams – and applied to the City Hospital to become a student nurse at their next intake in two months' time. Soon thereafter, in her final term at school and six weeks short of her eighteenth birthday, she messaged further to say that she had been called for interview. To coincide with her birthday, Sonny booked himself on a flight to Rio. He sent the visit dates to Maria, Sra da Silva and Amelia; each welcomed his proposed return, and Amelia booked him a room at the hotel. In that interim period, Maria relayed that she had been selected for a second interview.

    She subsequently texted that her application was successful, and a letter of offer would be sent out by the hospital board pending certainty of funds for her accommodation in the Nurses Home. It was Maria's intention that she paid the fees from her wages. Sra da Silva emailed him and asked that he contact the school by phone at his earliest convenience. Sonny made the call and in their lengthy conversation Sra da Silva expressed delight at Maria's exam results and job offer and said how it was 'quiet practice' for families to transfer the full amount to the hospital for that first year's accommodation – and that such may fast-track their letter of offer – she also expressed doubt that a wage-based source of funding would be acceptable. Sonny immediately made full payment to the hospital, and a week later Maria received her formal letter of employment.

Chapter 9

Sonny's flight from Manchester landed mid-week in Rio on an overcast morning. He made the familiar transfer to The Hotel Cristal and was checked in by Morena – who had no specific welcome for him. From his second-floor room, he rang The School of the New World and spoke to Sra da Silva; they arranged that he would visit the school at ten o'clock the next morning. He then sent two text messages, one to Maria which told of his intended visit, the other to Amelia to say that he had arrived. Within minutes Amelia rang him and suggested they meet up the following afternoon at the Frutos do Mar seafood café bar which sat midway between the hotel and her flat. As he laid on the bed, a towel beneath his wet hair after showering, Maria rang him and squealed a welcome.

    Sonny arrived at Maria's school and was invited by the receptionist to take a seat in an open-floored waiting area that lay out of sight beside the reception office. In what was a pleasantly sunlit space, he sat among perimeter chairs and waited. Within single minutes Maria stood before him and unleashed a broad smile, they hugged, and she broke into freely vented laughter. 'They've put us here,' she said and deftly palmed for him to sit as before, she took an adjacent corner chair, so that they faced each other.

    'I'm just so scared something bad happens now at the last minute,' she said. 'Something that takes it all away!'

    'Well, it won't,' he assured her. 'Like I said before, Maria, we're done with all that. It's our turn now!'

    The pair exchanged hopes and news until the receptionist appeared at the mouth of the waiting area, which signalled the end of their meeting. Maria herself then escorted Sonny to Sra da Silva's office, she knocked on the door on his behalf, supressed a giggle, and left him there to go in on command. Sra da Silva warmly proffered him to sit across her desk and smiled at him. She looked much as before, and he couldn't imagine her any different – or that she be in any other place.

'We always knew Maria had the ability,' Sra da Silva said. 'Which didn't mean, of course, that career opportunities would automatically follow. There would have been girls from relatively wealthy families who also applied for student nurse training, girls from well-funded schools in a city where people will bring influence to bear! I cannot begin to tell you how important this is, not just for Maria, but also the school. Our girls have to outshine the moon to be offered any such placement. That you have funded her Nurses Home accommodation was a hugely important factor. You are quite a special big brother!'

'Maria is quite a special little sister,' he replied easily.

'Well, she's been looking forward to you coming, and she could finally show her excitement, because... unfortunately, not all the girls have been quite as successful, Maria has had to curb her celebrations a little.'

During that meeting, Sra da Silva liberally planned his next visits, to incorporate Maria's last day of school.

Sitting at the hotel bar that evening, Sonny idly watched a televised football game – and felt bolstered that at last he had achieved something for his family.

Frutos do Mar was a popular café bar that had plate-glass windows made bright with cartoon food graphics and was centred among a parade of small general stores in a suburban street. Sonny walked there from the hotel and stood on the pavement at its front as he waited for Amelia. He was suddenly aware that they hadn't met for many months and, despite their updating emails and sporadic phone conversations, felt unsettled in case each thought the other had changed in some way. Minutes later any suchlike concerns fell away when Amelia smilingly walked up to him, and they greeted. Sitting then at a glass-topped table in the café they ordered beer and toasted their reunion.

Over the next few hours, they shared a seafood platter and strolled the nearby seafront as they caught up on each other's lives.

She was much taken with her university course and didn't regret the commitment to become a full-time student, even though her earnings were much reduced through only working part-time at the hotel and that her days were a circular route of work, uni and babysitting. In turn, he told how he had applied without result to Boca and Fluminense football clubs and had signed for another season with Northern Star. She asked about Maria and again delighted over what she already knew were her exam results and job success.

It was early evening when Sonny and Amelia walked to her flat block. At the main entrance they briefly hugged, and he went back to the hotel. In his room, after beer at the bar, he took off his shirt and again caught her cucumber-like fragrance.

Sonny remained in Rio for ten days. During that time, Maria received instruction from the City Hospital that she was to report to the Nurses Home at any ongoing point and be allocated her room before commencement of training due to begin in two weeks. In that interim period, she had to open a bank account for the payment of wages, obtain a certain type of footwear and provide next of kin details. On the rundown to her birthday, Sonny bought a Happy Eighteenth Birthday card which joyously depicted a gold-embossed number eighteen illuminated by a rising sun photograph; he wrote out the card and posted it to her, addressed to the school.

Throughout Sonny's stay, Maria was freely given day release and at eleven o'clock one Monday morning the pair chatted over an early lunch in a city pizza restaurant where she excitedly spoke of her upcoming new life.

'I just can't wait to get my uniform,' she gushed. 'Suki suggested I look in the storeroom for shoes!'

'Who's Suki, one of the teaching staff?'

'Suki da Silva!'

'Suki!' he said, somewhat amused.

'Yes. A bunch of us went to have a look and we found some.'

'We can pick up shoes today if you like,' he offered. 'Everybody else'll have new on, won't they!'

'No! I've cost you enough. I'll buy some with my first wage. I'm looking forward to that as well!'

'Okay, but if we see some! So, what do you think of Suki, then?'

'Oh, she's brilliant! One of the teachers once said that all those lines on her face aren't down to age, they're tear tracks cried for every child who's been through the school. I believe it. That's Suki!'

'So, where's everybody else going?'

'A bit fragmented, really. There's ten of us leaving, altogether. One or two haven't got anything yet, but Suki's letting them stay on until their eighteenth birthday. It's scary! We've all of us come through those years together, it's going to be tough saying goodbye, and to the school as well. We're all dreading it! Why is it always the good things that have to change, Sonny?'

'I wish I knew. All you can do is go forward the best you can. Leaving school is a big thing for anyone, it also means you're not a kid anymore. It's a day you never forget! And for both of us your school is our last link to the old life. So, that's a bagful of emotion for you!'

'It's our final assembly this week,' she said gloomily. 'I'm petrified! I tried to kid myself that I'll breeze it. But I know I won't. We can leave any time after that. Leave! It's been my home for over ten years! I've had ten magical Christmases there; Suki would read us Christmas stories and in the morning we'd all have a present at the end of our bed. How do I just walk away from it all, Sonny – from Sofia and Florence?'

'You take every memory with you, Maria. You never forget, and you never let go.'

She shook her head, eyes closed. 'Was it like that for you?' she asked.

'No. I just wanted it out of the way. For me it meant I was closer to coming home.'

'You had friends, though, didn't you?' she said, as though unable to bear the thought that he hadn't.

'They still are,' he assured her. 'Good friends, too.'

'You don't regret coming back, Sonny, do you?'

'No. This is where I always belonged.'

'And you don't regret finding me?'

'No. The only thing I regret is not being older – back then!'

'Will you come to the school when I leave, help me say goodbye?'

'Of course, I will. And I think this family owes Suki a proper thank you. I thought maybe we could get her something.'

'Yes, that would be nice. We've all done cards already for the teachers.'

'Well, Suki thinks a lot of you,' he said.

'Suki thinks a lot of everyone!'

'Does she have kids of her own?'

'No. Some say that's why she does what she does, but Suki's heart is pure gold, it's what makes her who she is!'

'We could get her something today! And for you I thought a laptop, and get you connected to the internet.'

'Oh, I can't let you do that, Sonny, they're pretty expensive things.'

'Well, everybody else'll have one – so I think you should. You'll need it for studies. And emailing me! What colour would you like?'

She laughed. 'The cheapest colour. Thanks, Sonny.'

That afternoon, they bought a laptop computer – chosen in white by Maria – and set up an internet service payable monthly from Sonny's bank account. They then went to a local branch of his bank and opened an account for her.

'I'm feeling all proper grown up,' she said smiling as they strolled the busy streets. 'Nearly eighteen, laptop, internet... bank account, pleased-with-myself expression!'

'Not done yet!' he said. 'We still need to get you your birthday present!'

'Sonny, you're not serious! You've just bought me a computer!'

'Ah, that's a work-related necessity. No, I thought maybe something in gold!'

'Not on top of everything else, Sonny – Goodness!'

'Well, that's the plan! An eighteenth is super special.'

'Just the shoes... and then no more!'

'In gold! you'd look pretentious!'

They strolled city centre stores where nothing much caught Maria's eye. As they progressed, she paused within the tight confines of a jeweller's shop – drawn to a small gold cross pendant on a fine gold necklace displayed beneath level glass. Sonny thought it the perfect choice and silently looked on in approval as she viewed it around her neck through an obligingly placed mirror. She, too, thought it perfect, he wouldn't let her see the price tag, and the shop carefully box-presented it; they placed it in a small, brown gift bag, put that in a plain white carry bag, and handed it to her, as she radiated delight.

'Now let's get the shoes!' he said when they were back on the street.

'Sonny, I've got the shoes,' she protested in laughter.

'Not new you haven't. And everybody else will have! Can't turn up in old! And then someone else can have the school shoes!'

Twenty minutes later they came out of a shoe store with a big, shiny white bag in which were Maria's new work shoes.

'We're doing well,' he said. 'Let's get Suki's present while we're on a roll!'

At a crystalware shop Maria saw what she believed the ideal gift for Suki da Silva – an oblong crystal block that had at its centre a blood red three-dimensional heart; they looked no further and bought it. For the other members of the teaching and support staff they bought small, cubed boxes of chocolates at a chocolatier's, all colourfully wrapped and tied with teased ribbon.

With only four days left at her school, Maria and Sonny took her packed bags to the three-storey Nurses Home at the City Hospital. There, she was formally inducted by the fifty-something home warden and made aware of the many rules and regulations. The warden then led the way to Maria's allocated room, number twenty-nine, along the first-floor corridor that had numbered doors along both its sides, and where the prevailing smell was that of cleaning product. On that occasion only, Sonny was allowed to accompany Maria and, in the company of the warden, both reined-in obvious glee that such pleasant accommodation was singularly hers – complete with tilt-out window that looked over a residents-only grassy area. Maria was furnished with keys; she left her bags on the bed and the pair made their way to the hospital taxi rank.

'Just leaving my stuff there hammers it home how imminent everything is!' she said as they walked across the neat grounds. 'I feel everything has moved on now... that I have! And I'm not sure I'm ready to let go yet! Do the impossible for me, Sonny... wind us back to the favela, just for five minutes, let me see everyone again and tell them all how much I love and miss them.'

'They know it, Maria, that's how we go forward.'

'I'm eighteen on Wednesday, do you know what I'd like to do on the day?'

'What?'

'Visit mama and Sofia's graves and lay flowers. Do you think we could?'

'I'm sure we could!'

Maria had not been told of Sofia's demise until after the burial and – accompanied by school staff – had only once visited her grave at The Sao Francisco Xavier Public Cemetery, a name with which Sonny felt an uncomfortable familiarity when she told him of it. She could recall at will the six-digit plot number.

Sonny arrived at the school on the morning of Maria's eighteenth birthday, and they met in reception. They hugged, he wished her happy birthday, and she thanked him for the 'lovely card', they then made their way across the grounds, without the jollity of previous occasions, to the waiting taxi. Partway of their thirty-minute journey they stopped at a florist, both selected flowers, and then continued onto the cemetery.

There, they walked through the stone archway of the entrance pavilion and waited at an enquiries window for one of the staff within to address them. Eventually a paunchy middle-aged man in grey jumper came over and offered them a vacant look through the hole-drilled glass window. Sonny held aloft the quoted plot number, as written by himself on hotel note paper, and enquired of its location; as the man stared at it, Sonny decided him to be the same automaton person he had previously spoken with on the phone. Duly directed, Sonny and Maria went in search of their mother's grave in the far reaches of the vast site among a matrix of bare earth pathways that fingered out beyond sculptured gravestones and neat plots, many with fresh or faded flowers, some adorned with teddy bears.

Beyond, in a gently rising field, a myriad of wooden crosses bore vertical numbers, each number hand painted in white. Painstakingly they found their mother's untended grave. Sonny felt a years-long journey had suddenly ended. Maria knelt, spontaneously she kissed her fingertips and pressed them against the wooden cross. 'We're here, Mama, we love you and we never forgot you,' she said. Tears filled her eyes as she looked over the barren plot, Sonny then beside her as he likewise knelt. 'Love you, Mama!' he said. 'I hope you and Paulo and Seve and Sofia and Florence are all together again.' The pair fell silent as each allowed distant memories to vent behind unfocussed eyes. Maria got to her feet, 'Let's clean this up before we lay the flowers,' she said.

They cleared the plot of its weeds and wilted tufts of yellow grass, which Sonny deposited on a large pile of already uprooted growth at the end of a blind path. With that done they laid their flowers.

'We're going to lay flowers on Sofia's grave, mama,' Maria said, 'and find where Florence and Seve and Paulo are, and lay flowers for them!'

The pair let their released emotions bring its own calm as they came away from the grave in pensive silence. As they then stood beside that of Sofia's in a neighbouring field, Maria broke down at the all-too-recent loss of her sister. 'Oh, Sofia,' she wailed, as the wretchedness of deep sorrow drained her of further words.

Sonny didn't want Maria to return to the school in her then state of anguish, and suspected their graveside visit might have been better postponed. He suggested they go on to a Botafogo pizza house that fostered a lively vibe. She welcomed the idea.

'I'm glad we went to the cemetery!' she said as they sat on soft leatherette chairs and looked over colourful menus in the pizza house. 'Somehow, I feel easier now... and I'll always take Sofia's cool hack on how to keep my stuff safe!'

'And how's that?'

'Put it in a shoe,' she said and giggled, 'you jam it in tight with a sock and lay it on a side like it's nothing. It's where I keep my chain,' she pointed at it beneath her t shirt, 'we're not allowed jewellery at school, or the hospital, so that's where it goes when I'm not wearing it, no one would think to look there, would they!'

'No, I suppose not – sounds like good advice!'

And we'll keep our word, won't we, and find where the others are buried?'

'For sure.'

'I don't suppose you've heard anything back yet from those clubs?'

'No. But in truth they couldn't sign me up anyway now, I'm committed for another season in the UK, but I won't give up!' Maria took on a blank expression. 'Just take anything, Sonny – it doesn't have to be football, does it? you could get a job anywhere!'

'I've got to play to my strengths, Maria. Anyway, after this, what say we find a nice bar somewhere and make a proper toast to your eighteenth, and then we'll get you home, you've had a heavy day.

Sonny arrived at the school, Wednesday mid-morning, on Maria's last day there and was shown into Sra da Silva's office by staff-member Paloma. Sra da Silva invited him to be seated across her desk and again expressed pride and delight over Maria's outcome. Maria, she said, was among the few in her year to secure formalised training and believed her to have laid a path for others to tread – and that the school could no longer be seen as a place of minimal education grudgingly funded by a temperamental government.

'I think the school can take credit for her achievements,' Sonny readily acknowledged. 'And I know she's been happy here. She has often spoken of your kindness, Sra da silva, and I would like to say thank you, for that, we are both very grateful to you.'

'Thank you.'

'How is she this morning?' he asked.

Oh, very, very emotional, as they all are when they leave. You never hear the piano at final assembly, only sobbing. Maria is a truly delightful girl; I predict she will be a very caring nurse with a long and fulfilling career in front of her. She is all packed and ready to leave, she just needs to call by here first and then you may collect her from reception.' Sra da Silva stood up and offered a hand. 'I wish you both every success,' she said. 'It's seldom I take pleasure when one of my girls leave!'

Sonny engaged the hand and again thanked her for all the years that she and everyone at the school had looked after Maria.

Maria came away from Sra da Silva's office as Sonny waited at reception. Helped along by half a dozen equally sobbing friends she looked exhausted; her face shiny with wiped-away tears as fresh ones spilled, she all but collapsed into him in despair. He took the singular holdall from her numb grasp, she hugged each of her friends and with Sonny's arm around her, the pair walked out of the school to the waiting taxi. As they passed through the gateway she turned around and quietly said, 'Bye, Florence, bye, Sofia, bye everyone.'

At the Nurses Home door, the journey done mostly in silence save for Maria's quiet sobs through escaped tears, he handed her the holdall.

'Do you want me to come round tomorrow?' he asked.

She nodded; eyes closed. 'Yes... I'll be able to talk better then. I'll ring you. Thanks, Sonny,' she almost whispered, and let herself into her new home.

Sitting at the hotel bar, over beer, Sonny contemplated the day – and believed that a significant upturn had been made in the fortunes of his family.

In his room the next morning, Sonny answered his mobile phone to Maria; from that call, he walked the near-mile distance to the City Hospital Main Entrance and waited on an outside bench. Maria soon appeared; she looked refreshed and smiled broadly at him.

'Come on,' she said as she practically scooped him up. 'It's roast beef dinner today. And I'm starving!'

They sat at a laminate-topped table in the expansive Food Hall of the hospital, where square pillars and heavy-duty carpet tiles diffused the hubbub of voices and clatter of cutlery from staff and visitors alike.

'So how was your first night in the bad girls home?' he asked lightly as his knife went through roast potatoes.

'Scary! I laid awake listening to nothing for most of it, just a few doors closing. I've never had my own room before.

'No, I don't suppose you have.'

'And I couldn't help thinking about my empty bed at the school – and the girls still waiting to leave – that must be the worst!'

'Yes,' he agreed, as though he understood.

'Amelia sent me a lovely birthday card to the Home!' she said. 'That was nice of her! Say thank you, for me, will you?'

'Oh, right, yes, I will. Mail already!'

'And I got the laptop up and running. It works brill!'

'Good. I'm just glad you knew how to set it up! So, have you got internet okay?'

'Yeah, it was straightforward, really.'

'That's handy, because the only net I know anything about is where a football goes!'

'Ah... different hard drive.'

'I see! So, how's everybody else seem?'

'I haven't really seen anyone much to talk to. I think it's a fairly big intake, though, because there's been people arriving all the time this morning, doors banging and *love you, mama,* stuff going on. One girl asked me if I knew where the laundry room was! I mean, who arrives needing to do laundry? but then I thought she probably just wanted someone to talk to.'

He nodded at her assessment. 'It's good it's not just you, though, that's fresh in.'

'Yes, it helps. But I'm not going to go burning up to people trying to be everybody's new best friend!'

He knew what she meant. 'No,' he said. He wanted to ask about her farewell meeting with Suki da Silva, but feared she might become upset, and so didn't. Maria herself raised the subject.

'Suki loved the heart block,' she said. 'She said for me to say thank you, she figured your hand was in it!'

He smiled. 'Oh, I've put you some money in your bank account, he said casually. 'Keep you going until payday.'

'Thanks, Sonny, but you really shouldn't, I have to make this work on my own!'

'Yeah, I know. It's just to cover a few canteen dinners – maybe even a pudding!'

'Thanks for all this,' she said. 'I wouldn't be here if it weren't for you.'

'That's alright. Anyway, don't blame me, it was you who passed the exams!'

'You fly out soon, don't you!'

'Saturday, and I shall leave you in peace tomorrow! so I'll see you when I'm next over. I've got my own seat on the plane now!' he goofed. 'The pilot comes over and says, *Yo, Sonny!*" They laughed away the moment, helped along by the unrelenting background noise of the Food Hall.

An hour later the pair stood at the Main Entrance of the hospital.

'I'm not going to blow this chance, Sonny!' she said. 'I owe it to all of us!'

'Keep safe, Maria. I'll be back whenever I can. Any problems, just let me know.'

They hugged, she again with tears forming, and he walked back to the hotel.

Amelia came on duty in the early part of that evening and over the reception desk Sonny told her how focussed and happy Maria was to begin her new life – and relayed her thank-you for the birthday card.

'Pleased for her,' Amelia said. 'So, what are you going to do with your last day tomorrow?'

'I know! where's it gone?' he complained. 'We haven't even been to the beach this time!'

'No, you're like some shooting star thing, in and gone!'

'A shooting star for Boca would be good! I thought I'd give them another ring tomorrow, actually; it might nudge them along a bit. Let them see I'm serious.'

'Good idea, I think you should.'

'Yes.'

He remained at the desk, and they further chatted but he didn't want to monopolise her whilst she was on duty and so came away when new guests arrived.

Sonny decided that to simply ring Boca FC might be to invite an all too easy shrug-off from some nameless person on the other end of a corporate phone. Instead, mid-morning, he took a taxi to the mile away Boca FC Headquarters and Training Ground and stood at an open-fronted reception desk in a broad foyer, accessed off the street through a wall of hinged glass doors. Immediately, from a well-staffed clerical pool, a smiling young woman came over to him from her workstation. He explained his visit and she invited him to take a seat along an empty wall-side bank of dated leatherette chairs that were set out alternately in the club colours of orange and white – he chose white as she made a mobile phone call on his behalf.

Fifteen minutes later, an athletic-looking middle-aged man, who's precisely cropped, silvered hair borrowed a hint of purple from his tracksuit, strode up to the desk and spoke with the woman. He made his way over to Sonny and without formality sat beside him with a deft twist that allowed face to face conversation. He introduced himself as Leon, assistant head coach, and asked how he may be of help. In that just-arrived waft of track suit, Sonny stated his case as Leon listened without interruption. Leon said that he had no personal knowledge of Sonny's earlier application, and for him to leave contact details at reception and follow it up with an email to Alberto Ferreira the club manager. Ferreira, it seemed, wouldn't be on site for the next two days but Leon said he himself would pre-empt the email when he next saw him. Sonny came away from the complex unsure if he'd made any real progress but nonetheless glad that he'd made his approach.

Back at the hotel, he went down to the gym, did a workout, and then packed his bag in readiness for his flight the next day. Early that evening, over the reception desk, Amelia smiled at him as he stood before her, his expression empty and fixed.

'You all set, then?' she asked.

'Amelia, I seem to be permanently all set, I'm in a loop of all set!'

'At least this time you've got Maria sorted before you go!'

'Yes, and to be fair I'm proper chuffed about that!'

'Well, there you are, then. No need to sulk!'

They both laughed at her admonishment – him a little sheepish.

'I think this coming year's going to be a big hitter for us both,' he said. 'You've got your degree exam, and I've got to make myself welcome on a football pitch.'

'Do you want me to book you a taxi for tomorrow?'

'Yeah, that would probably be best, ta, Amelia. It'll give me a time to aim for! Let's keep in touch!'

'Yes. Let's,' she agreed.

The following morning Sonny checked out of the hotel and again began a journey back to the UK.

Chapter 10

Sonny began pre-season training with Northern Star. There were a few new faces in the changing room, reinforced dogma was bandied about, and all-around hectoring threats made that the club wouldn't carry passengers. By then, he had heard it all before and knew that scored goals trumped anything said – and that those who did the hectoring were not the paymasters.

When the season got under way, Sonny set about enhancing his credentials as foremost striker for the club – he didn't disappoint, and pressure further mounted for him to sign a long-term contract. Emails from Maria said how she was loving nurse training and that everything was going: *really well*. Similarly, Amelia told how she was: *fully engrossed* with her university course and confessed to being worried that had he gained a placement with Boca they couldn't have spent as much time together as either would have liked.

One mid-week evening, Sonny took a call at home from Simmonds.

'Hia, Sonny,' Simmonds said in uplifted tone.
'Now then, Mark, how's things?'
'Soon to change, I think. And I'm getting all the blame!'
'What have you done, Mark?'
'Ah well, such explicit detail I couldn't possibly go into, but there is to be much disruption in the house, you know, the kind a baby always brings!'
'Whoa, great news, Mark! congratulations. I bet Sam's cock-a-hoop!'
'Yes, that was part of it! So anyway, she's had that baby shower thing that they do, and I thought, right, not to appear without couth myself, I'll shout up my own little wet in the Feathers, nothing outrageous just a few jars. It'd be great if you could make it, Sonny!'
'When?'
'Ah, that's the thing – two weeks on Saturday, seven-ish!'

'If I can make it, Mark, I will!'
'I'll settle for that! Kev reckons the next time you come in he's going to get one of those blue plaques for the pub!'
'I'll try, Mark, is all I can say!'
'Be good to see you again, Sonny!'
'And you, Mark. Give my congrats to Sam.'

Two weeks later, Sonny, fresh off the field of a won game in which he featured largely, walked into The Feathers at seven thirty on a Saturday evening for Simmonds' celebratory drink. Already gathered in the bar were friends of old – Sonny soon in their midst and noisy greetings exchanged. Banter, football talk, inane jokes about nappies and sleepless nights all featured prominent until old Justin purposefully ambled from his lounge table and stood beside Sonny.

'Sad news about Mr Johnson,' old Justin said to him in the paused jocularity.
Sonny's stunned gaze told how he knew nothing of it.
'Died on Thursday night!' old Justin said. 'I thought you'd have heard!'
Sonny was without response and stared at him as the group silently took on a collective look of dismay. Old Justin said nothing further and went back to his table.
'Sonny, I'm sorry, mate,' Simmonds said, 'We'd no idea!'
'No, I know you didn't, Mark. Just give me a minute, I need to make a phone call.' With that, Sonny withdrew from the group.
Minutes later Simmonds went out to the back yard where Sonny had gone to absorb the news and collect himself.
'You okay, Sonny?' Simmonds asked.
'Yeah, I'm alright. He was practically my dad, Mark! Always the good ones, isn't it!'
Simmonds unashamedly hugged him. 'He was proud of you, Sonny!'
'I hope so. Come on, let's go in, I don't want to sour the night. I want to hear about go-faster prams... happy stuff!'

On their way back through the crowd they paid no heed to old Justin's targeted stare from the lounge. Sonny wasn't about to let such terrible news impinge on the celebration of new life yet to come into the joyous world of Mr and Mrs Mark Simmonds.

Two days later, Sonny got a phone call from Simmonds, he'd asked him to ring if he heard news of Mr Johnson's funeral arrangements; Simmonds relayed that the service would be held in a week's time at the crematorium at Mr and Mrs Johnson's new location. Sonny went out and bought a black tie.

On the day of the funeral, Sonny went by taxi to the thirty-mile away crematorium. He had expected mourners to be few, given that the Johnson's were private people, but so large was the attendance that some listened to the service from the broad, entrance corridor as overspill. Sonny had already followed others into the main hall and stood wall-side, closer to the front than he felt comfortable with. Mrs Johnson, sitting along the first row of bench seats remained still throughout, she didn't look around and her shoulders were frequently overlaid by the comforting arms of others. When the service was over, everyone filed outside into a gardened area at the rear where people formed themselves into little clusters as they stood and chatted. Sonny recognised an elderly group among them from Cowton, they smiled at him and drew him into their company, so that he felt better at ease. When a sudden gap opened between those assembled, he found himself in the direct gaze of Mrs Johnson.

'Sonny!' she said, as though in enormous relief.
He immediately went to her; she lifted both her hands to his face, and he lightly hugged her.

'I'm so sorry, Aunt Mo,' he said.

'Oh, he would be proud that you're here,' she said. 'He followed your games all the time, he'd say, *He's done it again has our Sonny!*"

'Seems half the county loved him, Aunt Mo. What a marvellous service for him!' He almost said: *send-off* – but feared the brutality of the words and was glad that he hadn't.

'He was loved and respected by many,' she agreed solidly. 'It's wonderful to see you again, Sonny – and look at you, so tall!'

'It was your dinners, Aunt Mo, that's what did it!' he said smiling.

'Did you ever to go back to Brazil?' she asked.

'I did! Quite a few times, and I found family!'

'Oh, I'm so pleased! it did make me cry when you got upset – and I had no answers to give.'

'You and Uncle Phil gave me all the answers I ever needed, Aunt Mo, you gave me everything!'

He'd wanted to ask what she knew of him being brought to England as a child, but the day wasn't about him. Instead, he spoke warmly about his time spent with her and Mr Johnson – and let her introduce him to as many others as she wished.

Early into the football season, Sonny received a text message from Janice which said she would like to meet with him. He immediately rang her, but the call didn't connect so he texted back that he would love for them to get together, and included his email address, should her phone be the problem. Within the hour, he received her email to say that she was in Lusaka, she would be home in two days' time and would contact him then.

When, after two days, Janice rang him she sounded tired, her voice perhaps thickened with the onset of a cold or from airplane cabin air, nonetheless, they arranged to meet the following night at The Reindeer pub barely a mile from her parents' house.

Sonny tidied the flat throughout in case he and Janice moved on from The Reindeer and she stayed over. He changed clothes twice before settling on a black and white checked shirt coupled with dark blue jeans, and on what was a wet Tuesday evening, took a taxi to the twelve miles away Reindeer pub. The Reindeer was generally considered a well-to-do country-style inn and sat on the moneyed side of Tanlow, next to open fields, Sonny had always thought it a place where a booking was essential in the restaurant and certain tables were always reserved.

The venue suited him because he was less likely to be recognised, and those who did – unlikely to stare or monopolise him as might be the case elsewhere; it had been some time since he and Janice had been in each other's company, and he wasn't about to share her. He sat at a corner table, lager before him, in the fuchsia tartan carpeted front bar and waited. When Janice appeared, he was shocked. She had put on considerable weight, and her choice of kaftan-style dress did little to hide the fact; her face felt too moist for comfort when he stood up and kissed her on the cheek – her overdone scent that of rose.

'Janice, it's great to see you again,' he said. 'How's it going?'

'Oh Sonny, you too, yes, really good! I think I've seen you every day since I got back! Everywhere I look, there's Sonny beaming at me from bus shelters! How did this all happen I asked myself. Is this the same Sonny Lopez who was my so adoring boyfriend at school?'

She sat across from him and dropped her African-themed fabric handbag onto the chair beside her.

'It's great to see you again,' she said. 'You look fantastic. Please tell me you're not in love with anyone else. I'll sue!' She grinned at him, and he wondered if she'd already been drinking.

'No. No one since you!' he obliged, smilingly.

'Oh, that's so sweet. And how's life at the top, then?'

'Ah, you'd need to ask someone who knows,' he said. 'Maybe a jetsetter, someone who's just flown in from Lusaka! yeah, they'd know!'

'Oh, don't talk to me about Lusaka! I seem to spend half my life there dispatching out aid when I'm supposed to be in Geneva driving things forward from there!'

'Well... let me get you a drink?'

'A large dry white, please, Sonny, it's been a long day!'

He went to the bar and came back with a stemmed, bulbous glass of dry white wine.

'Ta, Sonny,' she said, as he placed it before her.

'So, when did you get back, then?' he asked.

'Yesterday... the day before! It's all melded into one really bad jetlag!'

'And is it all going to plan... you know...?'

'If there's a plan of any description, Sonny, then no one's blue-printed it to me!'

'But you're happy with it... the job, and everything?'

'I get a little stressed when I have to do other people's work for them and still be expected to do my own! But hey-ho, if that's what it takes to keep half the world fed!'

He looked into her pink-veined eyes, at a blank expression that seemed devoid of awareness – and at her round-tipped nose, the only remnant characteristic of the Janice he had been so in love with.

'Anyway,' she said, 'I want to hear your news! The last time I saw you, you were getting ready to go back to Rio and seek out family. And I've heard nothing from you since – naughty boy! Come on – spill!'

Sonny went on to explain all that he had encountered in Rio. He couldn't have made his story any more concise but found himself staring into non comprehending eyes that increasingly struggled to stay open.

'Tell you what, Janice,' he eventually said, 'why don't we leave this for another night and get you home in a taxi?'

'Okay,' she accepted tiredly, her drink untouched. 'Soz, Sonny!'

'Since when, did we ever say sorry to each other, Janice,' he said kindly. He went up to the bar and from a pinned-up list of taxi companies, made the call.

As their taxi waited outside her parents' house, Sonny and Janice slowly walked as one up the garden path to the front door; she mumbled a further apology, he saw her inside, went back to the taxi and continued his journey home. Sitting then on the sofa, beer in hand, he reflected on their short evening. He had looked forward to seeing Janice again – Janice that so special girl who was the first he'd ever kissed and made love with – not the one who had turned up that night.

Later that same week as Sonny idled at home one evening, Janice rang him. 'Sonny, I am just so glad you picked up!' she said. 'I wouldn't have blamed you if you hadn't! I can't apologise enough for the other night, I was so completely out of it, and thank you for getting me home, I'll be honest, it's all a blur. I felt dreadful when mum told me the state I was in!'

'Janice, I'm just glad you're okay,' he said.

'I'm totally fine, thank you. Much in disgrace, I know, but fine. Unfortunately, I got the call today to fly back out. I was hoping to make it up to you, can we meet when I'm next over?'

'Of course, we can!' he wanted to add that she lay off the sauce a bit – but didn't.

'Thanks, Sonny, I know I'm a rubbish friend! Promise you don't hate?'

'Promise forever!' he assured her.

'Thanks, Sonny. Bye for now.'

'See you next time, Janice.'

'Love you, Sonny.'

'Love you too, Janice.'

The line went dead.

'Oh, Janice!' he murmured as he put down the phone; it pained him that she had so quickly let go of her younger self. He wanted to revisit a certain grassy bank at their old school and see if she was still there.

Chapter 11

Sonny was called from training into Lou Gomero's office. Frustrated at Sonny's unwillingness to commit to a meaningful term of contract, Gomero put to him an updated five-year deal with a substantial financial package. Sonny immediately saw how the deal would easily outweigh anything Boca FC might offer, by then, though, he was twenty-two years old and the prospect of being twenty-seven and still not resident in Rio troubled him more than he wanted to contemplate. It didn't help that he'd heard nothing from Boca despite that he'd sent them his cv as advised by assistant head coach Leon.

Embarrassed that he'd continually declined everything offered, he came clean to Gomero about his reason for doing so. Briefly thereafter, management silence ensued. Northern Star then suggested that they contact Boca FC on his behalf and establish what, if any, their wishes might be regarding his prospects with them. They would also amend their own contract to that of three years duration and asked that if Boca didn't make him an offer before the following season, that he then sign the revised deal. Sonny accepted, much in the hope that Boca would be spurred into action once officially approached. In addition to this, he somewhat gingerly asked if he could personally contact Flamengo FC, another of the Rio clubs, to which Northern Star agreed. Flamengo responded to him with a generic email acknowledgement.

A week later Sonny was told in Gomero's office that Boca had expressed their gratitude at being consulted but were fully committed to their existing players and trainees and could not make any offer of employment to him at that time. The news shocked him in waves of disbelief and resentment: *Had they not seen his performances? Could they not see what an asset he would be?* In the changing rooms, he felt the eyes of everyone upon him, eyes that mocked through condemnation at what they saw as his wish not to be there. Any behind-the-scenes discussions were supposed to be confidential – in reality, such was rarely the case, as proven when fans held up a placard during a match that read: Rio 1, Sonny 0.

Sonny had never been exposed to ridicule. He'd known racial abuse and jealousies manifested across many years, but derision was something new to him. He perceived that it lay behind every smile and glance of those he encountered, and that every observed conversation was about him. He recognised, though, that neither self-pity nor anger would further his cause and so turned to that which would – he blanked his mind to the provokers and scored goals as though for fun. The issue was soon dropped by those who sought to criticise, lest they themselves become a target of it as the club pulled away on the leader board. The club itself put no pressure on him, they told him to continue as normal and to let them know in his own time how he wished to proceed beyond that season – and that many options were available.

A few weeks later, with numerous games yet to be played, Sonny got an email at home one evening from Boca FC. It said they had revaluated their position regarding a placement for him and would shortly put forward an offer. Elated at the communication he marched the flat, triumphant that he would endure no more wasted hope and that he was going back to Rio to assume his own country as a determined and long-overdue expat.

That next morning, Sonny was called into Gomero's office. Gomero had himself received a similar email to his, and the two men sat easy across his desk and openly discussed the possibility of Sonny leaving Northern Star. Gomero told him they were loath to lose him but would fully cooperate with any reasonable request from Boca, such as fitness and medical reports and goal form. The pair mutually agreed that until more was known they would keep the matter tight between themselves. Sonny thanked him and resumed training where his summons to the office hadn't gone unnoticed by others. He felt sure Gomero would maintain confidentiality but felt equally sure that word of it would soon echo throughout the stands.

Frequent telephone and email communications took place between Northern Star and Boca FC; with the result that Boca made a formal offer for Sonny to commence with them in four months' time. Their financial renumeration package, as Sonny expected, was far less than his current wage but he was untroubled by it and trusted to his own footballing skills that the initial figures were transient.

The deal would stand good on the basis that he remained uninjured or otherwise unimpaired for the remainder of his commitment games in the UK and that he arrived intact at Boca FC on the specified date. With news of it then publicly known a small element of disgruntled fans on the Northern Star terraces booed whenever he got the ball in a match, but he knew how to render them silent – he scored goals, and his name held good. Messages in support of him were even held aloft, and rhythmic chants of: 'Come back, Sonny, Sonny, come back' would break out on his every goal.

With club agreements fully in place, Sonny emailed his news to Maria and Amelia; they immediately replied, and each expressed their joy at his achievement. Maria, at that point, was nearing the end of her first year of training and said there was already much talk of flat sharing between students. Amelia, for her part, was very much: *head-down,* as she went toward her final exam in four months' time. She confessed to being a little stressed over it, worried that she might fail and have to re-sit, even though she was on top of her studies; she said it was a further spur for her that he'd come good with his: *thing.*

So that he didn't overlook or alienate Flamengo FC Sonny sent a polite email thanking them for their earlier message but would like to withdraw his application. In return he received an automated response, followed by a personal email in which they thanked him for advising them of such and wished him every success for the future.

At home one rainy Saturday night, Sonny received a call from Simmonds, in The Feathers with Freddy, and told the happy news that Samantha had given birth to a boy, who they named Cameron. Sonny loudly congratulated him in laddish manner. They concluded how Samantha might have timed things better so that others of them could have made the pub to celebrate.

The following week, Sonny got a phone call from Janice. He thought she sounded more like the Janice of old than her last manifestation in the previous year. He welcomed the call, and they arranged that she would come to the flat on Sunday for coffee.

On what was a sunlit Sunday morning, Sonny gazed out through his lounge room window which overlooked the gateway to the complex and waited for Janice to arrive. When she pulled up, driving her mother's white Mercedes, he pressed an opaque button on the wall-mounted annunciator panel inside his own front door, and let her through the then sliding open, metal gate. She parked in his unused numbered parking bay as he went down to the communal entrance; he stepped outside, and they hugged on the forecourt. Whatever weight she had previously and uncharacteristically gained was completely gone, her eyes were bright, and she exuded a keenness as she smiled broadly at him.

'Hi, Sonny,' she said. 'Ta for not making every plausible excuse not to be here!'

'Hi, Janice,' he said, and let her remark pass over him as though it hadn't registered. 'You look fantastic!' he added.

'Thank you. And you're looking outrageously fit!'

'Come on up, kettles on!'

He thought that to use the lift would have been both pretentious and unnecessary, instead he led the way up a carpeted concrete stairwell to the first floor, and along a silent corridor that had maroon, flowered wallpaper its length.

'What a lovely place,' she said, as they entered his flat where sunlight gave a welcoming glow.

'Yes, it suits,' he agreed in understated manner.

He made them both coffee from the freestanding capsule machine and they sat across a granite-topped table in the lounge window. She centred her cup on a cork coaster that had a faded, hunt-scene depiction, and looked over at him.

'Well, I made a big mistake, didn't I!' she said abstractly.

'Oh, would you rather have had tea?' he clowned, more to diffuse her discomfort over whatever was to come.

She smiled. 'You always were the least judgemental of anyone, Sonny. I meant, actually, me and that big-wiz charity job!'

'Sounds like you're no longer with them?'

'No, I'm not. And I've got my sanity back to prove it!'

'O-kay! so, it didn't work out, it's not the end of the world,' he remarked cheerfully.

'No, and at least I saw it early on.'

'Was it that bad?'

'It was like something out of a film. You know, where some naïve young thing gets drawn into a corrupt place step by step until they're part of it themselves. They offered up this fabulous ideology where you'd really be making a difference to something worthwhile. And then you see them... nice salaries, expenses and limousines, everyone on coke all the time, backhanders all over the place, and nothing else matters. They told me it's the only way to cope with the pressure, that I was blinkered by soft western thinking and woolly values and knew nothing of the real world. You know, I actually believed them too. Right up until I went to one of their targeted hotspots in Africa, we went straight from the airport to a top hotel nowhere near any area of concern – and we stayed right there. Then all these government bigwigs came to see us. I thought I'd be hearing logistics and water purification plants, but all I saw was handshakes where no one got anything unless they already had the power to take it. *Well, that's another visit done, guys,'* she mimicked, *'Good job! everyone back on the plane to Zurich now, for the after party!'*

Himself aware of how such things worked, Sonny let his gaze fall to the table.

'That's not all of them, though, Janice. They help kids living in some pretty bad places. I saw it myself way back, how they looked away from anyone in a uniform, they were almost as scared as I was. I never understood it. I just saw them as taking us away from home to somewhere we didn't want to go. And all the time they were trying to protect us! We were just simply in someone's way, and they wanted rid!'

'If I'd been given half a chance to do anything constructive like that, I'd have stayed with it.' She affirmed. 'But it wasn't like that for me, no one even spoke in those terms! Someone told me I was only there to raise the female quota and bring down the average age for the sake of the company's woke profile!'

'So, what are you going to do now?' he asked.

'At the moment, I'm working a till at Rootcropper in Danby, but I've applied to a farming research company as a project developer. They seem a decent outfit. They're based over here working with an agricultural college trying to come up with different grains that'll grow best in certain parts of the world. I quite fancy it!'

'Good for you!' he congratulated. 'You never were a quitter, Janice!'

'Yes... or is it no? Anyway, I've come to apologise for being such a cow!'

He laughed. 'I'm just glad to have you back, Janice, no apology needed here.'

'And I'm told you're leaving us – you finally got the call!'

'I am, I have! Only four years late but never mind.'

'Right, so you went back, you were hoping to find family, and I know you tried to tell me before, but how did you get on? And don't miss anything out – like the last time!'

He again told her of his visits to Rio, of how Maria was now a student nurse, and of the loss of their other two sisters, to which she closed her eyes and expressed heartfelt condolences – and he told of his struggles to find a football club there that would take him on but had finally managed to do so. They then talked and laughed at length over things familiar, of how their schooldays seemed so long-ago, of Simmonds happily married and with a new-born boy.

'It was just so written that contentment was always going to be his, wasn't it?' she remarked. 'Has he ever said a bad word about anyone?'

'You know, I don't think he has. Oh yes, there was that thing about you!'

'Shut up! I love the name, Cameron!' She giggled. 'I want one, a baby Cameron. What about you?'

'Yeah... one day.'

'Will he be a footballer?'

'Mm, there's worse things for sure.'

'I want a girl first... Annabel. She'll be a scientist,' she decided.

When the outdoor gloom became evident in the reflecting-back windows, she stood up, arched her back, and said, 'Right, well, I'd best go, you'll have the neighbours online! You make a nice coffee, Sr Lopez. It's very decadent of you!'

'We're open again tomorrow about four if you fancy another one,' he offered brightly.

'I can squeeze you in Tuesday, and I don't do washing up!'

'Me neither. Tuesday, then!'

He walked with her down to the car.

'Thanks for coming, Janice,' he said fondly.

'That's alright, it would lift any girl's day... doing coffee in the lair of a famous footballer. Why, I barely got out unsullied!'

'Well, there's always Tuesday's chance!'

Back in the flat, in uplifted mood, Sonny cleared away the two used cups. Sitting at the computer, he read emails, among them a request forwarded by Northern Star from the parents of a thirteen-year-old boy who had suffered a broken leg playing football at school, asking if he would kindly send: *Greg, a Get-Well-Soon card*. To simply intend to do so, Sonny knew, might be to overlook it, happy for the distraction, he sought out a pen from a kitchen drawer, jotted down the details, and went out to the nearby newsagent shop where he bought the card with envelope, and a stamp. At the lottery podium, he wrote an encouraging message in the card, signed it with untypical flourish, and posted it on his way home. Within the half-hour of his absence an email had come through from Maria which told that she had just heard his name mentioned on the radio as: *an exciting new signing for Boca FC*.

Late Tuesday afternoon, Sonny pressed to open the gate of the complex in response to Janice's in-car phone call to say that she was almost there. She parked-up as before and they again came together on the forecourt.

'Hi, Sonny,' she said, and delivered him a solid kiss to the cheek.

'Hi, Janice, how are you?'

'Buzzin! got an interview for that job!'

'Whoa, sounds promising!'

'Yes... I really want it now!'

They went up to the flat and sat on tall stools at the brightly lit breakfast bar – the lounge window table without appeal against the day's wilting light.

'So, when's the interview?' he asked as he made coffee.

'Monday!'

'Ah, you'll be swotting up, then!'

'I don't do swotting up, dear – intrinsic research... and then it'll be mine – all mine because I'm such a swot!'

'And so where would you be based if you got it?'

'York... quite commutable!'

'For sure! Sounds good.'

'Yes, could be both of us on a fresh start, you all set for yours?'

'Janice, I'm still coming to terms with me going back there for keeps! The only thing I know is I can't have it both ways – the heart in one place and the boots in another! I've lived that for years and it doesn't work. I've just got to go with a one-way ticket and a one-way mentality!'

She nodded, and remarked, 'Good focus.'

'Oh, and then score lots of goals!' he added.

She laughed, and he felt reminded of her confident charm and breezy appeal. Sitting then on the sofa, soon in silence, they leaned into one another as heavy rain let loose against the windows.

At nine o'clock that evening, they kissed goodnight at the front door of the complex. With one of his coats held over her head, in defiance of wildly blown rain, she hurried to the car, and he waved into diffused taillights as she drove away.

Again, happy in each other's company, Sonny and Janice seamlessly resumed their long-standing relationship. She was successful with her job application and the pair celebrated such with an evening meal at a steakhouse pub. They got back to his flat at eleven o'clock and she stayed the night.

Janice began her new job with an agricultural college near York and took up the staff accommodation offered with it. Despite little interest in football, she periodically attended weekend Northern Star home games, after which she and Sonny would return to his flat and resume their normality, as typically they laid entwined on the sofa. She loved her job, and he would keenly listen when she spoke of her working week and its objectives; it enabled him to hear about a world beyond football – where he himself played no part and could voice detached opinion without need of validity or merit.

Chapter 12

Just home from work one Friday, Sonny got a text message from Simmonds to let him know that Kev at The Feathers had planned a: *footy with tapas and raffle night,* to coincide with a televised England game to be played at the end of the football season. The match was a weekend friendly against Brazil, and Kev hoped to make it an event night in the pub which would raise funds for a local charity; any raffle prize donations would be welcome. An hour later Janice arrived at the flat and Sonny told her of it as he busied over mulligatawny soup and a twin packet of part-baked bread for them both; she read the message from his phone, sitting at the breakfast bar.

'Should be a good night,' she said as she put down the phone. 'Are you going?'

'Yeah, I'll go. What about you, you fancy it?'

'Yes. Chance to see everybody again – why not. Might even be able to hear one another if you lot can keep the noise down!'

As end of season approached, Sonny and Janice sprawled on his sofa, and he commented that he was just six weeks shy of his start date with Boca FC.

'It's finally happened for you, hasn't it?' she said. 'No dry run this!'

'No.'

'Any second thoughts?'

'A few jitters. I can't pull back the missing years, but I can sure lay claim to all the rest!'

'And what if you could pull back the missing years?'

'I don't regret anything of here, Janice,' he asserted, 'the Johnson's, our school years, the friends, football... You!'

'Oh, well that's okay then. As long as we haven't completely wasted your time!'

He understood the depth of the moment and that to make light of it would have been hurtful and shallow. He also understood how much he would soon be leaving behind, and how the component parts of what he always believed his interim life had protected and cherished him throughout the years.

'I'm nervous, Janice, I admit it. Who will I be in Rio, not the same streetwise kid I was, for sure. I can't even be certain I'll fit in! I'll have to be there two years before I equal my time here! I might not even sound or think like them anymore! And supposing I don't cut it as a player – get booed off the park, what will I be then?'

'It'll all come together in its own sweet time, Sonny. Don't rush things. What do you need to do about this place?'

'Just give a month's notice. I'll do it tomorrow. You never know, I might even see some bond money back if I leave it tidy enough.'

'I'll help,' she offered.

He pulled her tightly to him with an overlaid arm and kissed her forehead.

'Crawler!' she accused. 'You'll have to have a send-off night, you know, a few drinks, a few hugs, that sort of thing!'

'Mm, not sure about that.'

'Of course, you will!' she protested. 'You can't just go sneaking off! *Where's Sonny these days?*' she mimicked of imagined others, *'Oh, haven't you heard, he's gone to live in Rio. Didn't he tell you!'*

'I suppose,' he accepted. 'It's just seems a bit me, me, me!'

'Well, it's a bit you, you, you, who's going! No – you can't not do it. I don't want people speaking ill of you! How about the Feathers?' she suggested. 'That would work!'

'Yeah, that could be okay, so long as Kev doesn't start selling tickets for it, you know what he's like! Anyway, I say we go over the road to that Italian place before I agree to any more of your dubious schemes!'

'I've brought sandwiches – but okay, then!'

With the club's approval, Sonny donated a Northern Star shirt signed by the team for The Feathers footy cum charity event and he and Janice took it across there one mid-week evening. The shirt, then on display behind the bar, was deemed the star prize and generated much interest which ensured healthy raffle ticket sales.

On the night itself, Janice drove them both to The Feathers where they engaged with welcoming friends; Kev leaned over the bar and offered him an outstretched hand.

'Thanks, Sonny,' he said. 'And don't you go and win that shirt tonight, or there'll be 'ell on in here! Your first drink's on the house – pick your tap... hot or cold!'

Shortly, Simmonds and Samantha came in and added further of the noisy gathering.

'How's baby Cameron?' Janice asked Samantha.

'Sleeping like a baby,' Samantha said. 'And that way mum can watch all her programmes, and I don't get a right rollocking when we get back! The girls are all sat in there if you want to go through – leave these woodentops to their football?'

Janice laughed. 'A good idea!' she said and followed her through to the lounge room.

As though the sudden presence of both girls had Freddy aware that Sonny and Simmonds were in the bar, he swapped rooms and stood with them. 'Ayup,' he said, 'thank goodness you're here, got me away from that lot – those girls can talk!' Simmonds cocked a sideways glance at Freddy, and said to Sonny, 'Helen Robertshaw's got him right where she wants him!'

'No, she hasn't,' Freddy wailed. 'I just like everything kept sweet, that's all.'

Behind the bar, Kev pushed down a mid-air thumb in support of Simmonds' remark, which had Sonny laugh.

To evenly format the evening, Kev drew the raffle prizes before the live football began – the tapas supper scheduled to coincide with half-time. Soon, bottles of wine, gift baskets of soap packed in straw, boxes of chocolates and weathered-looking perfumes were bandied about to shouts of: *fix,* and: *swap yah!* When Freddy won yet again, booing broke out as he tauntingly held aloft a bottle of premium vodka.

In the lounge room, old Justin had before him a long strip of tickets laid across his usual table and nudges and sniggers were barely supressed at his sour expression as the roll call of numbers passed him by – his demeanour not helped by those seated with him who amassed their own winnings on the same table. Everyone approved, though, when the Northern Star shirt was won by a newly local man, there with his ten-year-old son. The boy was further thrilled when Sonny presented him with his prize and a spontaneous round of applause broke out for his win as photographs were taken. Sonny himself had bought a strip of tickets to further support the night, it suited him, though, that he didn't win anything.

With the raffle draw then over, chairs and stools were quickly re arranged by customers in the bar to better view the newly installed big screen tv which Kev proudly switched on with the held-aloft remote control. Those with little or no interest in the game, or wished distance from the more vocal element, relocated to any other free space. Sonny was engineered to sit front-of-house among friends, as the regular contingent leaned back against the bar, or tucked themselves into corners, beer cradled, from where to view. It was a full house, some there for the match, some for the supper, some the raffle and the occasion – others simply because Sonny was.

To the triggered cheer of nearly twenty thousand spectators at Wembley Stadium the two national squads trotted out of the tunnel and onto the floodlit pitch. Keenly, Sonny scrutinised the faces of the spilling Brazilian team, one of whom, Ernesto Vargas, he knew played for Boca FC. With no small measure of envy Sonny watched as they lined up – some similar in appearance to himself with black razor-cut hair and tanned skin – and proudly sang their national anthem. From the distant memory of when he and Enrique would routinely sing it at La Esperanza, he micro-mouthed the words.

When England scored the only goal of the first half of the match and the pub erupted around him, Sonny couldn't find willing jubilation and in timely manner felt reminded of who he was and why he needed to return home to Rio. As he then stood with Freddy and Simmonds at the tail end of the queue for the tapas supper, laid out on a line of tables on what effectively was neutral ground near the kitchen, old Justin sidled up to him and tugged him aside by the arm.

'You remember me telling you the grandson's a keen Northern supporter?' old Justin said.

'I do, yes.'

'Well, he's looking to get a start with them as an apprentice player – and I said I know just the man to talk to!'

'I hope he gets on,' Sonny said helpfully.

'I thought maybe a word from someone on the inside might be useful!'

'Well, they have their own selection process, Justin, they decide all that themselves.'

'Oh yes, but if they're struggling with a short list then perhaps a heads-up from one of their own might help get things in order,' old Justin hinted without embarrassment.

'Justin, I really have no influence over any of that. The club takes care of its own recruitment without anyone else needing to say anything.'

'Oh, come on!' old Justin derided loudly, which drew the attention of those nearby, 'Let's not kid ourselves, I can tell you the lad's shouted up your name from the terraces a good few times, I'm sorry, but I don't think it too much out of the way for a bit of reciprocal! And I'm sure you yourself have had the benefit of a word or two put your way in the past – let's not forget, we've all of us needed a helping hand at some point!'

'Justin, it's beyond my control,' Sonny floundered.

'Well, it's lucky this village didn't think it beyond their control when you were brought here empty handed not so very long ago. Perhaps you've forgotten!'

Behind the bar Kev quickly became aware of old Justin's rise in both volume and agitation, it was something he'd seen before and knew it would end with the man bellowing if it wasn't curtailed. 'Justin!' he said pointedly. 'I'll not have tonight spoiled by you! Get your tapas and get back to your own side!'

Old Justin knew better than to argue and simply did as he was told without any degree of self-consciousness.

'Sorry about that, Sonny,' Kev said.

'That's alright, Kev. We all know what he's like.'

During the supper break, Kev grandly announced that a preliminary sum of eight hundred pounds had been raised by the event for charity and a congratulatory round of applause broke out.

The second half of the game proved laborious as England failed to increase their lead and Brazilian players, perpetually it seemed, rolled on the turf and claimed foul. Openly shouted abuse punctuated the pub to a chorus of groans as arms were thrown aloft in protest; it pained Sonny to hear such vitriol levelled at his own kind. When Brazil drew level with a goal from Ernesto Vargas minutes before full time, Sonny drew up both forearms, fists clenched. Ongoing furore in the pub to a dismissed foul against England in the goalmouth somewhat concealed his animation but in that moment his heart had spoken its own truth – and he felt relieved to know it.

At eleven thirty, Sonny and Janice got into the car, and she drove them back to the flat.

'What was all that about with the old guy?' she asked along the way.

'He was badgering me to get his grandson on the youth team. He gets like that at times – big voice! Then next he'll want me to sign him a shirt or something.'

'And what did you think to the game? Last gasp goal by your lot! I caught you in the mirror when they scored!'

'I'll be on the same team as the guy who scored it in a couple of weeks! I think I'm starting to bounce off the walls a bit with it all. I just need to get on that plane, Janice, and scream away the years.'

'Not long to wait now, dear.'

Janice stayed the night and on Sunday morning, the pair sat about with mugs of unsweetened tea as they idly chatted and looked out at a blue-pocketed grey sky.

'Kev seemed happy enough with the night's proceedings,' she remarked.

'Yeah, standing room only – it got busy after that!'

'I think he's going to do that giant cheque thing with the charity people.'

Sonny chuckled. 'Yeah, that would be him. Big cheesy grin in the paper. Do you fancy going out somewhere for lunch?'

'Actually no! I fancy potato waffles well done through the toaster, and time it please, to go with a two-sugar coffee!'

Sitting at the breakfast bar they ate browned potato waffles and then took to the sofa.

'So, what's next week with the job, then?' he asked. 'And are you still liking it?'

'I love it! It's everything I studied for.'

'Ah, but what do they think of you?'

'Oh, they can't believe their luck!

'Which way?'

'The thank goodness you're here kind of way!'

'Do you get on with them? I imagine them striding about fields in silly shorts and big boots, all dead serious!'

'It's you lot who go striding about fields in silly shorts and big boots, all dead serious,' she countered. 'No, they're a decent bunch. I've only come across one ego, and that's only because he wears a bush hat – but he is from South Africa! the guy's a biochemist genius, and there's always a quirk comes with that. He drives around in a jeep.'

'Not got big horns on the front?'

'And they've given me a field assignment!' she boasted happily, in disregard of his comment. 'A project management job part-funded by the States. They've got a bit of a problem over there with locust. They rock up from your backyard and eat anything that's green.'

'They should go to Walmart like everyone else!'

'Now, do I make light of your daft football game?'

He smiled at her indignation. 'No, go on... I promise – no more mickey.'

'Well, it's quite a plum number, actually. In fact, the guy who trained me up when I started was expected to get it.'

'Oof, I bet that wet-fished him in the face a bit!'

'He was okay with it. Anyway, they're looking for a way to introduce something into the seed that locust don't like as the plant grows. It's been going on for years but it's getting more crucial as everywhere hots up. They've even had locust swarms in Italy can you believe! They normally zap them with insecticides, but not to have them there in the first place is better.'

'You're really in it for the good, aren't you?' he said.

'Why else would I have done the degree?'

'Good point! Go on.'

'That's about it, really. I don't want to bore you with heat-flow charts and bio formulae!'

'Sounds like an interesting job, got a worthwhile feel to it. Makes mine seem a bit trivial!'

'No... I won't hear of it. A footballer on the big bucks... trivial? Never!'

'Oh, so now who's taking the mickey!'

It was her turn to smile.

'And how's the accommodation bit going?' he asked.

'Can't fault it. It's separate from the student lot, noisy buggers! We're all in neat little terraced rows, you know, made from that yellow flinty brick, more windows than brick!'

'I bet your mum's pleased you're back?'

'Oh, yes, just so long as I don't turn up on the doorstep with a suitcase and a sob story!'

'Want to help me book a one-way flight to Rio?'

'Don't tell me you haven't got that teensy detail sorted yet!'

'My head's not been right for it, I'd end up somewhere geographically incorrect!'

'Have a look now, if you like?' she offered.

'Yeah, come on.'

They seated themselves at the laptop computer and he button-pressed it into service; twenty-five minutes later he was booked on a flight from Leeds Bradford Airport to Manchester to depart in two weeks' time, followed by a flight the day after that from Manchester to Rio.

'Now do you believe you're finally going?' she said.

'You know, I think I actually do. Email from Northern come through!' he said as he then noticed it on the screen. He read the message forwarded by the club from Greg's parents thanking him for sending a Get Well Soon card, and to say that Greg was beyond thrilled to receive it, and fully on the mend.

'Oh, that was sweet of you,' she said after he'd rang Amelia and told her of it. 'But how's Greg going to handle the news that his new best friend is jetting off to wear another shirt?'

'Could be the next old Justin!' he commented.

'You're doomed! Do you want to make a start cleaning this place?'

'Nah, I'll do it next week. Let's go out somewhere!'

'Yes. How about we take a stroll at Golden Acre and get a coffee from that chugabug?'

'Sounds right to me!'

Over the next few hours, Sonny and Janice wandered the damp woodland pathways of Golden Acre Nature Reserve and drank coffee at a mobile café in the earthy car park. They returned to the flat late afternoon before darkness set in; an hour later she drove out again and went home in readiness for the week ahead.

On Monday, Sonny sat across from Lou Gomero in the man's office where ceiling-panel lights beat back the greyness of the morning beyond his pitch-view windows.

'You go with our best wishes, Sonny,' Gomero said. 'It's been a long time coming for you, and I know with you it was never about the money. You've done this club gargantuan proud, and you can walk away with your head high. But I'll say again, if it doesn't work out for you over there – for whatever reason – come back. And who knows, you might even come back a better player,' he joked, 'if such were possible! Academic question, I know, but I take it you haven't changed your mind?'

'I've got to go for it, Lou,' Sonny said earnestly. 'It's everything I've dreamed of.'

'I totally understand. Well, you've certainly earned the respect of everyone here, and that includes the fans. On a personal note, you've been a revelation. You delivered at every level. There's kids out there clamouring to get a start with us because they've seen the way you did it! They'd give their right arm to wear that same shirt and be the man. You've shown them what's possible and you've unfolded the road map for them to get there! There's no such thing as a closed door here for you, Sonny. Come back and see us at any time!'

'Thanks, Lou. And thanks for the chance you gave me. If it weren't for you, I don't know where I'd be right now, not where I am that's for sure... or where I'm going!'

Gomero stood up and offered a hand across the desk. 'Go net for 'em, Sonny. You know where we are!'

'Thanks for everything, Lou,' Sonny said as he engaged the hand.

For the remainder of that week, Sonny readied both himself and the flat for departure. He arranged with Simmonds that they would meet for farewell drinks in The Feathers on the Saturday night, and Simmonds would discreetly invite others. Late Friday afternoon Sonny let Janice into the complex; the pair then sat in his lounge window as sunlight slid down the wall beside them.

'It's been a long countdown for you, hasn't it!' she remarked.

'Yes. I had to say goodbye to Lou on Monday, it was like saying goodbye to my own dad, whoever he was! I feel as though I've been doing goodbyes for years on account of back then. I know Leeds better than I do Rio! I need a factory reset! get home and believe I'm finally in the right place. *Sonny! where've you been?'* he mimicked of non-existent others. '*Oh, I took the long way home!* And anyway, Janice, how come there are more goodbye's than there are hellos?'

'Ah, those are the rules, you see.'

'Do you want to go over the road to that Italian?'

She shook her head. 'Can't be arsed. Let's do a takeaway.'

'Yeah, let's,' he agreed. 'I'll go for it. I've put a bunch of menus somewhere.'

From a shallow kitchen drawer, he brought out menus and they opted for Chinese food from a takeaway outlet that was only a few minutes' walk from the flat. He made the telephone order and pushed his feet into white slip-on trainers as Janice slid out plates and cutlery from drawers and cupboards.

'Who would put...? forget it!' she said and lifted a bottle of soy sauce out of an otherwise empty saucepan.

Within an hour they were sitting at the breakfast bar amid a sprawl of buckled silver cartons from which they spooned hot food onto pre-heated plates.

'I bet Maria's getting all excited,' Janice said.

'Oh, she doesn't know we're having Chinese.'

'I can just imagine how's she feels, big bro' coming home at last! Does she look like you?'

'Yes, I suppose she does now. Back then she was small and dumpy, belting around rough ground in a pink dress with a big shiny smile on her face.'

'She sounds like fun!'

'Oh yes. And she managed to keep hold of that, despite all the crap that happened to us.'

'Good for her.'

Janice stayed the night, and the following day the pair deep cleaned the flat. From a high shelf within the fitted wardrobe of the bedroom she brought out his wooden carvings and placed them on the window table in the lounge.

'What a gruesome collection of bug-eyed monsters!' she said in obvious distaste, arms folded. 'Do they come alive at night and do stuff?'

'Ah, that might explain the mess and the empties!'

'What are you going to do with them?'

'I thought I'd just spread them around a bit and let people think they belong the place.'

'But you made them – for whatever reason?'

'I did indeed make them. Why, what have you got in mind?'

'I was thinking Kev might want them for one of his charity auctions!'

'Can't see it, Janice. We used to carve them for the cruise ship tourists in Rio, they'll all be in garages somewhere in the States worrying spiders!'

'We're talking floggit, Kev... and handmade carvings by Sonny Lopez in his primal crayon years!'

'Well, if he wants them, he's welcome,' Sonny said with an easy shrug.

'Ring him!' she suggested.

'I'm not ringing him; he'll think I'm a right knob!'

'I'll ring him, then!'

While he earwigged nearby, she made the call and spoke to Kev.

'Yes, he wants them,' she said when the call was ended. 'But you need to sign them. That way he reckons some gullible... I mean... some art knowledgeable person will buy them!'

'And how exactly do you sign a lump of wood?'

'Standard method, dear, with a permanent marker pen from over the road – off you go, nothing with glitter!'

Sonny went to the newsagent shop and, unsure about the range of marker pens, came back with a few of various colour. Janice looked them over. 'This one!' she said. 'White on dark wood, that should stand out nicely.'

Sitting at the table, he signed the carvings; she then wrapped each with kitchen roll and put them into a polythene carrier bag.

'I've got some old trainers,' he said glibly. 'What do you think, you know, while I'm still pen in hand!'

'I think perhaps not quite yet! So, is word fully out now, then, that you're escaping?'

'Oh yes, everyone knows. I'm keeping away from the media stuff. It's probably riddled with all kinds of abuse! By my own hand no longer a Northern Star player – how dumb does that sound!'

'You see, suddenly you're not looking cool anymore on my cv, when did you say you were going?'

'I just want on that plane, Janice, my last goodbye said – in the hope that I said it right!'

'Yes, well, deep breaths, dear. Like me when I see the panini truck on a Friday lunchtime.'

As his final week of residence passed, Sonny gradually felt detached from the flat as he cleared any remaining clutter and wiped down surfaces until there was no further point. Late Friday afternoon Janice pulled up at the gate, he let her through, and the pair then sat at the breakfast bar with mugs of tea.

'So, how's your week gone?' he asked. 'And have you got my locust in turmoil?'

She gazed blankly at him. 'Good – and no. And you look stressed.'

'I'm okay, it's just the waiting, really!'

'What, for me to come?' she asked with an inane grin, eyelids batted.

'Yes!'

'Come on,' she urged, 'you've been on your own too long. Let's go out somewhere for a pub meal, grab some cans, and back early!'

The following morning the pair again walked the trailways of Golden Acre Nature Reserve. They returned to the flat a few hours later, slumped on the sofa and fell asleep.

'Right,' she said lazily when they'd roused. 'We'd best make a start and get ourselves all polished up for the Feathers. We don't want folks' thinking we've just rolled off a sofa – goodness!' She then stage whispered, 'I just hope the-you-know-tribe in the bag don't suss what's happening and run amok!'

Janice drove herself and Sonny to The Feathers and they walked in early that Saturday evening, him with bag of carvings in hand. Already standing in the otherwise empty bar room Simmonds, Samantha and Freddy were engaged in conversation as Kev leaned on an elbow behind the bar.

'He's here!' Kev said triumphantly and straightened up.

Sonny handed him the bag. 'Don't eat them all at once, Kev,' he said as Janice greeted their friends with hugs, Sonny then likewise with Samantha and handshakes and a ready grin for Simmonds and Freddy.

'Good of you to bear us in mind,' Kev said and stashed the bag out of sight. 'People still think you come in all the time, *Sonny been in?'* he generalised. *'Oh, you've just missed him!* It's good for trade,' he added with a wry smile.

'So... excited or nervous?' Simmonds asked Sonny.

'In equal measures, Mark. The head's doing its own thing without any permission from me!'

Samantha cast a quick glance at Janice who gave nothing away.

'So, what's new here, then?' Sonny asked.

'New... in Cowton?' Freddy said aghast. 'Yesterday's not even turned up yet! So, when you going?'

'Manchester tomorrow! then Monday to Rio,' Sonny confirmed.

Kev sucked in breath.

'Hi, Sonny! Hi, Janice!' Wendy welcomed as she joined the group. She smiled warmly at them both as they returned her greeting.

'Flies out to Rio on Monday!' Kev said.

Wendy looked at Sonny as though to commiserate. 'Aw,' she murmured. 'Well, that's a long way to go for a kiss and a cuddle!' she said to Janice.

'Isn't it!' Janice agreed. 'When he can get one here!' Laughter vented at her twist on Wendy's remark.

'I've always wanted to go there,' Wendy said. 'It's one of those places, isn't it? You know – everyone laid about on that white beach – and that sugarlump mountain – it just looks so utterly fabulous!'

'It probably is if you don't get shot!' Kev said.

'What a thing to say!' Wendy chastised.

'Well, in fairness, it does have a certain reputation,' Sonny remarked in Kev's defence.

'You'll get a few shots in yourself, won't you, Sonny?' Janice said.

'If I don't, I'll be hiring out deckchairs on that beach!' he predicted, which humorously saw off any further analysis.'

An hour later the room had filled with Sonny's well-wishers. Many wanted to be in his company and perhaps hear snatches of a life that bore no resemblance to their own. Only old Justin looked on with an expression of disapproval as he distantly observed and muttered to cohorts.

At the end of the night Sonny, somewhat overwhelmed by his own popularity, engaged with handshakes, hugs and kisses.

'I'm not going to say goodbye, Sonny,' Simmonds said to him. 'Because I can't. I'm just going to wish you well and say see ya later, mate!' Their handshake turned into a tight hug.

'Oh, that was a good night, Sonny,' Janice said as they drove back to the flat.

'Yes, it was... it was good,' he agreed, his thoughts steeped in goodbye exchanges with friends.

'And you were just going to go sneaking off without! But whatever you do when you get there, don't go hanging around that sugarlump mountain,' she giggled. 'Chance to get shot!'

Wendy's misnomer amused them both; any joy and satisfaction at their happy night fell away, though, as they approached the flat and the car's headlights picked out red graffiti newly sprayed onto the white stone wall of the complex – it read: *S. Lopez Go Home.* Janice groaned when she saw it, Sonny was silent in dismay. They pulled up at the gates, he got out and, in the glare of the headlights, stood at the foot-tall graffiti. He touched it, checked his fingertips and then went over to the gate and put in the entry code.

'That's the last thing you needed,' Janice said when she'd parked up and got out of the car. 'I hope there's no more of it anywhere! Do you think we should call the police?'

'Let's check round first,' he said glumly.

There was no further evidence of graffiti or break-in to either the communal door or his flat. As Janice visibly battled apprehension and annoyance at the outrage, Sonny took out a can of lager and bottle of white wine from the fridge, he poured the wine into a stemmed tulip glass and handed it to her.

'I'll ring the letting agent tomorrow,' he said. 'They'll get it cleaned up and they can send me the bill.'

'It just scares me that those morons know where you live.'

'Well, it's never exactly been a secret, Janice. Don't be bothered by that!' Which wasn't exactly how he felt.

In the morning, the pair sat about and eased themselves into a final tidy up of the flat. He reported the graffiti incident to the letting agent and booked himself a taxi to Leeds Bradford Airport for three o'clock that afternoon. Janice had wanted to take him, but he couldn't bear the thought of her making the journey and then driving home alone. She took the last of the bedding and towels down to the car, he emptied the fridge and put anything of use into carry bags for her to use, all else he put in a bin-liner which he deposited in outside bins. As he then stood in the lounge, Janice made a final pass with a damp cloth around the kitchen sink and worktop; she paused, eyes closed, and lips pursed. 'This is the one, isn't it?' she said, as her emotions surfaced.

He nodded. 'I don't know how to say goodbye to you, Janice,' he said emptily. 'There are no words good enough!'

'No. There aren't. So, I think I'll take the Simmonds' approach and say see ya later... And hope it's everything you want it to be over there, Sonny. You've had to wait an awful long time!' They came together and hugged tightly.

'Please always be safe,' he said.

'I knew I'd struggle with this,' she complained as she looked up at the ceiling, her eyes wide and pooled with tears. 'I think it best if I go now... I'm failing rather badly here!'

Hand in hand, they walked down to the car. They hugged in silence, she got in behind the wheel, the gate drew open, and she drove through.

Sonny had no desire to be alone in the flat, he didn't want to see the still-wet kitchen sink become dry after Janice's efforts, nor did he trust his own inner voice not to scream out his love for her. He gathered up his singular luggage, said, 'Thanks flat' and went down to the communal entrance. The taxi duly arrived and took him to Leeds Bradford Airport. Late afternoon, as dusk gathered, he made the short flight to Manchester.

That evening, in need of more than an overly floral-patterned hotel room could offer at Manchester Airport, despite runway vista, Sonny seated himself in a quiet corner of the lobby bar. He considered how Janice herself might be sitting alone at home, perhaps in the belief that, in the thrill of moving on, he'd let go of her. The thought was more than he could bear, and he rang her. She immediately answered and over the following half hour, detached from their moment of parting, they calmly spoke of their hopes for themselves and each other. They concluded with an exchange of affection. He felt a little easier as he then drank beer and obliged with an autograph for an awestruck boy who recognised him and had waited to make a timely approach as his mother anxiously looked on.

Chapter 13

Sonny arrived in Rio at noon during a tropical storm. He cleared immigration formalities and made his way out to the taxi rank beneath a high canopy that cascaded rain from its edges – as normally placid palms flailed beyond in a chaotic wind. The weather-impeded journey to the Hotel Cristal took half an hour as the driver, all the while, cursed such driving conditions, conditions barely beaten by slapping windscreen wipers. Along the way Sonny looked out at what little could be seen and tried to accept that he was finally home.

At the hotel, he was checked in by Morena for his reserved five-night stay, he resisted the urge to tell her that he was no longer a tourist, and was allocated a room on the second floor, accessed by way of stairs, as sign advised, due to the risk of lift-faltering power cuts in the storm. He then tried to shower away the thousands of miles worth of travel and, sitting in an enveloping velour chair, rang Maria from his mobile phone. His call went into recorded message mode, which he took to mean that she was either sleeping or at work. He left the brief message that he was at the hotel and would ring again later. Within the hour she had called him back and squealed delight down the line from the hospital ward where she was on duty – his own ready laugh triggered by her shrilled response. They arranged to meet at the Nurses Home the next afternoon when she'd finished her early shift.

Mindful not to sleep away his arrival day, Sonny went down to the hotel bar, ordered beer and a steak sandwich, and – perched on a bar stool – gazed out through closed bi-fold glass doors at the thrashing banana plant leaves and rain-plagued terrace. From there he sent a text message to Amelia which told of his arrival. She promptly sent back with: *Welcome Home!* and that she would be on duty at the hotel from six o'clock that evening and looked forward to seeing him again. Aware that he had become light-headed through his own scattered emotions, made more so by a singular beer and travel fatigue, he went up to his room and laid on the bed. Back-to-back dreams, which still had him in transit, soon claimed him.

Late that afternoon, he looked in the bathroom mirror and was unimpressed at that which looked back at him. He did thirty rapid press-ups, thirty sit-ups and took a shockingly cold sudsy shower that sloughed off any residual brain fog. Dressed in fresh clothes, he then felt more alert as he went down to reception where Amelia was already on duty. She looked up as he crossed the empty floor and with a wide smile, leaned over the desk and embraced him.

'Hi, Amelia,' he said, elated by her open welcome.

'Hi, Sonny, good to see you again!'

'Good to see you too, Amelia. I've been away a bit longer than planned.'

She laughed. 'I'm just thrilled for you that you made the team,' she said. 'I know how important it is to you.'

'I thought it would never happen! Now all I've got to do is justify that it has. How about you – the exams?'

'Sat the last one three weeks' ago! I'm just waiting for the results.'

'How do you feel it went?'

'I actually feel okay about it, I think I did enough to get through – and I'd be ecstatic if I just got a straight pass!'

'Too right! I know I would be,' he said, in awe of such a prospect.

'So, uni's all behind me now – and I'm back at work!'

'And is that here, then... are you doing part-time or...?'

'No, I'm here full-time. The hours are spread about a bit more than they were, but I don't mind that and if the exam comes good then it'll be time to look around and see what else is out there! How's Maria getting on?'

'She's loving it! First year over now. I'm seeing her tomorrow.'

'Give her my love.'

'I will.' He looked into Amelia's hazel eyes, at an engaging smile. 'I was hoping us two could go out somewhere and do a full catch-up?' he suggested.

'I think we should! I'm day off Wednesday; we could do something then if you like?'

'Great! What do you fancy, anything at all – beach day, a stroll out, a meal someplace?'

'Do you know what I'd really like to do!' she said.

'Go on!'

'Chill in sky park on the beachfront! It's a good spot. We could wander a bit, get coffee-faced, maybe a shrimp panini or two!'

'Well, that sounds perfect enough to me,' he agreed.

Later that evening from his room he sent two emails – one to Janice to say that he was battened down in the hotel in a tropical storm, the other to Alberto Ferreira to confirm his arrival.

The following afternoon, the storm then spent, Sonny walked to the City Hospital. He made his way to the Nurses Home, sat on a nearby bench, and waited for Maria. He had expected that she would appear from within the Home, instead she came along the pathway, centred among half a dozen chattering female others, all in nurse uniform. He thought she looked the happiest girl on earth. He stood up, she broke into a huge grin and hugged him. With an arm clamped around his she introduced him to everyone with her, and he found himself surrounded by eager smiles.

'Give me ten minutes, Sonny,' she then said. 'I just need to change.'

'No rush,' he assured her.

She went inside, amidst the group, and he again sat on the bench.

Fifteen minutes later she emerged in blue jeans, thick-soled white trainers and a black T shirt with rolled-higher sleeves.

'They all think you're gorgeous!' she complained. 'It's embarrassing!'

'I'll cope!'

The pair walked to the Hospital Food Hall exchanging their news along the way.

'I can't tell you how glad I am that you made that team,' she said over lunch. 'All I wanted was you home again and be done with everything of the past! I was looking out for jobs here at the hospital for you!'

'I had to use the tools I've been given, though, Maria. Nobody wants a nothing man!'

'I know, and there's no one benefitted more than me from it, Sonny, that's for sure! The waiting's all over with now, isn't it. You're back, once and for all, just like you said you would, you never gave up. You've beaten them!'

'We've beaten them! – I just need to re-acclimatise a bit and step back into old shoes. You can update me over coffee on everything I've missed since I was ten!'

'Okay.'

'So, how's it been for you here, then?'

'I love it like you wouldn't believe. I've done my first year now, and it just keeps getting better and better!'

'Do you get exams?'

'Oh, all the time, we have course work and theory to do as we go along, it's quite intense!'

'Do you pass?'

'So far! you can do them again, but I'm not into that – it would be like doing it twice.'

'And what happens when you qualify?'

'I'll be assigned a ward and be a permanent member of staff.'

'Do you get a say in where?'

'I hope so. I want to specialise in paediatrics, so I'd like a kid's ward. It'll depend on what's going at the time, though.'

'Soon be nineteen as well, hey!'

'Yeah, I know. How did that happen? I'm nearly as old as you now!' she marvelled, to which they both laughed. 'Is it very different over there in England?' she asked, as she trained her hair behind an ear.

'Totally. But they're good people, and they sure like their football!'

'Did you always speak English, was there no one else there from Brazil?'

'No, so yes, I spoke English. Do I sound any different?'

'No. You sound just the same.'

'Glad to hear it. So, have you got anything lined up for your nineteenth, then?' he asked buoyantly.

'There's a whole bunch of us going to Sammy's Chinese Buffet Restaurant tomorrow night. They've got a bar and a dance floor, and we're going to make a night of it! Are you coming?'

'Sounds like fun! But I don't want to get in the way of your girly do!'

'Oh, it's not a girly do! There's estates guys and half the hospital football team going! Bring Amelia! I'd love to see her again. We can dual celebrate – my birthday and your homecoming!'

'Timely! But I'm not poaching your thing. I'll ask Amelia for sure, and if she can't then I'll still turn up for it – if you think it's a good idea! but it's not our do, it's yours!'

'Okay! And I'll introduce you to Saulo.'

'Who's Saulo?'

'My boyfriend.'

'Oh, boyfriend! and where's he sprung up from?'

'He works here. He's in his final year as a trainee engineer.'

'I see. So how long have you been going out with him?'

'Three or four months now! He's twenty, he's very nice – and he likes football!'

'I'm looking forward to meeting him.'

'Good. So, are you and Amelia still hanging in there, then!'

'Seems so!'

'Well, be advised, Rio girls like their men pushy, and she's hanging on like crazy for you – so push like hell!'

'You know, there's still a rich seam of favela in you!'

'Well, don't worry, I'll share it with you!' she said glibly.

Back at the hotel, he sent Amelia a text message telling her of Maria's invite to Sammy's Chinese Buffet Restaurant. She replied that she would love to go.

On Wednesday, Sonny walked from the hotel to Sky Park and arrived just before midday. The open-plan park, narrow and well-tended, lay along the furiously busy seafront highway and had a contour of internal pathways that invited exploration beneath a canopy of aged trees. He sat on a low stone wall beside one of its many gapped entrances and waited. Within ten minutes Amelia in jeans and grey fleece top, the only passenger to disembark the bus that pulled-in at the park-designated bus stop, strolled up to him bearing a broad smile; they greeted and went into the park. At a café within its part-shaded grounds they ordered coffee and sat outside on retro tin furniture.

'Beats a shopping mall,' he said, as he looked over the tranquil scene.

She nodded agreement. 'We like it here; me and Juanita sometimes bring the kids. They call it swoopy park!'

'I can see the appeal. Are you still okay for tonight?' he asked.

'Most certainly!'

'Good. Looks like Maria picked the right night!'

'I feel as though I've known her for years, actually. And it was nice of her to invite me along.'

'Oh, she thinks you're marvellous.' Amelia laughed.

'And she's got herself a Saulo,' he said. 'I've been usurped!'

'By a Saulo!'

'Yes.'

'Her boyfriend, I take it?'

'Seems so.'

'Good for her! he's a lucky lad! And she's picked a good venue with Sammy's! It's renowned for top class Chinese food, it's one of the best in town.'

'I reckon we can still manage a Panini now, though,' he suggested, 'what do you say?'

'I say so too.'

Over the following two hours as they sat, and then strolled, Sonny and Amelia reacquainted themselves with each other. When, at the end of their afternoon, they went to the bus stop for her journey home they did so hand in hand.

At seven-thirty that evening, Sonny got out of a taxi barely a mile from the hotel at a modern white-clad residential block which had Amelia's flat among its three storeys. As the taxi waited, he walked up the lawn-sided path of the short, front grounds and pressed her flat number at an annunciator panel beside the main entrance. She soon answered through the integral speaker and said she was coming down. Moments later she emerged casually dressed in wide, black trousers and pink blouse beneath a black jacket, over which hung a cream shoulder bag. 'Impeccable timing!' she said as they touched cheeks.

The pair made the ten-minute taxi journey to Sammy's Chinese Buffet Restaurant which sat at a convergence of town centre roads and resembled a floodlit pagoda guarded by two giant stone lions at its front. Maria and her twenty-plus group of friends were already there when they walked in; she quickly saw them, excitedly rushed over and both girls squealed delight as they hugged. From her handbag, Amelia brought out an obvious birthday card in a purple envelope, along with a small, gift-wrapped present, both of which she gave to Maria – and further hugs were exchanged.

The three then went over to the rest of the group – sitting at tables from which aloft balloons were anchored in a reserved area of the restaurant – and Maria made a sweeping introduction to all of Sonny and Amelia, which drew returned cheery greetings and waves. Among them was Saulo, he stood up, which showed him to be quite short, and offered a hand to Sonny. Sonny thought it perfectly weighted as he engaged it and felt him someone who conveyed an honest open-faced confidence – and was reassured for Maria on account of it.

It was turned midnight when Sonny and Amelia went home by taxi after what they both agreed had been an excellent night; he saw her inside her main front door and then continued the short ride to the hotel. The following afternoon, Maria rang him, she enthused over the party and hoped that both he and Amelia had enjoyed it as much as she had. She was glad Amelia came and asked what Sonny thought of Saulo? in answer to which he gave his welcomed, full approval.

Later that same day, Sonny checked for emails on his phone. There were two. He read them in their order of arrival – which conveniently took away any decision on his part; Janice told him to keep in touch whenever the mood took him, and of how everyone was asking if he'd: *got away alright,* Alberto Ferreira had sent a:*Welcome to Rio* message, and a date in the coming week for him to attend Boca FC Training Centre, sign commencement papers and begin training.

Sonny suddenly felt a measure of urgency; the realisation that he was no longer a tourist without agenda had him go to an estate agent's office along from the hotel where he perused a selection of flats for rent that were within walking distance of the Training Centre. The options were numerous, and he got back to his room with several printed-off sheets of A4 paper that detailed those he thought of special interest. Amelia was on duty behind reception, and he had wanted to ask what she thought of his choices, but she seemed continually busy, so he garnered whatever information was available by way of the internet.

An hour later, he rang the estate agent and took up their offer of an immediate escorted viewing of a vacant flat. The top-floor property sat at the end of a dated, lime-washed three-storey block, each flat with stand-alone balcony that looked across a broad street to family-owned shops and mini supermarkets, above which traded small businesses; it all had a vibrancy that he liked. He accepted the terms and conditions of the unfurnished let and was free to move in whenever he chose.

Over the next few days, Sonny assumed occupancy of the flat. He could have bought outright something far grander, but his mindset was that his new life in Rio should be funded only by earnings made in Rio; he also felt a need to steep himself in street life and be reconnected with its vibe. Amelia helped him choose new furniture from a home store and dissuaded his interest in a gunmetal grey tubular bed and black leather sofa and chairs, though he baulked at her willingness for soft throws and scatter cushions. On her various days off work Maria, much enthused by it all, would call by, herself with kitchen or bathroom items for him.

'What did you have over there?' Maria asked on one such occasion as they sat with coffee at his new block-laid table. 'Was that a flat?'

'Yeah, it wasn't a bad one either!'

'But you still don't regret leaving – coming here? No second thoughts?'

'No. None at all.'

'Were you sad to leave... maybe a little bit?'

'I was there twelve years; that's two more than here! But I always knew I'd be back; it just took me longer than it should have. Now I want forty-eight hours out of every twenty-four just so I can catch up.'

'I'm glad you feel like that. I got bothered that you might let go – forget! Now I'm bothered you won't like it here anymore and regret coming.'

'That'll never happen, Maria. I've got my family and my country back, and I'm not letting go. I've got a lot to prove!'

'Who to?'

'Good question... that's what people say when they haven't got a proper answer. To myself, really, I suppose. If I'm honest I'm maybe a bit bothered that what worked on a football pitch over there might not cut it here!'

'Just be yourself, Sonny. Don't put pressure inside your own head! And forget that doubling-up stuff – calm down and let you be you – in real time.'

'You turned out well, Maria.'

She twice tapped her forehead with a forefinger. 'Favela,' she said. 'Same as you, and we don't ever betray that, do we!'

He shook his head solemnly. 'No... we don't, and you're right!' he accepted, somewhat embarrassed that he'd perhaps shown weakness.

'Oh, and guess what?' she said as though to alleviate his discomfort. 'The decision's been made for everyone about whether to move out of the home!'

'How do you mean?'

'They're closing it!'

'No!'

'There's to be no more intakes. We have to be out in three months.'

'Why?'

'They say it's for a refurb, but no one believes that. Everyone thinks it will never open again as a Nurses' Home, and it'll be offices.'

'Oh, that's not right, if they do that,' Sonny scoffed. 'They should be looking after the new intakes! So, what do you need to do?'

'Me and Monica are going into a two-bed flat that we've found, it's really close to the hospital and the rent's not much more than the home.'

'And there's you – bringing me stuff for here! So, who's Monica?'

'You met her on party night at Sammy's. Tall girl! close-cropped hair to one side, long on the other.'

'I remember her! never stopped talking the whole night.'

Maria wryly smiled at his glib antonym remark. 'She's really nice!' she defended of her. 'It was Monica who first suggested we find somewhere a while back.'

'So, when do you move out – in?'

'At the end of the month, and I'm all sorted with money, thank you, because I know you'd offer!'

'Do you feel ready – I mean, obviously you're going to have to be, but are you okay with it – you know, big move?'

'I'm fully okay with it!'

'Is it secure, decent area – walking back at night, and that?'

'Yes, it's really nice, lots of families there, and hospital workers, there are no issues!'

'Well, let's drink to that, then,' he said cheerfully, and raised his coffee cup to hers.

Chapter 14

On Sonny's start day with Boca FC, he walked the half mile from his flat to the Training Centre – his mind a blend of determination and uncertainty. He announced himself at the reception desk and was invited to take a seat among the same leatherette bank of before; he chose orange to remind himself that he'd moved on from the wishful purpose of that visit. Within brief minutes a heavy-set man in grey flannel trousers and lime green shirt, sleeves rolled back to reveal powerful black-haired forearms, strode directly up to him across the empty floor; Sonny immediately got to his feet. With a firm handshake the man welcomed him to Boca FC and introduced himself as Alberto Ferreira, the club manager.

He then led Sonny behind the reception desk and said to a seated staff member on passing, 'Ask Javier to join us in my office, will you?' Ferreira and Sonny continued through the reception pool and along a corridor beyond to where a planked door bore Ferreira's full name neatly etched in lowercase blue letters on a glass nameplate. The sizeable office within held no trappings of self-importance – a row of high-level transom windows, its only natural light source. Ferreira sat at his centre-positioned desk, beside which, on a featureless brown carpet, stacked cardboard boxes gave their ready smell to the room and a nipped invoice between the top two willingly registered any movement of air; he palmed for Sonny to take one of three chairs randomly placed on the opposite side of the desk, and the two men settled themselves.

'I'm grateful that you persevered with your interest in the club,' Ferreira said. 'I've been looking at your form with Northern Star – we should have had you onboard last season!'

Sonny refrained from saying that he had tried for such. 'I'm just glad to be here now,' he said. 'Thank you for the offer.'

Ferreira then keenly outlined his plans for the new season, until there came a knock at the door. Immediately, it opened and a very tall thin man in white shirt and grey suit trousers came in.

'Sonny, this is Javier Mantel,' Ferreira said. 'Javier is our senior accountant.'
Sonny got to his feet and the two men greeted. Mantel then placed down on the desk a folder that he'd brought with him – and seated himself on a free chair. Over the next half hour, he invited both Sonny and Ferreira to sign prepared legal text which contracted Sonny to Boca FC for a period of one year – to commence from the date of signing, and which he himself signed as senior accountant with the club. When all was completed, pleasantries were further exchanged, and Mantel left the office.

Sonny was given a guided tour of the facility by Ferreira and introduced to everyone they encountered along the way. In the changing rooms and gym, he met further members of the squad and was allocated a locker amidst a back-to-back row, each with blue door and integral lock – for which he was given a sharp brass key; he was sized for club wear, introduced to the physios, got changed into training strip and joined the players jogging around the pitch. He was there in earnest. A few analytical glances came his way, not engaging glances that sought to befriend him, more that there was an awareness of him. He recognised Ernesto Vargas, the oldest player on the team who paid him no heed whatsoever.

Early on Friday evening at the end of his first full week with the club, Sonny walked the few hundred metres from home to café bar Embutidos to meet Amelia, as they'd arranged by phone the day before – the venue chosen because it was within easy walking distance for them both. Embutidos was a long-standing establishment that wrapped itself around a street corner beneath striped sectional canopies, and aproned waiters prided themselves on a near theatrical level of service. As instructed by Amelia, Sonny selected 'a nice inside table' and waited for her. Within twenty minutes of him, she arrived, they greeted as he stood up and he was again reminded of her thought-halting fragrance.

'So, how's it gone for the footy star today?' she asked.
'Oh, I didn't like to ask him, he just seemed so busy!'

They ordered dinner and over the next hour, relaxed in each other's company. At eight o'clock they walked to his flat and Amelia stayed the night.

Over the coming weeks, Sonny settled into his new life. He trained robustly at the Training Centre, asked few questions and didn't allow himself to be drawn into club politics in the changing room. He saw Amelia at least once a week, which usually included a Thursday, a day when she had no babysitting duties. Clear of work obligations, they would go to Embutidos for dinner, or cook something in his flat, and at the end of the evening they walked to her block, a beer had along the way or called a taxi if the weather was bad. It was during those early weeks of Sonny's repatriation that Amelia was notified of her exam results; she had passed her degree with distinction.

On commencement of the playing season, the locker room instruction from Ferreira was that each man 'produce something if presented with the opportunity', head coach Neymar's mantra was always that they 'get the ball out to Vargas'. Vargas himself would stare insolently at the floor during suchlike moments. Not yet selected for teamplay and left on the benches for the early games, Sonny thought players often forfeited their own chances of success just to facilitate Vargas's goal rush – and Vargas himself never made accolade to them unless in a post-match interview. To the continued and fervent delight of the club's supporters, Vargas inevitably racked up his goal tally and was soon once again lead scorer for the team. Sonny, though, had never played with reverence to others and quietly suspected that conflict would soon come his way.

Sonny was brought onto the pitch for his first time of play with Boca FC one evening during their lacklustre performance against Libo, a club of equal standing. In a game which mattered to both sides, Ferreira, animated on the touchline, frantically waved him on in the eightieth minute in a downpour of rain. Teammates, anxious not to be caught in possession of the ball and risk further criticism from an already angry manager, quickly had Sonny in possession by way of a desperate back-pass close to the Libo penalty box. Vargas made a dash toward goal in expectation of a lobbing cross to then come in for him; the goalkeeper, aware of the game-plan, focussed his attention fully on Vargas. Sonny recognised the opportunity that this created and himself attempted a looping shot at an unguarded section of the goalmouth – he spun, slipped on saturated turf and miskicked the ball out of play. Thousands of Boca supporters rose as one and groaned in fury. Vargas beseeched the rain-silvered floodlit sky, arms spread wide and mouth soundlessly open as he remained statuesque in otherwise empty space. Minutes later the final whistle blew on a goalless draw. In the changing room, Vargas wasted no time before berating Sonny as others looked on.

'That game could have been ours!' Vargas ranted behind a pointing finger. 'I would have scored if you'd followed instructions. You'd better learn quick, big shot, or get back to your crappy little England!'

Ferreira came in at that moment and silence descended. Only the goalkeeper Stefan, Vargas, and Sonny, escaped his analytical anger. With his tirade over, Ferreira turned to Sonny, 'Come and see me in the morning,' he said simply. With that he walked out, and the team stared about in sullen mood. Gloomily, Sonny walked home and considered that his place on the first team might be the shortest on record.

The next morning, Sonny knocked on Ferreira's door and went in on command. Ferreira, alone in the office, looked up from behind his desk. 'Take a seat, Sonny,' he invited. Sonny did so and waited.

'How would you best sum up last night's game?' Ferreira asked, almost indifferently.

Sonny briefly considered an answer. 'I would say it was a scrappy game where both sides struggled,' he said. He wanted to add, *in bad conditions*, but that might have sounded like an excuse on his part and so left out the comment.

'For sure,' Ferreira agreed. 'I'll tell you something now! There are only three people who know what you did out there. You, me and Vargas. You saw an excellent opportunity and you went for it! It didn't come off... but you won't always slip on wet grass. It was a shot made of foresight and clever play. It's what I want to see more of. Our winning formula has always been to feed the ball to Ernesto, but there's a downside... it stifles individual play, and it's made us predictable. Youngsters are afraid to commit. You are not! You're going to take a hell of a lot of flak, Sonny, but I want you to double down and chase those shots on goal. I want to see flair, chances created and some fresh thinking. I don't want Ernesto to feel undermined, but neither do I want you hesitant in the face of an opportunity! I saw the way you played in the UK, and I want that individual style of skill-play here. So, that's your role. And as far as anyone else here knows, you've just had the biggest bollocking of your life, got it?'

'Thanks, Alberto,' Sonny said, much relieved.

Over the coming weeks, Sonny sporadically came onto the pitch as a substitute. He was yet to score, and sometimes idle booing broke out if goals were needed and he was brought on without obvious reason. It disappointed him that he was so readily disliked by his home crowd, but he remained unyielding in any match that he was involved in. Open resentment of him wasn't helped when sometimes a ball passed to him from Vargas came with side spin which made it difficult to control. In demonstration of the fact, Sonny occasionally let the ball bounce unchecked so that it wheeled aside, and everyone knew what Vargas had done. Vargas, though, seemed unassailable.

Despite an objecting home crowd, Sonny was brought onto the pitch one Saturday afternoon during a failing game against their historic rivals Vasco. As he walked to the touchline to take a throw-in, he again found himself the target of derisory fans who jeered him. He considered how Amelia, who was at the game, would feel by it – how she would be saddened for him, and that she deserved better than the spectacle. He looked over at teammates who seemed untroubled and recognised that they didn't see him as a principal part of any game plan and were happy for him to be the subject of blame because they were then kept one step further from it. He also recognised that simply to be in Rio, be in the team, was not enough; he had to succeed.

When the ball next came to him, by way of a deflected miss-kick, he brought it under control and feigned a long pass to Vargas who dashed forward to capitalise on the never-to-arrive gift. Sonny himself sprinted with the ball and easily sidestepped the few players who offered any defence. His shot on goal was practically unstoppable and the keeper simply watched the ball hurtle into the back of the net. Ferreira was on his feet in celebration; his player had finally arrived. Sonny broke into laughter. So easily, all along, he could have turned-on that skill – he'd waited long enough to vent his talent, and the wait was over. He put his arms above his head and made a letter A, in tribute to Amelia.

In the changing room, after their one-goal victory, the team sat about in silence as they awaited Ferreira's analysis. Only Hernando, their eighteen-year-old youngest player, congratulated Sonny on his goal when unashamedly, he said, 'Awesome goal, Sonny!'

'Thanks, 'Nando,' Sonny replied.
Ferreira came in and spoke quietly with Neymar and to one of the physios, he then went back out and allowed the result of the game to speak for itself.

An hour later as he walked home, Sonny got a text message from Maria, it read: *Congrats. What kept you?* Without breaking stride, he texted his reply: *Jetlag*. Back in his flat he received the text message from Amelia: *So proud of you. Well done. x.*

Sonny went through the rolling-on days of training in relaxed mood. For a Saturday afternoon game, he was picked to start against Fluminense A, a team in league ascendancy. Before a typically large and hugely vocal crowd he put on a display of footballing excellence as he took the ball passed an outpaced, bewildered opposition and scored a goal that drew incredulity across the stadium. He made his bent-arm accolade to Amelia, and many of the home crowd followed suit in blind celebration. Boca won the game, which almost didn't matter to those who knew they had been treated to something unique; Sonny applauded newly grateful fans as he came off the pitch and took an approving backslap from Ferreira.

That evening, Sonny and Amelia sprawled across his sofa and let calmness prevail.

'You're going to see pitch time aplenty if you keep on scoring like that!' she said. 'And I've told the gang not to boo you unless I do!'

'Okay.'

'They're calling me the A girl, now. I feel fame setting in!'

'I'll point you out next time.'

She giggled at the prospect.

On Monday morning at the Training Centre, Neymar took Sonny aside as everyone strolled off the pitch for lunch break.

'We've got a bit of an issue,' Neymar said.

'Oh, right,' Sonny murmured, almost in expectation of it at some point.

'Seems there's a bit of concern in the camp,' Neymar went on. 'A few of the team are under the impression that you've come with your own agenda, that you're not willing to follow strategy. And I think they've got a point! So, I'm going to remind you again of how we operate here. Alberto and I decide on pitch play. if we say go wide, you go wide, if we say drop back, you drop back. We don't want some maverick out there who simply does things their own way because they're of a mind to. There's a lot more at stake here than personal ambitions! We've got an important game on Saturday... we're down Marcus and Divo, and that could mean you see more pitch time. If you're brought on you follow orders... is that clearly understood?'

'Yes... understood,' Sonny said as he gazed back at Neymar, at barely supressed anger, and said no more.

Chapter 15

The Boca Saturday match was a home game against Sao Paulo Unido, a club of high achievement. It would be a prestigious win if Boca could procure it. In the changing room pre match nerves showed as players readied themselves, gold chains were kissed, and personal little rituals adhered to; Ferreira added to the tension by prowling between Neymar and physios to exchange discreet words. Shoulders were patted as players then assembled in the tunnel and trotted out to sudden clamour from a capacity crowd. Sonny again was in the start line-up. It irritated him that Neymar's instruction to all as they passed by was the familiar dogma, 'Get the ball out to Ernesto!'

Neymar's instruction proved counterproductive. Long-shot passes to Vargas were often intercepted, always to the blaming fury of Vargas himself. Halfway through the first half, Sonny's own contribution was minimal; Boca were two goals down and goalless. Upon then receipt of a wayward headed ball by Sao Paulo, Sonny kept possession and rapidly gained ground into their defence area with direction-changing, confusing strides. He feigned the goalkeeper to the far side of the goalmouth and with a tight, right-angled shot scored an uncontested goal as players mustered beyond. The home crowd erupted. Ten minutes from the first-half whistle, Sonny made a repeat charge, Sao Paulo by then, though, were alerted to the danger he posed. To his left Hernando made a support run and despite Vargas closing in on goal to his right, Sonny put the ball inch-perfect at the feet of Hernando. Hernando, in a flurry of desperation, miskicked and the ball went for dead. Sonny felt that the groans from fans could have dragged light from the sky.

In the changing room at half-time, Sonny expected a tirade of abuse from Vargas. Instead, Vargas remained sullen and left any criticism to Ferreira in his coaxing of the team. Ferreira, though, made no mention of individual play and urged them to step up their efforts and not take their 'foot off the gas!' Only Neymar registered any disquiet; set-faced he said nothing as Sonny filed passed him for the second half.

In that half of play, Sonny let his own tunnel vision take him into any space where he could create a threat on goal. He wouldn't be denied. Almost uncontainable, he scored again to level the match and spontaneously made his tribute to Amelia. Emotion broke loose throughout the stadium as both team managers then hurtled pitch-side and waved frantic instructions. With only five minutes of the game left, Sonny put together another threaded attack. He quickly found himself corralled by Sao Paulo players who aggressively closed in – and again he slid the ball to Hernando who was unmarked. Hernando made no mistake with his gift and scored their third goal. Perhaps jubilant even beyond that of the home fans, Hernando fell to his knees and, totally unheard, screamed at the sky. Five minutes later the final whistle blew on their victory.

In the changing room Vargas hauled off his boots and separately threw them at his locker door as others roundly celebrated their win. Through the broad open mouth of the corridor, Sonny was aware that Neymar and Ferreira were in deep discussion; alone, Ferreira came in and further lifted spirits with a fists-raised cheer.

An hour and a half later, Sonny stepped off the team bus at the Training Centre. Along the way Amelia had sent him a text message to say that she and her friends had themselves just got back from the match and were at the café bar Zuma. He rang her and she answered above a great deal of background noise.

'Well done, Sonny,' she said. 'That was some performance!'

'Thank you. It was either that or get a proper job!'

'And thank you for the accolade again, I'm getting above myself here!'

He laughed. 'You're very welcome!' he assured her.

'And it was good that you gave Hernando that second chance. He won't forget that in a hurry!'

'Oh, you never forget your first goal, he's a good kid.'

Their conversation was halted by a car horn repeatedly sounded by Boca fans who shouted Sonny's name through the car windows as they passed him.

'You okay?' she asked.

'Just my new fan base, a few weeks back they'd have run me over!'

'This time next week they still might!' she joked. 'Where are you?'

'I'm practically on you... in pavement terms!'

'That noisy lot's just gone by! I can see you!' she said. 'We're sat outside! Do you want to come over... We won't make a fuss... maybe just a bit!'

'Well, it would seem rude just to walk on by!'

'We'd have to boo.'

'I'll be there in a sec.'

Amelia met him part-way and they went over to her friends sitting at an outside table where he was greeted with standing handshakes all round; most of the names and faces he remembered from their two-years ago introduction in that very place. He sat among them and shared their joviality until Amelia's pre booked taxi pulled up at the kerbside. She offered him a lift home which he happily accepted – and gave him a neat exit from the group; as they then drew away in the taxi her friends stood up and each formed an A accolade, it had her laugh out loud.

'Do you want to meet up tomorrow?' he asked, during their brief journey.

'Yes! We could do; I'm day off.'

'Maybe do a beach thing, or lunch somewhere... or just a plain old loaf around?' he suggested.

'I'll ring you tonight and we'll pick one!'

At eleven o'clock the next morning, Amelia pulled up on her motor scooter beneath Sonny's flat as he waited for her along the pavement. Without getting off the quietly buzzing machine she half turned around, jabbed a forefinger toward the luggage back box and said, 'Dig out that helmet in there and stick it on!'

He did as she said and with the open-faced helmet then snap fastened, he straddled the tan leather seat as pillion passenger, and they sped away.

At the one-mile distant Copacabana Beach they parked up in the sea-facing, promenade car park, on the beach, they got down to swimwear and laid on hired loungers. Over the following three hours, almost in replica of their previous visit, they plunge-cooled in the warm waves, ate of skewered prawns and melon slices, drank coffee from corrugated paper cups, and willingly steeped themselves in each other's company.

Mid-afternoon, they went back to his flat. They showered together, rinsed away the sea and the beach, and shared his bed until dusk.

On Monday, Sonny had expected some sort of post-match analysis of their game against Sao Paulo, but it seemed everyone's thoughts had moved on, and the team trained as normal. Typically, Vargas didn't speak to him, Neymar stalked moodily about which created a measure of tension and not much was said about their impending game against Vasco FC that coming Wednesday evening.

On Wednesday afternoon, with little or no training done, everyone was called into the lecture theatre to hear format details of the upcoming game. Quietness descended as each player considered the challenge ahead – and what it could mean for their individual prospects. Hernando was particularly focussed. For him, a follow-on goal would rubber-stamp his presence on both the team and scoresheet. Neymar assumed command of the room and from a list of selected players on a clipboard, read aloud names and their position of play. Sonny was on the start line-up, as was Hernando. With the full list then called, everyone waited for the game plan.

'We have come too far now to make any mistakes,' Neymar said. 'Every game going forward is a must win! Vasco are flying high, and they need us out of the way. I want us on that scoreboard early in. To do that, I want our proven method in place... and let's get the game to the good before we start any glory-boy antics!'

Though perhaps temptation was strong, no one glanced at Sonny.

'I want every single one of you focussed out there tonight,' Neymar went on. 'I don't want us ten brilliant goals in if they get eleven flukes! If you cock-up... don't look for sympathy, and don't give any! Just crack on and get that result! Now, we're still down Marcus and Divo, and that means some of you will get pitch time where otherwise you might not. If that opportunity comes, you'd better grab it, big time, because it might not come around again! We've got a chance here to get into the top six and if we don't capitalise on it then none of us deserves to wear the shirt. You all know what you've got to do – and I only want those who do it! ... Bring back that win!' he said emphatically. With his message delivered, he stood aside by way of invite for Ferreira.

'Thank you, Alex,' Ferreira said as he stepped forward. 'I sense fresh belief in the camp,' he calmy asserted to the room. 'And we stand strong to make good with that belief. Tonight, let our supporters know that we are worthy of them, let them see who we are – let Vasco feel who we are! Alex has spoken well of his expectations; they are also my expectations, and I can add nothing further. Alex will now go through the strategy plan in detail; I would like you all to listen and learn!'

The coach journey to Vasco FC was done mostly in contemplative silence. There, the team changed into their away strip and sat on changing room benches as they awaited call up. Any glances between them were unintentional and quickly averted with a flicked expression.

Played in a downpour of rain, the first half of the game saw end-to-end passes without goal from either side. Boca's goalkeeper Stefan was frequently tested and made a succession of agile saves, some of which evolved from promising shots by Vargas on the Vasco goal that were then cleared and rapidly transformed into an attack by them.

In the dressing room at half-time, Ferreira sought to inspire his team without individual blame or criticisms levelled.

'It's coming!' he said. 'Everyone's keeping discipline, now I want to see an explosion of energy – burn their bloody house down! Ernesto's in machine gun mode and I want each of you right there with him on the trigger!'

The second half of the game began in similarity to the first. Vargas sent powerful shots at goal – all of which were either saved or deflected by a bunched and determined defence, Sonny even found himself in admiration of the man's ceaseless efforts. When one such strike by Vargas again met with a reflex lash-out by the opposition, the ball wheeled high into the night air; Sonny ran to where it might conceivably fall, and although he knew that football wisdom, and Neymar, and Vargas, and every sports journalist and fan in the stadium would have screamed that he first trap it and bring it under control he, nonetheless, swung his right foot into the arc of the falling ball, connected, and volleyed it into the back of the Vasco net. In the furore of thousands of celebrating fans, he stood in the floodlit rain and made his A accolade – to what was the only goal of the night.

On the coach journey back to the Training Centre, Sonny read and replied to two congratulatory text messages on his phone, one from Amelia at work, the other from Maria likewise on her hospital ward where staff and patients had gathered in the day room to watch the televised game; he allowed himself a tight little smile as the city fleeted by. At the Training Centre everyone dispersed in usual manner, and he took a taxi home. Not wishing solitude he sat on the balcony, beer in hand, and happily listened to neighbouring voices and televisions until silence bossed.

The next day at the Training Centre, a subdued atmosphere prevailed as everyone went about their routines. Latent tensions, however, found release at the end of the day. As Sonny wandered into the changing rooms, he was aware that some sort of abrasive conversation was ongoing between Vargas and Hernando. Hernando then made the comment that everybody had the same right to score if they felt they could. Vargas's reaction was both immediate and vitriolic.

'You score one goal and now you are the big expert!' he raged, his native Guatemalan accent apparent. 'I have scored more times than you have shit! No one has the right to score a goal... no one,' he bellowed. 'You have to make a goal – from nothing!' Vargas pointed a blind, accusing finger at Sonny. 'He gave you the ball to deny me! Ass-play like that will lose us the championship!'

'Giving you the ball all the time might!' Sonny said, despite the certainty of an anger-fuelled response.

Vargas, not in a mood for discussion, hurtled passed Hernando and the half dozen lockers between himself and the real target of his fury. 'You are nothing here!' he yelled into Sonny's face. 'You think you are something big – that you are the only one in the team! You try to stop me scoring goals because you give the ball away to a nobody kid and try to take my crown, but you will never! Everyone knows I am top scorer – and every year they know it more! Who are you? Who are you from your big-shot crappy England to come here and do whatever you like?'

'Who are you to say no one else can score a goal?' Sonny said in committed tone.

'I am the striker!' Vargas shrilled; his neck muscles proud as he glared at Sonny.

The raised voice of Vargas drew Neymar into the changing room. Concerned that things might escalate, he stood before the two men. 'Ernesto,' he said with some measure of urgency, 'I want everyone calm here. Alberto and I are already in discussion about team discipline. We are holding a full review, and the outcome will soon be known. The last thing we need at this point is any disharmony!' He palmed for Vargas to withdraw. Vargas down looped his stare away from Sonny and, in smouldering mood, went back to his own locker. Without glance at Sonny, Neymar returned to the corridor.

Two hours later at home Sonny answered his phone to Amelia. She quickly detected he wasn't in usual buoyant mood.

'You don't sound too happy?' she said.

'I'm fine... there was just a bit of a blow-up that went on in the changing rooms today, nothing alarming.'

His attempt at nonchalance didn't lessen her concern. 'Vargas?' she said.

'Naturally! He just won't let go of the pecking order!'

'Well, let's face it, Sonny, he's probably terrified of being usurped by young blood. He's been number one for a long time now, and he won't want to let go, will he! You've got to see it from his side, as well. And I know it's been reported in the press about tensions between Ferreira and the coach. Everyone is just so aware of how close Boca are to that cup final, a bit of panic setting in, I think! But you just keep on scoring your goals and you can't be wrong, can you?'

'I'm not too sure, seems to get me into trouble!' he muttered.

With most other clubs knocked out of the national competition, Boca's next mid-week evening game and that of the Saturday week predictably had them play against hugely strong opposition. In the first of those two games, Sonny again scored and secured a one-nil victory on away turf. For their Saturday afternoon match, a quarter-final at home, long-standing mid-field players Marcus and Divo resumed their places on the team. It dismayed Sonny that they instantly formed an historic playing alliance with Vargas, to the exclusion of teammates. Vargas scored twice to take the match two goals to one. At the final whistle, Neymar was jubilant. As Sonny came off the pitch, he thought many were those who again believed in old ways. In the changing rooms Vargas championed celebrations; Boca was through to the semi-finals.

On the rundown to their semi-final game, tensions became evident in both the playing and non-playing members of the club. Vargas was often in the company of Marcus and Divo, the three seemingly blinkered to anyone else, Neymar was bullish to the point of being unapproachable, Hernando focussed solely on training and conversations between the rest of the players became guarded, without attempt at humour. Should Ferreira pass through the changing rooms silence would descend lest he had something to say or be overheard or had a facial expression that could be deciphered.

On Thursday evening of that pre-match week Amelia arrived at Sonny's flat straight from work; the pair sprawled on the sofa, and he commented on the emotionally charged atmosphere at the club.

'I can imagine,' she said. 'It's all you hear anywhere, *Semi-final! Semi-final!*' What will it be like if you get through to the final?'

'How's it going at the Cristal?' he asked, as though to dodge the question.

'Good! But I've seen another a job that I quite fancy!'

'Oh yes! where's that, then?'

'They want someone in finance at Real World Television in Rio!'

'Whoa! that sounds interesting, are you going to go for it?'

'Yes, I think I will.'

'Is it a degree job?'

'Well, it's a requirement!'

'Sounds to me as though as though someone could be moving up!'

'Stay tuned to RWTR for further developments!' she joked.

Chapter 16

On the morning of their Saturday semi-final match against Rio Roco FC, the entire Boca squad gathered in the lecture theatre at the Training Centre to hear the team's address. Standing at a bare wooden podium Ferreira looked over the room as it quietened into silence, 'Okay, guys,' he began, 'know this! there can be no final for us – unless we lay claim to it today!... Things in our favour – a home game, a full squad, pride, determination, the ability to deliver! Things against us – nothing! I will not contemplate failure... you must not play failure! Remember, nearly-men are quick forgotten – they wash cars to support their families... Each of you must decide where your dreams lie, victory today – and in the final – will determine the house you live in, which school your children go to, it will let wives and girlfriends know they made the right choice when they looked to you for their futures! I believe this is the team I have waited for – a team that is not afraid to win! It is my unshakeable belief that we will do so – do you share that belief with me?'

The room loudly confirmed that it did, and Ferreira, adrenalin fuelled, vacated the podium to let Neymar deliver his own address. Over the next ten minutes, Neymar read out the list of players and their pitch position for the match. Sonny was in the start line-up, as was Hernando.

From the outset of that game in the sold-out Santos Stadium, the ethos of both teams was that of full physical engagement. Sonny made several attacking runs on goal but was industriously body checked or bundled off the ball before he could make good, on each such occasion Neymar, sitting at Ferreira's side along a red bank of high-backed seats, threw up his hands in frustration. At half-time, Rio Roco had scored the only goal of that period. In the changing room Neymar bristled with dissatisfaction as Ferreira urged on his players. Everyone knew that to concede another goal would effectively end their chance of glory; faces became set, and stares fixed as they came out for the second half.

Ten minutes into that half of play, Sonny's powerful long shot on goal was skimmed barely wide by the keeper who made a flying leap and deflected the ball around the post. As everyone then grouped for the corner kick Sonny noticed Neymar, postured hands upturned, in a leant-in verbal exchange with Ferreira.

'What was that about with Neymar?' Sonny asked Hernando after the keeper caught the corner kick taken by Divo.

'Neymar wants you off!' Hernando said.

As though by way of riposte to Neymar, Sonny produced a masterful long-distance goal from a curling shot that had the crowd on its feet in disbelief, Sonny made an A configuration, and applauded Ferreira. Within minutes, a bad-tempered foul by a Rio Roco player had Neymar run onto the pitch to remonstrate with the referee as a near-fight broke out between players. The fracas, in all its fragmented forms, took fully five minutes to be brought under control, at the end of which Neymar, to a great deal of booing, was escorted from the pitch by stewards.

The miscreant of the foul received his second yellow card and duly sent off. Boca took full advantage of the then imbalance of players and brief minutes from full time Vargas scored Boca's second goal which secured victory. The team's celebration at the final whistle – and in the changing room – told of deeply felt relief. Vargas grinned like a child rewarded; Sonny even felt pleased for him; he thought him someone from whom fear had fallen away. When Ferreira stood in the middle of the room and raised both hands all noise quickly died down.

'In this game, success does not come to those who wait patiently,' he said. 'It comes to those who take it by the throat! There is freshly oxygenated blood coursing through the veins of this club, blood enriched by victory! It flows through all of you. Let it take us forward! Now we have a winning team! and tell me if I'm wrong... but do I smell further victory here?'

Belief was vented that everyone did, and Ferreira fist pumped the air.

During the team's bus journey back to the Training Centre Sonny got a text message from Amelia. It forewarned him that the café bar Zuma, where she had just arrived after the game, was mobbed with inebriated Boca supporters, all in wild spirits, and that he would likely find himself the centre of attention should he turn up there. At the Training Centre, the team filed off the bus and made their way between corralling security guards, through hundreds of cheering fans, and into the confines of the facility. From its corridors Sonny rang Amelia and she quickly answered above the noise of her own background.

'Hi, Sonny,' she said eagerly, as she sought a quieter spot to talk. 'Well done, that was some fantastic goal and thank you for the accolade again! This place has gone nuts – get a taxi and don't even think about walking past here!'

'Sounds like good advice!' he agreed. 'How about I scoop you up on the way and we go to Embo's, or maybe straight to the flat?'

'Sonny, I'd be happy with either or both, you just say, I can't even think straight in all this!'

'I'll come by in a taxi and we'll take a look at Embo's, I'll ring you when I set off!'

'Okay, do that!'

Thirty minutes later Sonny's taxi pulled up beside Amelia, standing alone a short distance from the hugely overspilled bar. She got in beside him on the back seat and sighed deeply.

'What's it going to be like if you win that final?' she questioned as she hugged his arm and kissed his cheek.

The pair had dinner at Embutidos, which, apart from the sound of passing vehicle horns that randomly gave vent to Boca's win, provided calm at its inner reaches. From there, in the then darkness, they walked to his flat where they sat on the balcony and savoured the warm night air.

'Yan next door'll be out soon in his white vest,' he said quietly. 'He sits out and fires up the stinkiest cigars you've ever had whiff of, goodness knows where he finds them! He gets three days out of each one and you can tell which day they're on! Next door will take in their budgie!' he laughed. 'I absolutely love it!'

Five minutes later, Sonny's neighbour emerged in a white vest, lit a cigar, and sat out of sight on his part-screened balcony, Amelia turned to Sonny's shoulder and supressed her giggles.

'I applied for that television job,' she then said.

'Oh right! Come on, let's go in and you can tell me all about it.'

Laid entwined on the sofa they let the high tensions of their day further dissipate, as turned low music played on a radio channel on the tv, and she told him of her job application. She stayed the night.

In the morning, the two walked to the communal front door of her block. She invited him up, but he knew she had a two o'clock shift start at the hotel, he said such and they parted with a hug. On his way back, he bought a newspaper from a street kiosk, and sitting at home, pored over the sports-pages reports and opinions of Boca's win. He somehow felt detached from its analysis and dropped the skewed paper onto the table. Unsure if Maria would be at work – and aware that her tenure in the Nurses Home would soon be over – he sent her an enquiring text message. Twenty minutes later she rang him from her ward.

Thrilled for him that he had played so well in the semi-final, she said that both herself and Saulo had been present at the game. She explained how Saulo's scheduled extra workday that Saturday had been cancelled at the last minute, suspectedly because of the match, and so they themselves went. She then revealed that her and Monica had earlier that week moved out of the Nurses Home and into a privately rented two bedroomed flat – and invited him to come over later that afternoon.

Sonny took a taxi to Maria's texted address. He rang her along the way, and she was waiting at the kerb when he arrived at the low-rise dated block of flats, each with its own inset balcony, and the entire row matched by similar across a street that had thinly barked trees pocketed into the pavements at either side. They greeted and she led him up a central stairwell to her door along a communal corridor.

Within the flat, a faint smell of tea tree oil and hardwoods permeated an open-plan space made bright with daylight through glass-panelled doors that hinged onto the street-facing balcony. She went behind the waist-high kitchen divide, took out two bottles of beer from a tall freestanding refrigerator, opened them, and put them on a small table which abutted the divide on the lounge side. Sitting across the table the pair grinned happily at one another and touched together the vapour-weeping bottles. He felt reminded of a certain school desk but made no mention of it.

'We cheered you on yesterday,' she said humorously. 'Or you might not have scored that goal, you know!'

'I knew there was something!' he agreed. 'Well, this looks a nice place you've found yourselves!' he added, looking around. 'Where's Monica?'

'She's at work, she'll be back soon, but don't you go dashing off! She's not scary!'

'So, what do think of it so far?'

'I love it! I'll be honest, leaving the home was a bit of a toughie. It was one of those moments, you know, where you're saying goodbye to something that's proper solid and good. This place was on the notice board, can you believe I actually felt reassured by that, like it gave its approval!'

Ten minutes later the door to the flat opened and Monica walked in. She had grown-out her side-cropped fair hair, and a loosely layered hairstyle gave a more balanced look to her small head.

'Hi,' she said, as she crossed the floor with a leggy gait that bounced the raggy hem of her black trousers at the gingery carpet.

Sonny got up and proffered a hand. 'Hi, Monica. Nice to see you again,' he said. She looked slightly away and engaged the hand.

'Hi, Sonny.'

'Love the flat,' he complimented.

'Thank you. We like it.'

'Right, well, I don't want to be in anybody's way here,' he said. 'When you come home from work all you want is your normality – so I'll disappear now!'

'No need to go rushing off,' Monica assured him. 'I'm going for a shower anyway.'

'Well, I've got to get back. I'll catch up with you both later!' he said.

Maria walked with him down to the street.

'Are you coming to the final, then?' he asked.

'Oh, too right, we are! Saulo can't wait!'

'I'll sort you some tickets and drop them round.'

'Oh, that would be brilliant! Ta, Sonny, Saulo'll be chuffed to bits over that – tickets from the hand of Sonny Lopez!' she said grandly, to which they both laughed.

Chapter 17

It soon transpired that Boca would play Puerto Barrios FC in the National Cup Final. Barrios was one of the wealthier clubs in Rio and general belief was that they would lift the trophy. Barrios, though, had only narrowly beaten Flamengo to secure their place, and had shown a weakness in defence. It was perceived quite possible by many in Botafogo that Boca might seize the day.

The two-and-a-half-week countdown to the Cup Final saw intensive mood set in at the Training Centre. Both Marcus and Divo crafted an ongoing display of bravado as they went about their routines; Sonny suspected it a sham to feign seniority or perhaps to nudge selection, Hernando, mildly irritated by their antics, said little, upcoming striker Renato, even less. Mid-morning on the Friday of the then two-week buffer, Sonny was called off the field by Neymar who himself had been approached by Lilian from the administration office. Lilian, a middle-aged HR officer, with company lanyard and retained spectacles around her neck, waited at Neymar's side as Sonny wandered over to them.

'There's someone to see you in the office,' Neymar said simply.

Sonny went with Lilian who seemed to have some urgency about her stride, though he didn't know whether such was usually the case.

'Who is it?' he asked as they made their way over a red asphalt running track.

'The police,' she said in constructed light tone.

'What do they want?'

'I really don't know.'

Lillian knocked on Ferreira's office door and they were called in by Ferrira who was sitting at his desk, a troubled look on his face; across from him sat two men, one a forty-something uniformed police officer, cap loosely in hand, the other a swarthy thin-faced, slightly younger man in plain clothes.

'Sonny, these two gentlemen are from the police department,' Ferreira said. 'They would like a private meeting with you. This is Sonny Lopez,' he said as both men stood up.

'Good morning, Sr Lopez,' the man in plain clothes said. 'I'm detective Gomés, and this is officer Rocha. Officer Rocha nodded to Sonny, reinforced with a slow blink.

'Lilian, if you'll kindly show the gentlemen to the Pressroom,' Ferreira said. 'And mark it engaged.'

Lilian led the three men along the corridor to the vacant Pressroom. She switched on the lights and stood back as they filed in. 'If you need anything, press zero on any phone,' she said.

'Thank you, Sra,' Gomés said.

Lilian left them and closed the door after her. In the quiet coolness of that narrow room the trio seated themselves at a grey melamine workstation beside a gallery of deep windows which overlooked the sports field.

'If we can first establish a few facts, Sr Lopez,' Gomés began. 'Can you confirm that you are the brother of Sra Maria Lopez?'

Sonny felt his skin instantly cool at the question.

'Maria is my sister,' he said. 'Why?'

'I'm afraid I have some very distressing news for you, Sr Lopez,' Gomés went on. 'Obviously you are unaware of events?'

Sonny stared at him. 'I don't know of any events!'

'Sra Lopez was attacked as she walked home from her hospital shift last night,' Gomés said. 'I'm sorry, but she died from injuries sustained in that attack. It is a murder enquiry.'

Sonny let his head slowly tilt downwards; without focus his gaze went to the floor, he sighed involuntarily. He had no other response and simply stared as he was buffeted by waves of shock.

'I'm sorry,' Gomés said, 'but I must ask, were you aware of any difficulties she may have been having, debts, perhaps boyfriend troubles – street or neighbour difficulties?'

Sonny was without answer, he wasn't about to let-in what he'd just heard – as though choice to defer was his, he remained silent and still.

'Anything you can tell us might be useful,' Gomés pressed him.

Sonny shook his head as tears formed.

'When did you last see Maria?'

Sonny struggled to recall. 'Sunday,' he said.

'And when did you last speak to her?'

'Then.'

'Did she have any concerns about anything?'

Sonny caught the movement of officer Rocha discreetly writing in a notepad placed on the thigh of a crossed-over leg.

'No, she didn't, Sonny answered. 'She was happy, she was always happy. There was nothing wrong!'

'Did she ask for a loan, anything out of the ordinary?'

'No.'

'Formal identification of Sra Lopez has already been made by the hospital,' Gomés affirmed. 'There is nothing you need to do at this point. If you have no immediate information, however trivial, that you can recall then we'll leave now and continue with our enquiries. I apologise for bringing you such tragic news, Sr Lopez!'

Sonny brought the man's face into focus, 'There's nothing.'

'When we know more, we'll contact you,' Gomés said. 'As next of kin you'll be able to collect any possessions of Sra Lopez that you may wish to claim. If you remember anything at all in the meantime do not hesitate to ring.' He took out a calling card from his jacket breast pocket and placed it down before Sonny. 'This is my direct number. You have our sincerest condolences, Sr Lopez.' The two men got up and made their way out. Sonny remained seated and let tears seep through tightly closed eyes. 'Not you Maria,' he whispered in anguish. 'Please, not you!'

An hour later Sonny went home by taxi. There, unable to put together any coherent thought, he sat on the sofa and waited numbly for some measure of rationale, or a sent person to bring news and reason and impossible comfort. Late that afternoon he answered his phone to Amelia.

'Oh, Sonny,' she sobbed, 'I'm so sorry! I've just heard the horrible, horrible news, where are you?'

'At home.'

'Is anyone with you?'

'No.'

'Do you want me to come round?'

'I don't know, what are you doing?'

'I'm at work, but they can manage without me, I'll come now, yes?'

'Yes.'

Within twenty minutes, Amelia was sitting beside him, her hands clasped with his as she tried to lessen his pain through shared grief. When she left three hours later they saw that beside his door someone had placed a small posse of flowers with a tied-on card which read: *Our thoughts are with you, Sonny.*

Sonny rang Ferreira the following morning and told him he wouldn't be coming in for that day's training. Ferreira offered his deepest condolences and said for him to take as long as he wished to recover from such dreadful news. In despair Sonny gazed over the silent flat and tried to bring about some acceptance of fact. He repeatedly made coffee, sometimes with milk and sugar, sometimes with only the one, sometimes with neither, until he rejected the not-wanted taste altogether and threw it down the sink. It pained him greatly that his much loved and equally loving little sister who had smilingly overcome every vicious detriment in her short life – and whose very ambitions he had seen rise to fruition – was gone. He anguished that shortly he would stand at her grave when it wasn't her turn to go, and that she was the wrong person to be so brutally taken. When he couldn't stand to be alone with tormenting thoughts any longer, he pushed his feet into trainers – simply to go anywhere and be somewhere else. As he stepped onto the street his phone rang from Amelia.

'Sonny, have you heard?' she said.

'No! what?'

'I've just been told it was on the news; they've taken the boyfriend in for questioning – unnamed!'

Sonny was without response.

'Where are you?' she asked.

'I've just come out to try and clear my head.'

'Well, I'm no good here at work. Do you want to meet up?'

'Yeah,' he said defeatedly.

'Sky Park in half an hour, yes?'

'Yes.'

Sonny and Amelia sat mostly in silence, hands loosely clasped, on a bench at Sky Park as they let the afternoon hours pass them by. There were no further news reports of Maria that day.

At ten o'clock the next morning, Sonny, at home, answered his phone to detective Gomés who told him that a suspect in Maria's murder had been arrested and charged. The suspect was flatmate Monica Ramos. Gomés said Maria's body would soon be released for burial and that if he wished a private funeral for her, to contact an undertaker of his choice, an approved list of which could be obtained from the front desk of Botafogo police station; the undertaker would then liaise with them in a prescribed manner. Also, if he wished, and with police consent then in place, he may arrange for access to Maria's flat and claim any relevant items that belonged her for his own keeping. Gomés instigated an automated text message to Sonny which quoted a reference number to that effect; it came through as he spoke. With gathered presence of mind, Sonny asked what had possessed the flatmate to do such a dreadful thing? Gomés told how Ramos had confessed to a jealous rage when she found out by way of gossip at the hospital that Maria and Saulo were to marry in the coming year. Ramos had lain in wait for her to come out of the hospital that night and committed her premeditated crime, she then went back to the flat, showered and watched tv. Conviction, Gomés predicted, would undoubtedly follow.

In answer to Sonny's question of whether Saulo had fallen under suspicion, Gomés explained how Ramos had concocted a story which alleged both Saulo and Maria were conspirators in the theft of hospital drugs which they sold to fund their planned wedding. The story was meant to cast wide the net of suspicion and at the same time, in a further act of revenge, besmirch both Maria and Saulo's good name. Police, though, found no such thefts had taken place and the story not plausible because as a student nurse Maria wouldn't have had unsupervised access to hospital drugs – Ramos had put herself in the frame with her lies and when pressed at length, had broken down and made a full confession. Everything in her life was perfect, she had claimed, until Saulo came along. Sonny thanked him for his call.

For fully fifteen minutes Sonny stared out from his sun-warmed balcony and anguished how Maria had by then missed two, forevermore additive, days of her so-meaningful life and that there could be children on a hospital ward who looked in vain to see her smiling face, still fresh in their minds. Knowing that Amelia would be at work he sent her a text message which told of his call from Gomés. She soon rang him and said she somehow felt better for knowing that Saulo was not involved.

Straight from Amelia's call, Sonny walked the three-quarter mile distance to Botafogo police station where, across a screened counter, he asked a uniformed officer for their approved list of undertakers. From a shallow drawer of a countertop tin stack the officer, without a word, took out a printed sheet of A4 paper and slid it beneath the screen. Sonny then showed him the reference number on his phone, sent him by Gomés, and asked if access could be arranged to the referenced property that he might collect certain items.

As Sonny held aloft the phone, the officer, unhurried and expressionless throughout, entered the number onto a computer keyboard and awaited completion of the resultant print-out. When the printer fell silent, he took the delivered sheet from the spill tray and slid that, too, under the screen, at the same time, without looking, he waved away other members of the public who had presumed to stand at the desk.

'This is the authorisation permit you will need for the letting agent, all the information is on there,' the officer said in routine manner. 'Make arrangements directly with them. It is no longer a police matter.' He looked away as though in wait for Sonny to vacate the counter. Sonny scooped up the two sheets, said 'Thank you' and left.

    Sitting on a square-cut log bench along a pedestrianised shopping street, Sonny studied the short list of undertakers and rang that nearest his own address – Sanchez Funeral Directors. In professional and sympathetic tone, the woman who answered stated the company's willingness to assume the burial service and asked that he visit them to formalise the request; he was made an appointment for one o'clock that afternoon. He then rang Maria's letting agent and, after a long conversation, oft paused by them, it was arranged that someone would meet him there at the flat the following morning at ten o'clock. With that disquieting prospect in place, he sought out the premises of Sanchez Funeral Directors and duly kept his one o'clock appointment. Fábio Sanchez, an elderly man, himself thanked Sonny for his consideration of them in the matter and foresaw no problems with the instruction.

    Later that afternoon, Sanchez's office rang him and confirmed they had contacted the hospital mortuary and relayed how Maria's body would be released for burial in two days' time – and in accordance with convention there would be no service fee to pay because Maria was an organ donor. The funeral would take place at three o'clock at the Sao Francisco Xavier cemetery for which they had posted notice online, as was customary. Sonny thanked them for letting him know and took comfort that Maria would be laid to rest in the same cemetery as Sofia and their mother. Standing on his balcony, as though to remain liberated from enclosing walls, he texted Amelia the developments. She immediately rang him and said she would come over as soon as Juanita got in from work; two hours later she walked in and they tightly hugged.

    'Why don't you leave the flat visit thing for another time, Sonny?' she reasoned. 'That can wait, you've got enough going on right now! And then just let someone go in for you and store it all somewhere until you're ready. It's the last thing you need to put yourself through!'

'It's not that! She has a cloth doll, and two more that belonged our other sisters. I know she'd want them buried with her.'

'Have you told the funeral people?'

'Yes, they know all about it. I just need to get them there.'

'I'll be glad for you when this is all over with, Sonny. I really will. It's just too awful for words.'

'I feel like I want to ring her and say, What the hell's going on?' He looked up at the ceiling, in abject misery.

'Do you want me to come with you tomorrow?'

'I would love for you to come with me tomorrow!'

'I have the whole day free,' she said, which he suspected was a lie but was grateful for it and didn't argue. He told her of Maria's gold chain, of where it might be, and that, along with the dolls, he would like to retrieve it. 'I'm desperate to do the right thing,' he said, 'but I just don't want to have to go in there searching through her room.'

'I'll go in, and if they're there, I'll get them,' she assured him.

'Thanks, Amelia.'

'How does anybody deal with this stuff?' he asked.

'They have to. Did you know Maria was an organ donor?'

'No. I had no idea. But that's just so her! Give life to others when hers is over. Nineteen and she carries a donor card! Who does that?'

'It's a fitting epitaph for her, Sonny, isn't it!'

He nodded. 'If anyone's lucky enough to get her heart, I just hope they can live up to it,' he said.

The following day, Amelia pulled up on her motor scooter along the traffic-busy street beneath Sonny's flat as he waited for her on the pavement, empty sports bag in hand. He put on the crash helmet, slid behind her as pillion passenger, and they drove the short distance to Maria's address. Already there standing outside the door to the flat was a thirty-something man, dressed in a royal blue linen suit, who intently watched their approach down the corridor.

'Morning,' Sonny said to him as they neared. 'I'm Sonny Lopez, and this is Sra Lemos. We're here to collect a few items that belong to Sra Lopez.'

The man nodded politely at Amelia. 'Sra Lemos,' he greeted. He turned his attention to Sonny. 'I am Sr Cortez, and I represent the letting agent of the property. If I may see your permit, please, Sr Lopez.'

Sonny produced the document. Satisfied, Lopez fetched out from his jacket pocket a singular latch key ringed to a utility tag and opened the door of the flat. He stepped inside; Amelia followed – prompted by Sonny who kept his scope of vision narrow as he, too, then entered. In the stilled gloom Cortez strode across the floor and drew open heavy curtains at the balcony so that daylight had its immediate impact. Leaden with discomfort, Sonny's gaze went to the table where he'd sat with Maria – and thought it so long ago. Amelia read his pain and gently asked him, 'Do you know which is her room?'

Sonny nodded toward a closed door and said, 'That one.' Amelia went over, opened it, switched on the light and went in. Minutes later she reappeared holding a colour-faded, much crumpled plastic bag, she pulled it open and said, 'I think these might be them.'

He peered into the bag, 'Yes,' he said and lightly took it from her. He placed it on the table, carefully lifted out each of the three threadbare cloth dolls and set them down. 'Yes, that's them,' he confirmed. 'I actually remember their names.' He pointed at each one. 'This was Sofia's, Clarissa, Florence had Rosa, and Maria's was Zafira.' He closed his eyes at the loss of his sisters and their collective long-ago happy childhood.

'And this,' Amelia said, and opened a hand to reveal the gold chain. 'Shoe!' she all but whispered.

Sonny nodded, with a slow blink. 'Come on,' he said. 'Let's get them where they need to be.'

'If I can just record the items, please, Sr Lopez,' Cortez said as he stepped away from the balcony doors.
Though irked by the request, Sonny waited while Cortez photographed the items on a mobile phone. When Cortez put forward a hand to perhaps further separate the dolls, Sonny objected. 'Don't touch them, please,' he said, his voice light and filled with sudden emotion. Cortez himself moved to alleviate any need.

With the photographs taken, Cortez asked, 'Are these the only items that you'll be taking today, Sr Lopez?'

'Yes.'

'In that case, if I can just pass onto you the landlord's request that the flat be cleared, please, of all personal items by the end of the month so that the property can be serviced and re let. Feel free to contact the office at any time and we will arrange access convenient to you.'

Sonny put the dolls back into the plastic bag -- the chain into the breast pocket of his shirt, as he considered a response. 'Thank you, Sr Cortez,' he said, and zipped the bag into his own. Amelia went over to Maria's door and closed it; she engaged Sonny's arm, and the pair left without further comment.

With Sonny again riding pillion, Amelia drove to the funeral parlour where they met Fábio Sanchez. The man greeted them with professional solemnity and led the way along a narrow uneven corridor, into his small office. He invited them to be seated at two upright chairs before his enclosed desk – upon which was a slimline computer screen, keyboard and wireless mouse – Sanchez took his own charcoal grey, office chair opposite.

'We are tending to Maria now, Sr Lopez,' he said. 'She will be most beautifully presented. I believe you have brought some items that you wish interred with her?'

Momentarily stunned that Maria lay in the building, Sonny lifted out the crumpled bag and held it aloft, 'These three dolls in here,' he said.

'Of course,' Sanchez agreed, and reached across for it.

From his shirt pocket Sonny teased out the gold chain, 'and if she could wear her chain?' he added.

Sanchez delved into a drawer of the desk and produced an envelope, obligingly he held it open beneath the chain and Sonny let it spill from his fingers. 'And, if I may say... a lovely gesture,' Sanchez commented. 'Would you like the dolls to be on display within the casket?'

Sonny was without answer.

'You may leave that to us with every confidence, Sr Lopez. I have here some possessions of Maria's to give you.' He opened a lower, desk drawer and brought out a vertical, sealed A6 envelope. 'These are the things she had on her person when she sadly passed,' he said and handed it to Sonny. 'You are a young man of high standards, Sr Lopez,' he complimented. 'Perhaps whilst you are here you might care for a private viewing? It will only take a few minutes to complete the presentation for you.'

Sonny wasn't in any way prepared for such inevitability – but knew it wasn't something to be ducked, and that Brazilian custom dictated the coffin be open throughout the service. 'Thank you,' he said with steeled commitment. 'Yes, I would very much like a private moment with Maria.'

'Then, if you'll excuse me,' Sanchez said and stood up. He took the delivered bag and the envelope that contained the chain and left the office. Amelia reached for Sonny's hand as they waited. Single minutes later Sanchez reappeared in the doorway.

'If you'd both care to follow me,' he said.

Much subdued, Sonny and Amelia followed him further along the corridor and into an ante room that was furnished with cushion-backed chairs around walls that hung with prints of cherubic figures and waterfalls. Discrete loudspeakers provided calming ethereal music and a low table with a ceramic vase of fresh yellow flowers commanded centre space on a busily patterned carpet.

'Please take a seat, Sra Lemos,' Sanchez invited.

Amelia sat beneath a high-level false window which gently coloured the room with a backlit depiction of light rays. Sonny suspected she chose it that she be on the blind side of the only other door, which Sanchez then opened and palmed for him to go through. 'Take a moment to pay your private respects, Sr Lopez,' he offered.

Sonny went in and Sanchez closed the door after him. Blank of mind, in a windowless room, Sonny looked upon an ebonised coffin, beneath which dark velvet draped over unseen support and went down to the carpeted floor. The coffin, elaborately padded with soft, grey material, was open its top half and dimly lit by tall pedestal uplighters in each corner of the room that reflected their light off the ceiling. He thought it a place of serenity and caused him no distress as his gaze sought refuge in the dolls that were positioned at Maria's shoulders. Gradually, he looked upon her face; he thought it a face of beauty and peace.

'Hi, Maria,' he quietly said. 'Say hi to mama and Seve, Paulo, Sofia and Florence for me.' He noticed the gold chain around her neck and squeezed the side of the coffin as though to be as one with her. 'If ever I have children of my own, they will know of you, Maria. I hope you're happy in your new favela – I'll see you all there one day when it's my turn to come home. Bye till then, God bless.'

When he came out of the room and closed the door, Amelia saw his emptiness and tightly hugged him. As they then left the premises, Sanchez offered his own personal advice, 'Mourn in deep sorrow today, Sr Lopez – that your tomorrows bring happiness anew.'

Amelia drove them back to the flat where they sat on the balcony in silence, and he allowed tormenting thought to lessen in the afternoon's sunlight. He felt easier that he'd seen Maria at peace; acceptance finally took over and he knew he could better cope with her tomorrow funeral. He rang Ferreira and told him he would be back at work the day after next. Ferreira hugely welcomed the call and again offered his deep condolences and wished him every strength for the day ahead.

Sonny and Amelia arrived by taxi for Maria's funeral at the Sao Francisco Xavier cemetery and made their way into the

Reception Hall for the service. There, Maria's coffin, open its head section, was displayed, surrounded by flowers, at the centre of a singular domed space, and in a one-directional route a gathering number of mourners filed passed and freely wept as they viewed.

Some, overcome with grief, had to be supported by friends and ushers. The attendance swelled to over a hundred, many in hospital uniform and all in a state of deep sorrow. Sonny and Amelia joined with them as they likewise paid their respects; he was heartened to see the three dolls and chain in place. Heartened too, that Sanchez had afforded him his private farewell to Maria and deemed it a precious moment for which he would be forever grateful.

As Sonny and Amelia then sat along the first-row bank of wooden chairs a mourner stood purposefully before him. It was Suki da Silva. He immediately got to his feet, and they greeted. Her very presence faltered his voice as he expressed gratitude that she was there. She offered sincere condolences from both herself and the school and spoke of her deep sadness at Maria's passing. She went on to say how Maria had been an inspiration for everyone, that her achievements had been widely noted and had gone some way in keeping the school viable. In her own words, Rio had lost a golden heart and acquired an angel.

Suki da Silva was the first of many who approached him and gave solace. Saulo, there with family, hugged first him then Amelia. 'I'd only just asked her to marry me!' he said distraught as he stared vacantly at Sonny. 'She said yes! She wanted to tell you herself... in person! we planned to get married next year when I'd finished my training... I just can't come to terms with what's happened! How can this be real?'
Sonny marginally shook his head, eyes closed – and found himself without answer.

At day's end, Amelia tipped back her head on Sonny's sofa. 'It's done!' she said wistfully.

'Yes,' Sonny said, sitting beside her.

'So many people loved her, didn't they. That was her tribute. I don't think I'll ever forget poor Saulo's face, perhaps more than anyone he's been denied her.'

'Yes,' Sonny agreed. 'He has... and the kids they'll never have! Suki da Silva had it right with her analogy.'

'If you manage to score in that Final, Sonny, make an M!'

Sonny reported for work the following morning at the Training Centre where a determined mood hung over the facility as everyone set about their workload with vigour. Only Hernando offered his condolences, for which Sonny thanked him.

On the Friday morning the entire team was called off the pitch to go into the lecture theatre. Ferreira took the podium and silence ensued.

'In just over a week's time we step into that Final!' he said with honed gravity. 'And I believe we are a team poised for victory. But belief alone will not lift the trophy! We are fully fit, fully capable, fully everything – we must capitalise on that! I want eleven men who can play as one – or alone – each with vision, all with hunger! Give me that and the rewards will follow. On Monday I will have a ten-minute meeting with each of you in my office, we will discuss tactics and the role you will play. You won't all see pitch time! But those on the bench may be called upon at any moment – be ready! And now I'm going to tell you all a hard fact! we have more at stake than mere pride and glory – revenue through victory will further enable us to invest in state-of-the-art facilities, more staff, and better renumeration for our players so that we keep hold of a winning team! If this sounds like a good plan to you, let me hear a Yo!' The room resonated with 'Yo!'

Each player's name and their allocated ten-minute meeting with Ferreira had been written on a whiteboard and set up to be viewed as they walked into the changing rooms on Monday morning. Those who came out from their own meeting said nothing of it and the day progressed in guarded fashion. Sonny's slot was at eleven o'clock, he duly knocked on the door, was called in by Ferreira, alone in the office, and invited to take a seat across the desk.

'Good to have you back, Sonny,' Ferreira said as he looked on approvingly.

'Good to be back, Alberto,' Sonny replied.

Ferreira leaned back in his chair as though to consider his next words. 'Out of the entire squad, Sonny, you are the player I can least afford to lose,' he said. 'You are the ace in the hole for any game. But you will start the Final on the bench.' He looked at Sonny to allow the news its impact. 'The logic is simple,' he resumed. 'We all know you've had some personal trauma to deal with, and yes, you've missed a couple of days training – justifiably so! But I am in no doubt that you are fully fit and committed to victory – this is purely a tactical decision. I wanted every player to mimic your vision and attacking style, to take chances and not care if it came to nothing, because next time they might prevail. With the exception of Hernando, players are still reluctant to commit to that level of risk, they are afraid of blame and failure, and a lot of that is down to the Vargas factor. In the Final, I want Vargas, Marcus and Divo force-fed up front with the ball by everyone because that's been the standard format, and everyone's in sync with it! If you're on the pitch, then that familiarity might unravel! So, this is how play will run, I shall give the status quo its head. If we go up, then I'll let it continue. If goals fail to materialise, or we fall behind, then I shall bring you on, and at that point, Sonny, your task is a singular one – bring home that trophy!'

Sonny understood Ferreira's thinking, understood that him being on the pitch might destabilise a focussed team – until he was needed, at which point there would be no Vargas factor to overcome.

'Bring me on, Alberto,' he said, 'and I'll give you your Yo!'

With all one-to-one meetings concluded tensions lifted and players began to open-up to each other again. In that countdown week to the Cup Final game as Sonny jogged around the running track Hernando caught up with his easy lope and ran beside him.

'So, what do I tell myself to come good in the Final, Sonny?' he asked, in need of answer.

'You tell yourself not to panic, 'Nando, turn boos into cheers and not to flatter the boo-boys with so much as a sideways glance! Just be yourself and play to your skills,' he asserted, as he perhaps reminded himself.

On Saturday morning on the day of the Cup Final, Sonny walked past heightened security, through the vocal early crowds of supporters, and into the Training Centre where he immersed himself in ongoing preparations. Trigger-ready players sitting along slatted benches paid little heed, beyond measured greetings, to anyone else as they wave-pushed heady liniments into leg muscles, adopted breathing techniques to calm themselves and willed personal glory.

When called as a collective by Neymar, the team boarded the bus and went to the Santos Stadium along a route that flowed with thousands of supporters on foot, and in cars and coaches that streamed club scarves – the journey punctuated with impassioned shouts and horns blared by those who recognised the in-transit team bus.

With everyone gathered and ready in the changing room, Ferreira addressed his team.

'The coursework is done,' he said. 'The mocks are over; now it is time for the final exam – time to graduate!'

The players, each with kitted-out child in hand, walked in single file from the tunnel to a spontaneous roar from the crowd. Sonny took his place on the substitutes bench from where he absorbed the spectacle of marching bands and the all-around fervour of the occasion. On the terraces a small section of Boca supporters showed disapproval that he hadn't taken to the pitch.

From the start whistle, Barrios laid siege to the Boca goalmouth. They played as though with more players and Boca was soon in survival mode. From the dugout, Ferreira engaged in up-down arm-waving theatrics as beside him Neymar ever rapidly chewed gum, mouth agape and head bobbing. On the pitch Hernando, Boca's busiest player, raced into any viable position for his chance at goal, but no meaningful passes came his way and those between Vargas, Marcus and Divo were industriously intercepted by a bullish Barrios.

With half-time nearly upon them Barrios scored what seemed an inevitable goal to have Boca heads down and goalless in front of increasingly frustrated supporters. Sonny found himself strangely disinterested as he looked on – he knew, though, that it wasn't simply churlishness on his part, more that he was needed on the pitch and yet remained on the bench in a losing Final.

A change of player to begin the second half for Boca was announced and to a cheering crowd, Sonny took up position on the right wing in place of Divo. Sonny knew he had to perform, with less time in which to do it; but he also knew his own frame of mind – that it was a blend of anger, of pent-up emotions and of the need to do what he did best. The ball that he hooked out of the air with a heel was never meant to be his, nonetheless, he took possession of it. He didn't look up or care who shouted, waved or screamed – he simply made for the Barrios goal as the crowd bellowed its will. In what was his fifth minute on the field he sent the ball in a straight-line drill into the back of the net and scored Boca level. With his face set to the sky as teammates mobbed him, he formed an M with touching fingers and mouthed, 'For you, Maria!'

His goal had him subsequently two-man marked whenever he made a break into open space – something which almost saw Hernando on the scoresheet when Sonny, not in possession, drew his markers away and Hernando powered a long shot on goal that beat the keeper but hit the post to then be cleared by a frantic defence. Hernando agonised at his miss – others, though, including Ferreira saw fresh talent unleashed. Barrios, in a state of angst at the near reversal of earlier fortune, quickly regrouped and ramped-up their aggression.

Repeated saves by Boca's on-form goalkeeper Stefan kept them at bay until the final whistle blew, and the game went to extra time. In the first half of that period Barrios, much energised by substitute players, mounted a relentless onslaught and regained the lead with a scrappy second goal. Player discipline then broke down in the second half as Barrios stalled for time and, in a stadium, ripe with hysteria, Marcos was brutally fouled near goal with a scything leg sweep by a Barrios defender who was immediately given the red card and a penalty awarded.

In considerable pain, Marcos was stretchered off and in the ensuing melee Vargas was shown a yellow card for continually chest barging the aggressor. When some level of control resumed and stewards had cleared the pitch of missiles hurled by both sets of outraged supporters, Marcos was substituted by Renato. Vargas duly stepped up to take the penalty – which Sonny thought justified because Vargas had seldom failed to score from a penalty. The Barrios goalkeeper, however, showed small regard for statistics and to euphoric acclaim made a fingertip save which tipped the ball over the crossbar.

With less than ten minutes of play left, Barrios, a man down, found themselves without composure, their ploy then to roll on the ground when so-much as nudged and claim for foul. After one such typically awarded free kick Sonny intercepted a Barrios pass and looked up as Hernando, then in expectation, rapidly covered ground toward goal. Vargas, likewise, sprinted on the opposite wing; without hint to any player, Sonny made his choice and long-kicked the ball, stride-perfect, into the path of Vargas who, of the two teammates, was less man-marked. Vargas scored a velocity-driven goal that saw the stadium pause its sanity. The final whistle blew on a draw and the game went to penalties.

Ten minutes later, Vargas stepped up to take Boca's first penalty kick. That he paused slightly suggested his earlier miss weighed upon him; the keeper perhaps sensed it and feigned to either side in tormenting preparation. Vargas went for glory and scored. Barrios, too, secured their first attempt with a confident shot into the top right-hand corner of goal. Sonny, who had no previous form on penalty taking, was next to take the spot and the keeper went about his distraction tactics. Sonny adopted the Vargas technique and put the ball under the roof of the net to score. Barrios' next attempt saw Boca keeper Stefan make a blocking save from an overly cautious kick. Hernando looked at no one as he stepped up.

Desperate not to send the ball soaring over the crossbar and be forever damned – or maybe to bring in unpredictability – he powered the ball hard and low, barely above the turf; it could potentially have been saved but the keeper went the wrong way, and Hernando scored. At their next attempt Barrios completely missed, and the taker sank to his knees. Boca was only a fourth goal away from the trophy; the challenge fell to Renato. Renato had good form under pressure and his body language bristled self-belief as he stared down at the spot-placed ball – his worthy penalty kick then duly saved. Barrios had two remaining chances; both needed as goals. They were denied at their next attempt by Stefan whose save gave Boca its victory.

The on-pitch celebrations, media photographs, interviews and the crescendo of the Cup presentation, done to cannoned orange and white ribbon and smoke, took nearly an hour to conclude. At its height Ferreira loudly hissed into Sonny's ear, 'I don't want you even to consider playing for anyone else, Sonny. Your future is right here!'

From the stadium, the team went to the Training Centre where the club's employees, over eighty strong, gathered in the commandeered Sports Bar. There, emotions ran free as success was further celebrated; in the animated throes of it all Sonny found himself standing next to Vargas who beamingly offered him a high-five – with which he happily engaged. At some point in the proceedings Sonny left the bar for the relative calm of the corridor and rang Amelia. She had been present at the game but had to take-up home commitments for the evening. She told him how thrilled she was for him, that she felt proud of his match winning efforts – and that his tribute to Maria had made her cry.

At two o'clock in the morning, Sonny left the Sports Bar revellers to their ongoing party and took a taxi home. He had drunk far more than accustomed to and knew he should simply have gone to bed. Instead, he sat on the sofa, clawed open a can of beer from the fridge and fumbled out his phone from a pocket. His focus gathered on the phonebook listings and when mind and vision agreed, he called Janice. After a series of fluctuating whines and shrill notes there followed a lengthy silence, he thought the connection had failed and then Janice spoke. Her voice spilled with surprise as she welcomed his call, and their words tumbled into each other's.

They talked at length, and she told of how nothing much had changed, that people often asked after him, that she herself was happy and had, on occasion, met with 'the gang in the Feathers'. It was a world which he was pleasantly reminded of. 'I miss you!' he said spontaneously. 'Miss you too,' she replied. She then asked after Maria and whether she had finally accepted the reality of him coming home? The innocent question had him briefly stunned. He realised that not communicating news of Maria's tragic death had left them both open to future difficulty.

He told her of Maria's passing; Janice groaned in shock and offered remorse-filled condolence – and concern for him. He apologised and said he hadn't meant to upset her. Suddenly clear of mind, he reset the mood and asked if it was okay if he rang again at a future agreed time – she assured him that it was, and they ended the call on a subdued note.

Sonny awoke four hours later – still laid on the sofa and with his phone beneath him; on the coffee table was the untouched can of beer from earlier. Momentarily, he felt his face prickle as he flash-recalled how he'd phoned Janice. It troubled him that he may have spoken foolishly in drink, and that on the back of a glib social call he'd given her the dreadful news about Maria. He went through into the bedroom as he agonised over the issue and wondered if he should again ring and apologise if he'd caused her upset. He decided to do nothing until fully recovered; he got into bed and slept for a further two hours. When he awoke, the matter was soon again on his mind – he checked his phone and read a text message from Janice which expressed her great sadness at his loss.

Over the following few hours, Sonny drank coffee and attempted to shower away a hangover. In the brightness of the Sunday afternoon, he looked over the balcony. His neighbour Ivan, under a stilled billow of cigar smoke, idly stood at his balcony rail and lolled a brief gaze at him without acknowledgement. Sonny was happy for such uncomplicated normality.

    Called in by his wife, Ivan disappeared and on the next balcony along a boy, aged about ten, distantly looked across without obstruction at Sonny; the boy darted indoors and quickly came back out wearing a Boca football shirt, he then stood fixedly proud and resumed his stare. Sonny knew his name was Felipe because he'd often heard his mother in full voice as she shouted him up from the street for mealtimes. Sonny offered him a wave and Felipe eagerly waved back, moments later Sonny's phone rang on the sofa, he went in and answered it to Amelia.

    'Hi, Sonny,' she said. 'Are you recovered yet?'

    'Amelia, I don't know if I'm recovered or still up there! How are you?'

    'Fine, thank you, just about to set off for work, actually – can't think what the topic of conversation will be? – so you're own your own today, hot shot!'

    'Well, I wouldn't be any hot shot company that's for sure!'

    She laughed. 'The best thing you can do, Sonny, is get yourself down to Embo's for a good steak, have a few beers and an early night!'

    'That sounds like good advice. You know what, Amelia! I think that's exactly what I'll do!'

    'Good boy.'

    'Have a good shift, I'll ring you later!'

    'Do, and don't forget the early night bit!'

    On his way out to Embutidos he passed Felipe's mother in the communal hallway as she pulled closed the door of her flat, Felipe standing beside her. 'Great shirt!' Sonny said to him.

    'Thanks, Sonny!' Felipe gushed and beamed up at his mother.

The little exchange lifted both Sonny and Felipe.

    Sitting in Embutidos, Sonny's demeanour further improved when he received a text message from Janice which read: *Ring any time Sonny. Stay strong and keep in touch. All my love, Janice. x.*

Chapter 18

On Wednesday evening of the following week, Sonny went through his many unread emails. One, forwarded to him from his club, particularly had his attention, and read: *Hi Sonny, my name is Enrique Moreira, I believe you may be the same Sonny Lopez I knew at a school called La Esperanza. If not, then please disregard this email with my apologies. If you did attend that school and remember me, then perhaps you might care to meet up. Should you not wish to do so then I fully understand. I will be leaving for Florida soon on a permanent basis and thought I'd make contact with you before I left. Can I suggest a daytime beer if appropriate at the Cantalupe Cafe on Botafogo beach, or elsewhere at a time of your choosing, I would be most glad to meet with you again. Best regards, Enrique.*

    Sonny read it several times – each time in attempt to find some implausible facet. He knew there was intrinsic risk in glibly going along with it and that it may be a hoax, nonetheless, he was enthralled. The possibility of again seeing Enrique was something he couldn't dismiss. He rang Amelia and told of it her. Immediately, she urged caution, to the point that she wanted him to discuss it with Ferreira so that some measure of security might be put in place for him. Sonny's response was that there was no security in place when he walked to and from work each day.

    To protect his own email address, Sonny sent his reply to Enrique from the Training Centre the following morning. He proposed they meet at the suggested venue the next day at three o'clock. At lunch break he went to the office and checked his email account. Enrique had confirmed the meeting.

    Just before three o'clock in the afternoon, Sonny wandered onto the pink stone-flagged apron of the Cantaloupe Cafe. Locally referred to as dove park, the Cantaloupe Café sat next to a newsagent kiosk midpoint along the beachfront promenade – its popularity ensured by an oasis-like setting alongside grassy picnic areas with municipal benches where flocks of white doves resided to be fed with seed readily bought from the kiosk, or with crumbs brazenly taken by the birds themselves from the café. Already there sitting at an outside table and unmistakeable to him, was Enrique. In return, Enrique instantly recognised him and stood up, arm aloft. The two friends came together with a firm handshake; for Sonny the years fell away as they grinned in unison and spoke each other's never-forgotten name.

'Thanks for coming, Sonny,' Enrique said. 'This is a day I thought I'd never see!'

'Me too, Enrique, I'm in shock!' Sonny replied as he looked into the open face of Enrique, who stood as tall as himself.'

'It's great to see you again, Sonny.'

'Great to see you, too, Enrique! I think we've got a bit of catching up to do.'

The pair seated themselves at his table and ordered beer from a white-shirted waiter who came over to them.

'Glad to see you're doing well, Sonny. They couldn't keep us down could they! They tried... but no!'

Sonny agreed with a sombre nod. 'No, they couldn't. How's it been for you?'

'After Esperanza... I had a big mountain to climb,' Enrique said, 'but I climbed it! Do you still remember it all, back then?'

'Everything!' Sonny replied solidly. 'It'll stay with me forever; I've never forgotten any of it. How about you?'

'Exactly that. I remember you and me planning to get away before they took us, we nearly made it too. I remember shouting, *Run, Sonny,* but it was too late. They hauled you away and one of them took a swipe at me with a baton.' He shook his head, almost in disbelief. 'The last thing I saw of that world was our football just sat on the pitch where we left it. I knew they weren't taking us to the same place but for weeks I kept looking out for you.' He paused, as though the memory was still raw.

'I know I cried, Enrique. Them hitting you like that. We were just kids!'

The two fell briefly silent as the waiter brought bottles of beer paired with glasses on a tray, he set them down on the table, swung the redundant tray by a thigh and moved away.

'I don't know what happened to any of the other kids,' Enrique said, 'I never saw or heard of anyone after that. I don't know if you did?'

Sonny shook his head. 'No.'

'So, what happened to you?' Enrique went on. 'I know you came from England to join the Boca squad, and congratulations on that, that's some achievement... and some final, as well... I watched it... I knew it was you!'

'Thanks.'

'So, was that where they took you, then, England?'

'Yes. I didn't know it until I got there.'

'What was it like?'

Sonny recounted his life and upbringing in his new homeland as Enrique listened intently and periodically asked of further detail – how soon he had learned to speak English, about his school and of his treatment throughout at the hands of others?

'It sounds like a fair place,' he commented when Sonny had talked the years through.

'Yes. It was,' Sonny agreed. 'I think I was pretty lucky, really. How did it go for you?'

'A bit different! They took me to some kind of holding place, like a barracks, or something. Just me. I was there a few days, then some old guy in a battered truck came and took me away. I asked him where we were going. He told me to shut up and never ask anything. We drove up into the hills to a cigar rolling factory that he owned. I had a bed in a makeshift dormitory where the men workers stayed, there was another one for the women. I was put to work rolling cigars from the bare leaf, if I loused up, the old guy would scream and threaten me with a horse crop. No one even looked up. For them it was a wage, the only way they'd ever see money, and everyone worked a twelve-hour shift to get it. On a Sunday they all went home with their wages to the villages, sometimes the hill bandits would swoop and rob them along the way. It was the most miserable, rain-soaked place on the planet – and I just wished you were with me to make some kind of escape plan.'

'I wish I had been there with you,' Sonny said in support. 'Better still if you'd been with me!'

'Yeah, I think that would have been better,' Enrique agreed. 'Hey, do you know what I used to do on Sundays?' he said with a smile. 'There was no one to play football with, and I didn't want to hang around anywhere near the old guy, so I used to wander off into the scrub with a cigar-knife and carve iguanas from bits of wood and pretend I was back at Esperanza!'

'That's what I did! I had a bagful!' Sonny traded gleefully. 'I did! I had loads of them! When I came back, I wanted to go and see if the place was still there, but a town hall guy warned me off the idea. He said it was demolished to make way for some new conference centre – and that was why they cleared us all out. He reckoned it was now an abandoned site full of criminal types and not to go there.'

'He was right!' Enrique confirmed.

'But why did they have to do that to us,' Sonny questioned. 'They could have just put us somewhere else?'

'Yeah, well, I heard something about that! The fact was they didn't want us at all, not anywhere. They'd already taken us off the streets and they didn't want us back there. They put the word out to charities and world aid groups that a whole load of homeless kids would soon disappear unless someone stepped in, and construction companies were told that if they didn't come across to help with relocation funding, they wouldn't see any of the building contracts. As a problem – we were history!'

Sonny nodded, as though everything of it made sense. 'So, how long were you with the cigar guy?' he asked.

'A long time! I never kept track because in truth I never really wanted to know! But then Vera came along – and she changed everything!'

'Ah...'

'And she packed one mighty punch!'

'I think we met the same girl!' Sonny joked.

'Hurricane Vera, actually,' Enrique said, smiling again. She was a maximum strength hurricane, and she hit us full-on. If you were in her path, you went with her.'

'That kind of girl! It's been a long while since I was in the worry path of a hurricane,' Sonny reflected.

'Well, we were on first name terms! She took the tin roof off the warehouse, then the walls, and then the dormitories went. She cleared the site. It hit when everyone was there, and the old guy just went nuts; he was screaming about getting tarps and ropes around the stock... everything was already airborne! People were running for their lives. He got caught full-on with a barn door that was spinning through the air – and that was him gone! When it went calm everyone knew they wouldn't see wages there again and they started sifting through the wreckage for anything valuable. Then they all scattered away, they even pushed the truck off its side, back onto the wheels and drove off in it! And I'm stood there thinking *What do I do?* There was nothing to stay for. And if I did, some emergency services bunch would only put me somewhere else that I didn't want to be! I wasn't a kid anymore; I was fourteen and six foot tall – and it was time for change. I looked around at all this total mayhem and I thought *Come on, Enrique* – do something for yourself for once. And you know what, Sonny? the answer was right there!'

'Get back to Rio?' Sonny suggested.

'No. I did consider that because one of the workers had taught me boxing,' Sonny nodded a similarity as Enrique went on, 'and he reckoned I could have made it good if I got myself to a proper boxing club. But I'd be on the streets. I fancied the idea for sure – but no. By then, the one thing I'd learned – apart from boxing – was how to roll cigars, and tobacco leaves were laid about like everywhere, some of it still in bales. I started to gather it up and hid it away between roofing sheets that I dragged off into the bushes. By the time the flashing lights people arrived days later I'd put together any amount of it. They combed the site for casualties and found the old guy under the door. They took him away in a body bag. I watched them go from the shrub – my head wanted to scream *I'm here,* but the heart said not to! It was like I'd made my own first real decision. When they'd gone, I dragged out a cutting bench from the debris, I was scared that the workers or robbers would turn up and do a raid for stuff, so I stashed it well away, including food from the old guy's wrecked house, and then I started rolling cigars under the open sky. Only this time, I was doing it for me.'

'That must have been one scary experience, Enrique – end to end!' Sonny pondered. 'You held up better than I would have. I feel a bit embarrassed now. I think in comparison I got the feather bed treatment! So, what did you do then?'

'I made my cigars and just kept on going because I knew it could end at any time. But no one bothered me, no one turned up... and I needed to crack on because the stock was out in the open, bugs had ready access and if it got wet it would rot.'

'That was some serious challenge, Enrique, out there on your own like that,' Sonny marvelled. 'I would have cracked! I absolutely would! Where did you sleep, even?'

'Night-time was the scariest bit for sure. The old guy had a scrap truck that hadn't moved for like thirty years, it was just dumped out of the way. I slept in there; it felt safer than out in the scrub! It's where I kept my cigars, and at least it was dry!' He nodded, smiling, 'I can still smell the cracked leather seats and that cold Bakelite steering wheel!'

'Wow,' Sonny muttered. 'And so did you just keep on rolling cigars, like every day?'

'Oh yes! That was my way out.'

'That's got to be a skill!'

'Well, there's no market for a rubbish made cigar, that's for sure. But by then I'd been doing it for four years, so I knew the game. It's all about knowing which leaf to use, filler, binder, wrapper and then rolling it perfect. When I'd done about a hundred, I tried to figure out where best to sell them. The old guy used to sell to some outfit that banded them up, you know, with the posh sleeving, and they sold them on to whoever – but I was out of that loop! I thought about setting up a box stall near the docks, maybe where the cruise liners pulled in, you know, like they did with our carvings – but then I'd be in the full glare of every robber in town, they'd just help themselves to my cash. Well, a couple of miles away there was a main road petrol station, one of those twenty-four-hour RoadRite places, you know, corn dogs and coffee to go, bit of a supermarket. I figured that might work. So, I made a cardboard sign, *Hand Made Cigars. 6R,* and off I went with just twenty in case I got jumped, and set-up next to the station forecourt, I half expected them to come out and chase me off, but they didn't. An hour later, I'd sold my first cigar.'

'I bet that really lifted you?'

'It did! The guy was a trucker, he said, *It had better be good!* But I knew it was. He did, too, he came back later and bought a bunch. At the end of that first day, I'd sold my twenty, I went into the shop and bought a bottle of water and a ham baguette! I remember the staff smiled at me. That's how it went on. The truckers were my main customers; they'd buy a handful and just chuck them in the door pockets. Pretty soon everyone was calling me the cigar kid. I was there every day, then I'd walk back to my secret place with the cash. Anyone could see I was on my own, so I never went straight there, always in a foxy way and then I'd hide the cash in the ripped roof lining of the truck!'

'And how long did that go on for?' Sonny asked, greatly intrigued.

'A few months – like that. But things had to change. I was getting to the end of my stock, and I was rolling cigars until it got dark just to keep up. I needed a grower who cured his own leaf and would sell to me in small amounts, and that wasn't easy because a lot of the farmers were contracted to the big cigar companies. Well, I found my guy, in fact I married his daughter, Maribel!'

'Whoa, Enrique, you're married!' Sonny exclaimed. 'How well have you done!'

'Yeah, it came good. Anyway, before then, I started renting a lock-up place just down the road from the service station, it was a tiny brick-built affair – no windows – which was good – and it had electric. There was a row of them, all empty, I think the farmers used to trade out of them one time with watermelons and that, but not anymore. I told everyone I was eighteen – and no one questioned it. I ferried down my gear and moved in. It was the safest I'd felt since Esperanza – in my own place behind a locked roller-shutter door! I don't know if they knew I was living there, but it was out in the sticks and folks just did what they had to, they wouldn't have cared – there were no rules to it, and they got their rent. At night I would turn out the light and listen to the traffic zipping by, it used to rattle the tin door – but so long as it kept right on going, I had nothing to worry about.'

'I'd have been scared witless,' Sonny openly admitted.

'I was! With the truck, I could have seen someone coming from miles away, and I'd have been out of there and into the scrub in a flash. In the lock-up there was one door in and no back door out. But when you're on your own there's no one to turn to and say how scared you are. Anyway, trade was good, the new stock was first class, and Lourenco would drop it off for me in passing. I started to make decent money – which came as a big surprise! I opened a bank account in town – being eighteen, of course. Well, it wasn't long before I actually was eighteen and dating Lourenco's daughter Maribel... we got married. Sunlight kissed both our lives that day. She worked for her dad and there was nothing she didn't know about growing tobacco – nothing! I moved into the house and started selling my stock through shops in town. The next thing, I was putting my own band on every cigar and that's when I learned if you want to make real money in the cigar business make them dammed good – and make them look damned expensive!'

From the chair beside him, he brought up a brown polythene carrier bag and stood it between them on the table. 'Brought you these,' he said. 'I doubt you smoke them – but they're yours anyway now!'

'Hey, Enrique, that's not fair – I haven't got you anything!'

'That's okay, I never thought you would. I just wanted to give you something to close the circle on all those years. Anyway, open it later... I know what they look like.'

They both laughed easily, and Sonny put the bag on the chair beside him.

'Thanks, Enrique, I appreciate it. So, where are you now with everything?' he asked, keen to know.

'Well, at one point we had a proper factory unit and forty staff on the payroll!'

'Wow! I feel like I underachieved here!' Sonny complained.

'No, I don't think you did. Then, next news, we had a baby boy, Luiz, then Tais came along.'

'Oh, one of each, straight up! Tell me you've got photos, Enrique?'

Enrique brought out his phone, he swiped it through and handed it across for Sonny to view. Sonny stared at the screen, at the two bright-eyed children who smiled back at him. 'Oh, just look at those guys, Enrique,' he said in admiration. 'You are the luckiest man on the planet!'

Enrique laughed in appreciation as Sonny shook his head and handed back the phone.

'Yeah, things came good for us. Maybe a little too good actually because suddenly we weren't under the radar anymore. You make money in this town, and everyone wants a slice of it! So, a bit of advice for you here, Sonny – you being a newbie in Rio – trust no one! We had the town hall guy who issued the fire certificate, the town hall guy who issued the business licence, the police chief who said commercial burglaries were on the increase and if we wanted the extra patrols then a partway cost needed to be met – we had to pay them all. We went along with it, of course, because we had no choice.'

He paused briefly, and then added, 'But a couple of things happened that changed everything. By then, Luiz was at starter school. There was an attempted ransom snatch from the school grounds – not on Luiz thankfully – and it really shook everyone. It was the new crime. Soon after that Lourenco became ill, he died in hospital. Maribel's mother had died years earlier and there were no other family members. So, we sat down one day and considered our future, the future of our kids. We decided to apply for a resident's permit for Florida, just to see what happened – it was approved. It wasn't just the corruption and crime thing here that was a consideration, Maribel had noticed over the years how the farmland was changing, it had become drier and any rain more likely to flood at crazy times so that we lost the topsoil. Tobacco isn't a plant that copes well with that. The big outfits dug in extra drainage; they used specialist feed and grew more under cover – we didn't have all that. Even the curing sheds were becoming more difficult to keep at the right temperature and humidity. I knew it would be a heartbreak decision for Maribel, so I let it sit for a while. In the end, we decided to make the move. She and the kids are over there now.'

'So, when did they go?'

'They've been there two weeks now, we all went, I had to come back and sort out a few key details, quite a lot of the staff wanted to transfer to the new owners, and then some dotted line bank stuff.'

'And then do you go over?' Sonny questioned.

'It's all done! I go as soon as we're finished here!'

'You're joking!'

'No. I'm on a flight to Miami tonight. I booked as soon as I knew we could meet this afternoon!'

'Enrique! After all this time – and it's goodbye again!'

'Yeah, I know, but at least this time, Sonny, there's no one swinging at me with a baton or dragging you away. I put my calling card in that bag by the way, drop me an email sometime. A risky question, I know, but did you ever manage to find your sisters?'

Sonny told him about Sofia, Florence and Maria, to which Enrique offered his deepest sympathies. Over the following hour the pair then traded happier stories of their time together at La Esperanza, until the mellowed sunlight had Enrique look at his watch. 'The sand's about through,' he said, 'and I need to pick up a bag at the hotel. It's been a real pleasure meeting you again, Sonny.' He stood up, 'I'll get the tab.'

'No way, Enrique! It's been the absolute best seeing you again. I never forgot our time back then, for years after, all I wanted was everything just as it was, and I always wondered what happened to you and where you were now. I'm pleased for you, Enrique.'

'Well, I reckon we both made it through okay. Thanks for coming, Sonny. Take care.'

'All the best, Enrique... thanks for remembering.'
The two friends shook hands, Enrique smiled and walked away.

Chapter 19

A few weeks after Boca's Cup Final win, Ferreira strolled into the changing room at the Training Centre and announced that The Christmas Gala Party Night would again be held at the Hotel Cristal and as usual, husbands, wives, boyfriends and girlfriends were invited – in response to which ribald humour did a tour of the room. He also announced that individual staff appraisals would soon begin, and a low grumble broke out.

That evening, Sonny told Amelia of the impending party night as she pushed a wooden spatula through a wok of stir fry in his flat.

'I used to love those do's,' she said. 'I always made sure I was on duty that night. They're just so... glitzy!'

'Well, this time you'll be soup-side with the good guys! And hey, wouldn't it be funny if someone thought you were on duty, you know, *Excuse me, miss, but my room hasn't been cleaned!*' He laughed at his own imagined scenario.

'Oh, yes, that would be... so funny,' she mocked. 'Not quite as funny as a stir fry over someone's head, though!'

At the scheduled time one weekday morning, Sonny had his one-to-one appraisal with Ferreira. Ferreira looked at him across his desk, smiled and said, 'When you walked in here that day, Sonny, I had no idea what was to come! My only regret... that I didn't bring you in sooner! Now my only worry is how to keep you here. So, time to discuss T's and C's!'

During their half-hour meeting, Ferreira put forward a contractual package that he hoped would entice Sonny to remain with the club. Flexibility within the offer allowed options and choices in terms of commitment and salary. Ferreira asked him not to give a hurried answer but to 'take it away in all its forms' and give his response before the imminent close of season. The numbers, he said, could always be adjusted.

When Sonny got home that afternoon, he rang Amelia and shared his news.

'You earned it, Sonny,' she affirmed as infants shrilled in her near background. 'You played a key role in that trophy, everyone knows they'd have struggled to make it without you, there's no way they'll want to lose you!'

'No, I'm more than happy with it.'

'You don't sound too thrilled, though!'

'No, no it's not that!... to be honest I think clearing Maria's flat looming up's been on my mind a bit. I just don't like the thought of going through her stuff, but if I leave it any longer, they'll just bin everything!'

'It's one to deal with, Sonny. You know I'll help.'

'Yeah, I know, and I can't tell you how grateful I am for it, Amelia. There's not even much that I want! She always hated that she had nothing of mama's, no little things she could hold and connect with. If ever I have kids of my own, I want them to know of their aunt Maria and let them touch and wear the things she owned – bangles and beads... that's all it is!'

'I understand that, Sonny, but we need to go through everything... there might be bank letters and confidential stuff. She had a laptop – it could have bank account details on it! You can't just let it all go; goodness knows where it could end up! Ring and catch them now and make the appointment, I'll go with you whenever they say and let's get it done!'

'You sure?'

'Just do it!'

'Right, okay, I'll do it now! I'll call you back.'

Within ten minutes of his immediate phone call to the letting agent, Sonny relayed to Amelia confirmation of his appointment with them at Maria's flat the next morning – she told him that she would pick him up fifteen minutes earlier.

Amelia pulled up on her motor scooter as Sonny waited for her on the pavement. He got onto the pillion seat, and they sped away to Maria's address. There, Amelia backed the scooter against the kerb, and they made their way into the block – Sonny with empty sports bag in hand. Much as before, Cortez was standing along the corridor beside Maria's flat. The three exchanged minor greetings and went inside where the balcony curtains remained open from their visit of three weeks earlier.

'If we can follow the same procedure, please, Snr Lopez, and allow me to record all items you wish to remove,' Cortez said. Sonny's nodded agreement belied a hint of disdain.

'Come on, Sonny,' Amelia gently urged, and led him into Maria's room.

In the neat little bedroom Sonny gazed uncomfortably around unsure of how to begin. Amelia, with the benefit of familiarity, unplugged the laptop computer that sat on the dressing table, she folded it closed and handed it to him. 'Take that through and give him something to do!' she said. 'And have a look around for any mail while you're there!'

Relieved to do so, Sonny took the laptop and placed it on the dining table, 'We'll be taking that!' he said to Cortez. He then picked his way around the lounge and kitchen in search of mail; he didn't find any and re-joined Amelia. In his stretched absence she had gathered a pile of loose papers on the bed.

'One or two payslips there,' she said, 'her nursing certificates, some tax advisories, and that's all I can see really of the legal stuff – best just to bag it and sort it later!'

He did as she said, and she continued her rummage. With various items of fashion jewellery then also placed on the bed she said, 'I reckon that's about it, Sonny! There's any amount of clothes and shoes and handbags...'

'Let's just take these and go,' he said.

They put the items on the dining table and Cortez laboriously photographed them as Sonny looked out through the balcony doors at wilted plants in glazed pots that sat on age-dulled floor tiles; among them a narrow-spouted watering can, visibly full of water. He stepped out, soaked each pot with green water from the can and brought it inside so that any wind couldn't render it a nuisance.

'Right, that's everything recorded!' Cortez said. 'Will you be making further visits, Snr Lopez?'

'No. we're all done,' Sonny replied. 'That's it.'

'In that case, I'll just make a quick disclaimer, and then we can be on our way,' Cortez concluded.

Sonny felt the finality of the moment. On impulse, he again went into Maria's room. 'I'm so sorry, Maria,' he quietly said; he came back out and closed the door as though to protect her privacy.

'If you'll just sign here, please, Snr Lopez,' Cortez invited, and slid an A4 sheet of paper, a pen laid upon it, toward him on the table.

Irritated that Cortez had assumed authority over Maria's possessions Sonny signed the handwritten paper without looking it over. With all effects bagged, Sonny and Amelia then made their way out. She dropped him off at his flat and continued onto her own in readiness for her afternoon shift at the hotel.

With an empty afternoon before him, Sonny strolled the seafront and considered the contract options Ferreira had given him. His own uncertainty, over something which should have been celebratory obvious, troubled him, and that to agonise over contract length, wages, or the minutiae of detail was to behave like a pandered-to child. As though to instigate advice from afar, he sent Janice a text message which outlined his good fortune and that he was on the cusp of a major decision. Within the hour, she texted back. She congratulated him on his achievement and said he had fulfilled his dream – and for him to go forward as best he saw fit.

Through having back-to-back appraisals, Ferreira was unavailable the following week for Sonny to discuss any aspect of a contract. Meanwhile, the team mood within the Training Centre became subdued, and Sonny quietly wondered if players avoided speaking glibly so not to reveal a satisfaction afforded them for the next season. Only Hernando seemed his usual chatty self.

At the end of one suchlike day, Amelia let herself into Sonny's flat as he laid on the sofa.

'I hope you're not in any kind of po-faced mood!' he said without stirring.

'No! You would have noticed by now!'

'Well, just about everyone else was today, anybody would think we'd lost that final not won it!'

'Sorry to disappoint – no mood here,' she said solidly. 'Anyway, make me a crunchy coffee and I'll put you in the know!'

He made coffee, carefully floated demerara sugar over its creamed surface, and placed it before her on the dining table as she looked on from a bare-wood chair.

'Right, go on, then,' he said, sitting opposite.

'Well, for starters, it's appraisal time!'

'Yes, got that.'

'And party night's coming up!'

'Yep!'

'So, the stress levels are getting peaky. And there are two very important factions doing the peaky-ing!'

'The directors and the players?' he suggested.

'No,' she dismissed with a shake of her head. 'The wives and the girlfriends! A good appraisal means good prospects – and a good table on party night! and party night is about as close it gets to a green-eyed monster got loose!'

'It's a dinner dance!' he protested.

She sucked in breath through pouted lips. 'Oh, no, no,' she said, suitably aghast. 'Let me tell you about this particular dinner dance. The wives who talk to one another will say, *Oh, I'm not bothering much this year; I'm just going to turn up in whatever.* Then they come wearing the only dress like it in Brazil and all the other wives boil behind a smile as they compliment one another. The hairdresser appointments are top secret – booked weeks in advance; jewellery, oh dear! And then there's the killer subject of seating. It goes like this; the directors and top management are on the same tables – and the closer yours is to theirs the better your prospects. We had to put out the place names only one hour before the event began, and if anyone contacted us to ask about it, we had to say *Sorry, I don't know!* Are you getting a measure of this now, Sonny?'

'Why can't us guys just meet up in a bar somewhere,' he said. 'What is it with you lot?'

'You have to earn us, dear boy... and then there's the keeping-us, bit!'

Early evening on The Christmas Gala Party Night, Sonny got out of an onward booked taxi at Amelia's flat block. He pressed her number on the main entrance intercom panel and was asked up via the integral loudspeaker by someone he took to be her sister Juanita – and remotely allowed entry into the building. Through unfamiliarity, he took one of the four lobby lifts to the first floor where halfway along a corridor that had modern, timber doors to either side, each with inset spy glass, he pressed the tactile doorbell of their neatly wall-numbered flat. The door was opened by a slender young woman, perhaps slightly older than Amelia, who looked back at him with a welcoming smile and stood to one side.

'Come on in,' she invited as though introduction wasn't necessary. He stepped into an immediate lounge that was furnished with tan leather furniture and had fabric toyboxes pushed up against a wall, generously covered with cartoon posters. She closed the door, 'I'll tell her you're here!' she said, her smile ongoing. She left him there and returned moments later, arms then folded. 'She's ready,' she said, and was followed into the lounge by Amelia herself. Dressed in a mid-length peach ruched evening dress matched with ankle-strapped shoes and white clutch bag – her hair perfectly teased with tendrils around her face – he thought her beauty time-stealing.

'Wow, look at you!' he complimented, somewhat clumsily.

'And at you, too – in a suit!' she replied, equally impressed. 'Without logos or stripes... and proper shoes!'

'Oh, there'll be no one looking at me, don't you worry – or at anyone else for that matter!' he said, still awestruck.

'Well, I'm ready for them if you are!' she said.

'Your taxi awaits!'

Amelia touched cheeks with the other girl in passing. 'Don't wait up, Juanita!' she said and led Sonny into the hallway, where variously along its length other residents stood at their own doors as though to view the emerging pair.

Sonny and Amelia walked through the specially lit, Boca FC themed, foyer of the Hotel Cristal, watched by Morena behind reception. At a podium before the lounge area, badged staff checked their names against a list and then welcomed them through to where party guests were gathered in chattering clusters – and kept an eye out for newcomers. Sonny spotted Hernando and girlfriend Felicia – their near-to-entrance position on the outer fringe of the crowd hinted that they too had just arrived – and he and Amelia went over to them; delight showed on the face of Hernando and the two girls were soon chatting freely. Felicia, in petrol blue evening gown, herself possessed grace and beauty and repeat glances through the crowd often found both girls.

When the floor manager made an announcement for guests to make their way to the function room the chatter fell away, glasses were deposited and a slowly moving procession quietly formed. At the double-door entrance to the refreshingly cool room the seating plan was set out on an easel and guests briefly faltered as they sought their own names. Within, a spread of ten-seater round tables were laid with white linen covers on which sat wine glasses, precision-placed silverware, flowers, carafes of water, already opened bottles of wine and a scattering of glitter that caught the wandering dots of coloured light from high-mounted robotic emitters.

Beyond the tables a polished hardwood dance floor was corralled by a scaffold gantry of lights – not yet illuminated, and along a side wall a marble-topped bar had before it a line of uniformed staff in readiness for service. Sonny, Amelia, Hernando and Felicia sat at the same table, glad of it they engaged in breezy conversation as the room filled. As Sonny then glanced around at the impressive spectacle he felt reminded of Amelia's earlier words when he saw Vargas and unsmiling wife Guilhermina, her black hair backcombed, positioned close to the table from where Ferreira, his club director wife Yara and other members of senior management oversaw the room.

The evening progressed in ever louder and indulgent manner. When meal service was over, and with the Cup Final

trophy grandly displayed at his table, Ferreira stood up and made a celebratory speech. He presented awards to those called upon – dutifully applauded by all. A backdrop screen then loudly played the season's highlighted moments in which back-to-back goals featured prominent to sound-enhanced stadium cheers.
Throughout, the club's official photographer circulated freely and, as drink held sway, guests posed and clowned when in photo-shot. When the dance floor lights came on and booming music let loose – the room was ready to dance.

    At some point in the proceedings, as Amelia and Felicia busied themselves on the dancefloor, Sonny made his way back from the bar with beer for himself and Hernando and was intercepted by Ferreira. Ferreira let him deliver the beer and then led him off to his own table where he introduced him to wife Yara. Sonny, aware that Yara Alves Marques Ferreira owned the hotel and was the major shareholder director in Boca FC, had never met or seen her before and was surprised that she looked slightly older than her husband. She smiled and offered a hand; Sonny engaged it and was instantly aware how she exuded mesmeric wealth and glamour. He also sensed the scrutiny of others, which included Vargas and Guilhermina.

    'It's a pleasure to meet you, Sra Ferreira,' he said dutifully.
    'Are you enjoying the night?' she asked.
    'Absolutely, it's fantastic! I'm so glad to be here!'
    'Well, we're glad to have you here, Sonny!' she said approvingly. 'I'll be meeting with each of our new signees over the next couple of weeks, so we'll be able to talk further then, in perhaps quieter surroundings!'

    Sonny knew he had paid his homage and smiled. 'I look forward to it,' he said, and went back to his own table. As he passed Vargas and Guilhermina, the pair yet to leave their seats, Vargas stared blankly toward the dancefloor – she found something of interest to examine on a turned-over forearm.

    At two o'clock in the morning, Sonny and Amelia got into the back of a taxi and went from the hotel to her flat. Along the way, hands held, she lolled her head against his shoulder.

'What a fabulous night,' she said tiredly. 'I like Felicia, she's fun. And ours was definitely the best table! What did Yara have to say?'

'Oh, just come-hither stuff, really. She's got power... I think she just wanted me to know it.'

'They call her the dragon lady at the hotel.'

'Yes, I can imagine. She's meeting all the new guys shortly. We'll see what she has to say then!'

'Best be on your guard,' Amelia advised.

As the taxi waited, Sonny walked with Amelia along a silent empty corridor to her door where they unhurriedly kissed goodnight.

Chapter 20

Sonny arrived at the Training Centre on Monday morning to the news that with immediate effect Neymar had left the club and taken up the role of head coach at Sando Paulo FC. It was openly rumoured he had been unhappy since Sonny came and had felt undermined by Ferreira's reluctance to rein him in. Sonny was unperturbed by it and suspected that not too many other Boca players were either, with the exception perhaps of Vargas.

During that same week, Sonny was called off the training field by stand-in head coach Leon and escorted by front-of-house staff member Tamirés for a meeting with Yara Ferreira. Yara, in yellow-trimmed blue blazer, white trousers and blue silk scarf, got up from her freestanding chair as Sonny was shown into the pitch-side private box. It immediately struck him how small she was. Yara dismissed Tamirés with routine politeness and invited Sonny to sit at a similarly mid-placed chair, her unnecessary movement about the room done, he believed, that he fully appreciated her heady perfume. Yara resumed her own chair with only carpeted floorspace between them.

'This will not take long, Sonny,' she said. 'And mostly all I want you to do is listen!'
She looked at him as though to establish that he understood; his blank return gaze and fractional nod indicated that he did.

'I have a concern regarding our offer to you,' she said. 'Now, I'm not in any way troubled by whatever the renumeration package or the specifics! My concern is that you may be unaware of certain facts. Facts which, should they come to light at a later time, may have a negative impact on your commitment to the club.' She again looked at him to allow her words gravitas. 'Alberto is an excellent manager,' she went on, 'he saw your potential quite some time ago and you proved him right. He's an excellent husband, too... except he has a singular failing! He likes a pretty girl! It's always been so.'

She shrugged as though in weary acceptance. 'I put up with it. A while back, he took up with one of his prettiest to date and they began what was quite a long affair. I say was – because it is now over. He has no idea that I know, which is foolish of him because my spies keep me well informed. Sadly, this particular girl was newly off the back of a personal tragedy, her fiancé was a stevedore – he was killed in a dockside accident when a crane toppled onto him. They were due to be married, and she'd just found out she was pregnant when the accident happened. She received no compensation. She had the child, a girl, and as soon as she was able, she looked for work. She is an exceptionally bright young woman; she knew what she wanted – and how to get it! She took a job as a receptionist at the Hotel Cristal. That was where she bagged Alberto, they met when he spent time there doing promos. I can always tell; he started wearing his diver's watch and favourite shirt – white – no collar! Feathers were definitely preened. Anyway, that's where it began.'

She briefly paused as though in reflection of her own analysis. 'He bought her a little motor scooter to run around on,' she resumed, 'biscuit cream, I believe is the brochure colour! To her credit she began a part-time degree course to secure her own and the child's future, Alberto kindly paid for her to go full-time at university! done, no doubt, by way of a few season tickets to certain university individuals and the occasional private box at the ground. By now, I'm sure elements of this will sound familiar to you?'

Sonny stared down at the carpet. 'Elements of it... yes,' he said. 'Other elements no. Does your person have a name?'

'It is, of course, Amelia Lemos – your Amelia Lemos.'

'Then I think we hold different beliefs of the same person!' he said. 'My Amelia Lemos has no children of her own. She shares a flat with her sister who has two infants, and Amelia helps look after them. I think someone has let loose their imagination! A bit of embellishment maybe, or misinformation for whatever reason!'

Yara looked fixedly at him. 'I do not do misinformation!' she said. 'Yes, I'm sure Juanita would very likely struggle without her, she is a single mother herself. I confess I don't know why, though I did hear that the father was just a street punk. Maybe he preferred that to being a dad!... Amelia found herself with a newborn, Cássia, without any means of support, so she and Juanita moved into a flat together – it seems the arrangement worked out to satisfaction! But she had more about her than to settle for that and applied to work here at the club, no doubt in order to bag herself a player. There was no vacancy at that time, so she went to the Cristal fully knowing of the ownership connection, as perhaps you yourself were aware when you first checked in! I don't blame her. Only it was Alberto she bagged. He keeps a motor yacht moored at the marina – they would spend time onboard together!

And then you came along!... she got her degree, and that was the end of their mutually useful little fling. So, you might think that, as unsavoury as it may be, it's all history, and that I'm just a vinegared old hag, out for revenge! Perhaps I am. I employed her... and she borrowed my husband as a thank you! But the last thing I want would be for you to go head down should all this come out later – which, of course, it surely would – and your allegiance to us then sour!'

Sonny again studied the carpet – in need of measured response. 'I'm surprised you allowed her to continue at the Cristal?'

'Oh, I wanted her there! She's good at it, and that way I kept an eye on them both – nothing unknown! I don't employ the unproductive, and those I pay I control, even when they don't know it – in fact, it works best that way!'

'Have I been taken for a fool?' he asked vacantly.

'Well, no! you haven't actually. I have... so has Alberto, but that's his own doing. He managed to keep you at arm's length for a season or so, to protect his little indulgence, but then you applied to Fluminense – not in our best interests that you go there – Alberto was decommissioned by Amelia because she had no further use for him, so it was all change! And in the end, she was only trying to give her own child some security. For that she is blameless – much to be admired, really! And I don't doubt for a second that she loves you. I saw it for myself on party night, and I'm sure that at some point she will tell you about Cássia.'

'But you thought you'd tell me first!'

'I owe Amelia Lemos nothing! And I don't want her to be of any detriment to this club.'

'So, no vinegar, then?'

'Perhaps just a dash!'

Early that evening, Sonny erratically wandered the flat and analysed everything Yara had told him. At seven o'clock Amelia walked in; she stared at him and read the heavy mood as he stared back.

'What's wrong?' she said.

'How's Cássia?'

'Oh, I see... the all-knowing Yara has spoken! Well, Cássia is fine, thank you for asking.'

'Why all the lies, Amelia?'

'Name one!'

'Cássia, Ferreira... all of it!'

'Cássia is a truth, a very beautiful truth, she is not a lie – and don't you ever say that again! What went on between me and Ferreira pre-dates you – and what I never told you can't be a lie can it? He took from me, and I took from him. To keep Cássia fed and housed, have her happy, safe and warm every single day, I would have done anything, and always will. Well, I'm financially sound now, I owe nothing, and I've earned any job that I get!'

'So, when would you have told me?'

'About Cássia? – as soon as I felt I needed to! Ferreira? – one day, when it mattered... he didn't! And before you judge, perhaps you'd like to hear some truths! Cassia's dad was called Marcos! Just a regular guy who was the love of my life and who worked every hour to fund our futures together and died doing it!'

'You could have told me, Amelia, maybe you weren't living a lie, but you knew that I was!'

'Well, now you're not! So, what's really the big upset, am I too much baggage for you now?'

'We could have talked all this through a long time ago, Amelia. I feel like I've been chumped!'

'Well, don't worry, Sonny, you haven't! Perhaps you'd like to tell me how I should have felt that day when the absolute joy of being told I was pregnant was followed by the news that my fiancé and child's father has just been killed at work, *And we're so sorry, Miss Lemos, but there's no compensation to help you!* Tell me the game plan of how to deal with that particular kind of day, Sonny!'

'You never gave me the chance, Amelia! you let me believe Cássia and Christiano were both Juanita's – why did you do that, what difference did you think it could possibly have made between us – where was the honesty?'

'I never said any of that – I never would! You believed what you wanted to believe. And let's not forget it was you who sought me, not the other way round! So, I suppose this is the end of us? Yes, of course it is! Because we don't do what we have to, do we, we must always play nice, mustn't we!' She turned around and left.

He wanted to go after her – but anger and hurt wouldn't let him.

After a sleepless night, Sonny rang the club and told them he was taking a few days off from training. In need of open space in which to clear his mind he walked the seafront where maelstrom waves matched his mood. There, he untangled his troubled thoughts and brought about some measure of rationale so that he could better see his way forward.

Sonny's initial urge had been to leave Boca FC and re-apply to Fluminense; when his anger waned, he re-evaluated and considered that the behaviours of others shouldn't be allowed to orchestrate his future. He trusted to personal confidence that he could look Ferreira in the eye and feel only indifference for him.

The following week, Sonny faced Ferreira across the man's desk and calmly told him that he was ready to sign a one-year contract. Ferreira nodded deeply and said he had hoped for a longer term but was nonetheless delighted at the news and that all new contracts would be drawn up over the coming weeks – and if Sonny elected for a longer term of commitment, to let him know.

'Our new head coach, Tomas Sousa, is very experienced and approachable,' Ferreira enthused, 'so you shouldn't have any problems there, and Ernesto could be down to his last few seasons on the pitch!' he looked at Sonny as though to suggest that the mantle of a departed Vargas could fall to him; Sonny, though, wasn't drawn to comment.

'Right, well, welcome to Boca!' Ferreira rallied as he stood up and offered a hand over the desk. 'You have made the right choice of club!'

Sonny shook the hand and smiled. 'Thanks, Alberto,' he said.

Sonny left the office full in the belief Yara had said nothing to her husband regarding Amelia. He thought him someone who had easily moved on from an indiscretion as though blameless.

Over the coming weeks Sonny heard nothing from Amelia and neither did he contact her. At home one evening he sent an email to Janice. For a while he'd wanted to let her know of his contract decision with Boca but had sensed some distancing from her in their last exchange and so allowed time to pass before he sent his news. Fully three days later he got her reply: *Live your dream, Sonny.* she simply emailed.

It was in that post-season period that Monica Ramos made a court appearance charged with Maria's murder. She pleaded guilty. Conviction duly followed with sentencing set to follow that.

When the new playing season began, and fixtures came and went, Sonny established himself as lead scorer – Vargas and Hernando each in turn followed. The replacement head coach, Tomas, had about him a relaxed authority which saw players want to please rather than comply through intimidation and among them a fresh willingness was noticeable – there were no favourites; Vargas himself seemed calmer perhaps because of it. Initially, the home crowd expected that Sonny would make his A symbol whenever he found the net, those who pre-empted it with their own imitation soon realised it wasn't to be – and let it wane.

Sonny and Hernando became good friends. Occasionally, Sonny would make social visits to his and Felicia's hillside home where the three of them would sit on the patio overlooking the ocean far below and make easy of a Sunday afternoon. By then Felicia was pregnant; the couple radiated happiness and Sonny told them – almost in earnest – that the pair could laugh away bad weather. It was a source of puzzlement for Hernando that Sonny, who much admired their spacious home, still lived in his rented flat. When Hernando suggested that he 'take a look' at a nearby house newly up for sale, Sonny smiled and said, 'I can't walk to the Training Centre from there, can I?'

'He'll move when he's ready!' Felicia defended of him. 'When the right girl comes along!'

Sitting on his own balcony one empty evening, beer in hand, Sonny pondered Felicia's words. She had effortlessly summed up his life and he was aware how easily time slipped-by when everything was in the loop of football games. Through natural gift and determined effort he was successful at what he did but was yet to know the fulfilment he'd always hoped would come with repatriation.

As the season progressed, Sonny increasingly focussed on his game. He sometimes scored multiple goals in a match and was often instrumental in the goals of teammates, which saw Vargas warm to him so that any animosity between them fell away and an easier atmosphere pervaded the changing room as matchday success repeatedly came their way.

Sonny attended Hernando and Felicia's baby shower at their home. Many of the Boca team were also present – as was Amelia; she and Felicia had become firm friends since the Christmas Gala Party Night of the previous year. Both Yara and Ferreira had politely declined their invitation. As Sonny stood among those gathered on the patio his gaze found Amelia as she likewise looked at him. Determined not to appear soured he went across to her.

'Hi, Amelia,' he said. 'How are you?'

'I'm good thanks, Sonny, how are you?'

He nodded. 'I'm good.' Cautious not to say the wrong thing he nodded again.

'Well, you're certainly making your mark on the scoresheet!' she said.

'Thank you. How's things at the Cristal?'

'I imagine things are much the same, I don't work there anymore!'

'Oh, I didn't know that!'

'You remember me telling you about that tv job?'

'Real World Television Rio?' he recalled.

'I got it!'

'Oh, fantastic, well done.'

'Thank you.'

'So, how's that working out, then?'

'I love it, it's proper hands-on with the running costs of the station, I'm involved with the budgets for the shows and all the advertisement revenues, I get to see the studios live on-air, it's such a buzzing place!'

'I can so see you there!'

'And I hear that you and Vargas are finally getting along!'

'It's true! he hasn't attacked my locker for ages now, it's almost boring!'

She laughed. 'Do you still get into Embo's?'

'I was in there only the other night battling a steak!'

'Good for you!'

'I'm going to be looking out for you now on that channel. You could be the RWTR girl! Tough to do with the hands, but…'

They both laughed – again comfortable in each other's company.

The following day, Sonny jogged around the running track at the Training Centre and thought about Amelia. She had freely engaged with him at the party and a pathway to reconciliation seemed open. He bore her no grudge or ill feeling despite the depth of her secrecy, but to try and resurrect what they once shared would be to make a full and obvious statement of commitment to her – and such, he knew, would have been a falsehood on his part; he made no contact.

One mid-week evening toward the end of the playing season, Sonny got an email from Samantha Simmonds. She had never emailed or texted him before and as such it possessed gravitas; he thought that perhaps something had happened to Mark. He opened it and read: *Hi Sonny, hope you're well, this is my third email to you, I deleted the other two. All good here, so don't panic. Mark doesn't know I've sent this, and he'd be sodding miffed if he did. There's something that no one is telling you, and I think it's wrong. I've decided not to care that it's none of my business, so here goes. Janice had a baby boy last January. The child is yours. She won't tell you herself. Apparently, she didn't want to step on your lifelong dream to return to Rio and she didn't want you to stay in the UK or come back unless it was for her. I'm pressing send now before I delete again. Hate me later. Love, Sam. x.*

Sonny read the email several times, he then read it piecemeal, one sentence at a time, even in reverse order until he knew that no ambiguity existed in its meaning. He looked at his watch – which conveyed nothing to him – and rang Janice. After spells of electronic squeals and silence, she answered.

'Hi, Sonny,' she said on a perfectly clear line. 'How are you?'

'Janice, I'm fine. How are you?'

'I'm fine too. I hear you're doing well; I assume you're still over there?'

'I am... indeed, I am. Was there something you forgot to tell me, Janice?'

'Oh, there's probably lots of things I forgot to tell you, which particular one did you have in mind?'

'I'm told I'm a dad!'

'My, the jungle drums have got internet now!'

'Am I told right?'

'Yes. You're a dad. His name is Jaren.'

'So, when were you going to tell me?'

'I don't know, I've had a busy year.'

'How is he?'

'He's totally gorgeous.'

'Good! You coping okay?'

'Coping nicely!'

'Janice, I'm feeling a little left out of things here, a bit disincluded!'

'Is that a Brazilian word? only, I'm learning Portuguese, and I've not come across that one!'

'You're learning Portuguese?'

'Yes, I want Jaren to know his heritage language.'

'Do I have any useful role at all to play here?' he said tersely. 'I've missed his first year! You should have told me about this, Janice, I've not seen him... he hasn't seen me... Where's the heritage in that?'

'Yes, well, as unfair as it may seem, Sonny, your wants, wishes, and sentiments were not the primary concern here! Your life is in Rio, it's what you always wanted, it's what you've got, and I wasn't about to damp-squib it for you, for all I know you could be married, maybe with a child of your own over there – what's here is what you walked away from... remember!'

'Well, I aren't, I haven't, and it wasn't like that either – I would never walk away from a child of mine, I resent you saying that – is that what you're telling everyone, that I left you in the lurch?'

'No, and surprised as you may be, your name hardly ever crops up anymore!'

'I bet it crops up with your parents!'

'Don't you dare bad-mouth my parents, Sonny, they've stood by me right through this!'

'I would have stood by you right through this... if I'd known! When did you first know?'

'A couple of weeks before you left, actually! So, what was I to do? *Oh, don't go and fulfil your life's dream, Sonny, I have such news!*'

'So, when would you have told me?'

'I don't know, if you'd have come back – then, otherwise... at some point or other.'

'Janice, did it not occur to you that such a thing would trump everything else? He's my boy!'

'Yes, it wasn't really a good time for analysis. It was a time for making good with what I had to deal with!'

'Right... so where does this all this leave us now?'

'It leaves me and baby Jaren right here, where it leaves you, I can't say. But we're not coming over there, Sonny... so don't even suggest it!'

'I was thinking more me coming over to you... with your permission, of course!'

'None needed, but be aware, you don't turn up here and expect to ring the changes! I decide what happens on every level – have no expectations of anything!'

'You've really dug deep into that steel persona, haven't you, Janice!'

'Where Jaren's concerned, Sonny, steel is warm butter!'

'I wish you'd told me, Janice.'

'Well, now you know, so let's just to go forward from here, shall we... one step at a time!'

'Email me some pictures of him, will you?'

'Okay.'

'Can we do a conference call, maybe tomorrow?'

'Yes, we can do that, but don't expect too much from Jaren, he won't shout daddy or anything – he's not yet one!'

'When's his birthday?'

'January tenth.'

Within an hour, Sonny was looking at multiple photographs of his son – and hating every mile that lay between them.

Over the following weeks, Sonny and Janice spoke by phone on a regular basis. He had wanted to fly immediately to the UK, but she had objected on the grounds that she didn't want him to come into baby Jaren's life only to then fly out again. Over those weeks, through text messages, ever-lengthy phone and conference calls, Sonny rediscovered a truth that had always been.

Sitting in Ferreira's office Sonny told him of his decision to permanently leave Rio at the end of the season. Ferreira looked crestfallen and blankly asked why; when Sonny explained, Ferreira nodded a deep understanding, 'I would have liked a son,' he said.

He went on to say how Sonny would always have a place on the team should he return and that he had been an inspirational game-changer for the club. Sonny came out of the office reminded of similar words said by another – and felt elated that he'd made the first real step to being with his son. In the changing room he showed Hernando photographs on his phone of baby Jaren; by then, Hernando and Felicia were parents themselves to a baby girl who they named Luciana. Hernando joked that Sonny had typically scored first in becoming a dad before him.

Sonny played his last game for Boca FC one sunlit Saturday afternoon. They had already been knocked out of the Challenge Cup competition despite their steeled efforts, and that Sonny's personal goal tally had set a best-ever season's record for the club. Determined to leave with a worthy display of football, he scored a masterful goal that drew open arms from Ferreira who sprang to his feet to make the accolade. At the full-time whistle Sonny was applauded by the entire Boca team as he in turn applauded them and the fans. When the stadium scoreboard flashed up the digital message: *Thanks Sonny*, the home crowd, many in tears, showed their appreciation and gave a standing ovation that followed him off the pitch.

With all club commitments cleared, Sonny booked a flight to the UK and gave notice on the flat – the furniture, it was agreed, would remain. He arranged with his bank for a contribution to be made for the upkeep of the graves of Maria, Sofia and their mother, and visited the three graves to pay his final respects; standing at that of Maria he made an apology for not finding the resting places of Seve, Paulo and Florence, and said that he was leaving Rio to be with his son – who he promised would learn of his family tree.

On his last day at the Training Centre, Sonny knocked on Ferreira's door and was called in. The pair exchanged gratitude's, and Ferreira presented him with a Boca FC shirt signed by him and the team. Sonny shook his hand and expressed thanks that he'd been allowed to wear it. With the shirt neatly folded in his sports bag, Sonny made his way out of the facility and said goodbye to many as he left, and walked home.

Early that evening, in his then spartan flat, he was suddenly tempted to seize up his luggage and take a taxi to an hotel at the airport in advance of his flight the following night. He calmed his mind against it and instead went to Embutidos. When he got back two hours later, he rang Amelia; she promptly answered.

'Hi, Sonny, I was hoping you'd ring before you escaped,' she said.

'I couldn't leave without!'

'Congratulations!'

'You mean... on -'

'On being a dad! Baby Jaren I'm told.'

'Thanks, he's nearly a year old – I've not long found out!'

'Us women, hey!' she commented. Nice that he's going to have you now, though. Are you and his mum still good?'

'Yeah, we're good.'

'She's a lucky girl! Is her name Janice by any chance?'

'Yes! how did you know?'

'You called me it in the flat one time without even realising! I didn't say anything, but I figured whoever she was she had a piece of your heart.'

'I never meant to be judgemental, Amelia. There was just so much I didn't realise about my own stuff! We had it good for a while, though, didn't we?'

'I think we can say we tasted the wine!' she agreed. 'And I think maybe we grew up a little bit together.'

'Yes, I think we did. I wish you all the best, Amelia.'

'Thank you. I wish you all the best too, Sonny, have a safe journey through life.'

Standing on his balcony early the following morning Sonny gazed over a clear sky and waited for his pre booked taxi to arrive. When it drew up near the main entrance, he said, 'Thank you, flat' and went down. Along the way to Galeáo International Airport he watched as Botafogo fleeted by and reflected on how not so very long ago, it seemed, he had arrived wanting to pull back every footstep of the missed years and embrace his birthright; he felt it something now fulfilled. The journey took them passed Sammy's Chinese Buffet Restaurant – he glanced over its frontage and blocked out painful memory.

In the mall-like departure terminal at the airport, Sonny bought a hand-sized football in the blue, yellow and green colours of the national flag. Sitting then in an open-fronted bar, beer before him, he sent Janice an update text message and shut out any troubled thought as he eased into sedentary mode.

Four hours later, his boarding call was announced. He walked down the sloping airbridge onto the aircraft and slid onto a grey leather seat, at which point he deemed himself no longer in Rio – his farewell completed.

Chapter 21

Sonny's flight touched down in Manchester and he made the disembarkation trek along a broad galleried skywalk to the railway platform for his train to Leeds. Three hours later in the darkness of a cold wet evening he arrived in Leeds and took a taxi to Baxters, a national chain hotel that sat on the outer reaches of the city in the direction of Danby. His pre known late arrival suited him because he would then overnight in the hotel and not turn up at Janice's parents' house looking dishevelled – it also meant he could slough off travel fatigue, shave, shower and be better prepared in the light of a new day for whatever lay in store for him. From his room, he sent Janice a text message to say he was at the hotel. She texted back that she would see him tomorrow. He suspected a tightening of her resolve to remain in control of all things baby Jaren.

    In the morning, Sonny extended his hotel stay for a further two nights, to allow himself mental space, and asked the intrinsically pleasant receptionist if she would phone for him a taxi to Tanlow, incorporating an enroute stop at a garden centre. He waited in the expansive foyer and twenty minutes later the taxi drew up beneath the tin profile clad canopy that overhung the hotel entrance, and which offered a continental look and rangy cover for smokers; he got onto the front passenger seat and was soon among traffic on wet main roads. From North Leeds Garden Centre, he bought a Blue Marguerite potted plant – at the gateway of Janice's parents' house, he generously tipped the driver.

    With the paper-wrapped plant encircled by an arm, Sonny walked up the lengthy front garden path between steel-blue hydrangeas of the Georgian brick-built detached property, its every sash window with stone lintel, and the iron fall pipes, and timber gutters all painted evergreen. He had walked Janice there many times over the years – been the relentlessly powering legs on her pushbike as she perched on the saddle behind him, her fingers at his hips as he cycled her home, and in later times when he and their friends had picked her up or dropped her off in their cars, sometimes when she'd had too much to drink and once when he had to pay a cleaning charge to an irate taxi driver because she'd been sick on the back seat, but he'd never been into the house – neither had he met her parents. He felt nervous about their reaction to him – nervous that Jaren might cry at the unexpected sight of him, a stranger.

At the already open, aged lean-to porch he pressed the white plastic disc of the doorbell and heard its melodic chime within the house. Moments later Janice pulled wide the front door. He stared into her bright eyes, at a guarded expression, and instantly thought himself a fool that he'd ever left her.

'Hi, Sonny, how was Rio?' she said as she waved him inside to where the trace smell was that of old gloss paint.

'Hi, Janice,' he replied, and swiftly kissed her cheek. She welcomed the gesture but ever so slightly turned her face to distance her mouth. 'It was interesting,' he said. 'So, what have you been up to while I've been gone?' She laughed, and he felt better for it.

'How's Jaren?' he asked.

'Fast asleep! Come on, we can have a minute before he wakes up!'

She led him along the hallway, which narrowed at a panel-boarded staircase, and they went into an airy front room that held no clue to a baby in the house.

'So, what's that growing out of your arm?' she asked.

'It's a plant for your mum!'

'She'll like that, she's very planty! Where's mine?'

'And I got Jaren a football!' he blustered, suddenly embarrassed, and brought out from his jacket pocket the ball that he'd bought at Rio airport.

'He'll like that. Where's mine?'

'I didn't think a dinner date somewhere nice would wrap-up well!'

She laughed. 'Crawler! Let me put that over here.' She took the plant from him and placed it on a dark-wood table that had a medieval look about it.

The pair then sat in heavy armchairs either side of a fireplace that housed a lit coal-effect gas fire. He might not have known it was gas fuelled but for the almost inaudible hiss detectable in their moment of silence as they looked across at one another.

'Right, you go first,' she said, 'and I want to hear all about it... you got on the plane...?'

Over the next twenty minutes Sonny summarized his time spent in Rio. With his story then shared he said, 'And the last time I saw you, you were waving goodbye through the back window of your mum's car, and inventing smart-corn that would turn up the nose of any passing herd of locust! any joy?'

She laughed at his flippancy, and it pleased him that she was so unchanged.

'Well, I gave them a stay of execution for a while, but I'm back on the case, working from home, they're flying scared again now!' She paused and held up a finger. 'Jaren's awake!' she said. 'Come on, let's go through, grab your toys, mum's there with him.' She sensed his sudden unease and asked, 'You okay?'

'I'll be better at half-time.' He gathered up the plant and followed her.

'Hi!' Janice said loudly as they entered the spacious farmhouse-style kitchen – which instantly drew animated giggles from the infant in romper suit standing in a spar-sided cot against a wall. He giggled more when he fully saw her and his lightly tanned face exuded joy. Standing with her back against the Belfast sink the not unkindly gaze of a middle-aged woman in navy-blue cardigan, rested on Sonny.

'Mother, this is Sonny!' Janice said and went to the cot.

Sonny strode up to her and offered a hand, she smiled warmly and engaged it. With unashamedly grey hair in a bobbed style, and slight of figure, she radiated an inner confidence – a trait, along with her round-tipped nose, passed on to Janice.

'Hello, Mrs Parker, pleased to meet you,' he said. He swung forward the obvious plant. 'I hope you like these?'

'Oh, a Marguerite!' she said knowingly. 'Always a favourite of mine. Janice must have said!'

'He got lucky, mother!' Janice called out.

Her mother took the plant from him, and her smile broadened. 'Thank you,' she said.

Aware that Janice was then at his shoulder, Sonny turned to her and met with the open stare of Jaren in her arms.

'Daddy's here,' Janice said, and bounced him a little to jolly the moment.

Sonny stared back at his son; at what he believed the most beautiful infant face he'd ever seen. Anxious not to lose the moment, he said 'Hiya' and waved at him. Jaren didn't respond except to look unsure at the waved hand.

'Daddy's brought you a football,' Janice said.
Sonny produced the ball and poised it on a trio of fingertips in front of Jaren. Jaren stared at it, knocked it out of his hand and giggled hugely.

'This could be a long game!' Mrs Parker said as Sonny retrieved it.

A tall thin man then appeared in the kitchen doorway. He was taller than Sonny, his face almost flat sided and his black hair – much balding – combed straight back; he wore an unbuttoned beige cardigan over a country shirt, which Sonny thought comfort wear solely for the benefit of the wearer.

'Dad, this is Sonny,' Janice said.
He and Sonny shook hands firmly, both men with a look of sincerity.

'Pleased to meet you, Mr Parker,' Sonny said.

'You too, Sonny!' he replied.

'I think it's time for a cup of tea!' Mrs Parker suggested in timely manner.

With Jaren happily occupied in a playpen beside them, the four seated themselves around a bare wood table, its straight edges hollow chamfered.

'So, have you any plans?' Mr Parker asked of Sonny, as they positioned mugs of tea before them on placemats.

It was a direct question to which Sonny truthfully answered, 'Yes! I'll not be going back to Rio. And me and Janice have a lot to discuss!' It was the nearest he could say to *you'll know when we do!* With the thorny subject of intentions then quelled, the conversation lightened. Janice's parents soon realised that Sonny presented no menace to their daughter or grandson; relief plainly showed and pleasant conversation took over.

At some point, Mrs Parker suggested that Janice and Sonny take Jaren into the back garden to 'air his lungs'. Sonny recognised that the three of them would then share their first time together. They sat in the garden among old plum trees where leafless branches segmented the weak sunlight; when black twigs dislodged by crows fell onto Jaren's pram, Janice lifted him out and handed him to Sonny while she picked at the bits and shook out the open-weave baby blanket. Sonny looked down at him in his arms and gently kissed his forehead.

Over the following week, Sonny, Janice and Jaren were seldom far apart. With Jaren asleep in the evenings Mrs Parker would urge the pair to 'get out of the house for a while and go for a drink or a meal somewhere'. It was on those occasions that he and Janice held hands again, found one another again, and knew that theirs was a love very much beyond its youthful fact. Sonny moved into the spare bedroom of the house. He cherished that he was there whenever Jaren woke up and that he raised both arms for Sonny to then lift him.

Sonny, Janice and Jaren spent a week at a static caravan park along the North Yorkshire coast. Jaren played on the beach for his first time and Sonny held him aloft at waves edge and swung his feet in the chasing water which had his giggles as continuous.

On their final night there, Jaren asleep, Sonny took out a can of lager from the fridge, he paused as his thumbnail hooked the ring-pull and put the unopened can on the worktop. He turned to Janice and said, 'Let's get married, Janice?'

She looked at him without obvious emotion. 'See, it doesn't actually go like that, Sonny!' she eventually said. 'You don't pose it like it's an idea to beat boredom on a slack night, or you've just been told by some guy in a pub it's a good way to beat the taxman! Perhaps you'd care to try again?'

'I love you, Janice. I always have; I always will. Will you please marry me?' he said with conviction.

'I love you too, Sonny. Yes... I'll marry you! What kept you?' she said, as they hugged deeply.

With their news relayed, they arrived back at her parents' house on a Friday afternoon, and hugs, kisses, handshakes and laughter filled the hallway. Janice and her mother swept Jaren away to his cot and stayed with him in the kitchen; the two men walked to The Reindeer pub and celebrated with beer.

On Monday morning, Sonny rang Northern Star club manager Lou Gomero. Gomero was delighted to take the call, and they arranged a meeting for the next day.

At Northern Star's ground, Sonny made his way to the reception desk and exchanged cheery greetings with familiar faces along the way. There, a member of staff made an internal phone call to Gomero and invited Sonny to 'just go straight in'. Gomero got to his feet as he entered, and the two men shook hands.

'Good to see you again, Sonny,' Gomero welcomed solidly.

'Good to see you again, Lou.'

'That was a seriously impressive couple of seasons you had over there!' Gomero said in admiration as he ushered him to sit guest-side of his desk, and himself resumed his own high-backed executive chair.

'It was a slow start,' Sonny pondered when settled, 'but yes, it got better.'

'Sonny, I know you've left there, and what I'd like to hear most right now is that you want to come back... and I don't care how slow a start you have!'

'Lou, I want to come back,' Sonny confirmed.
Gomero nodded deeply as though in great relief. From a lower drawer of the desk, he lifted out a bottle of whisky and two shot glasses, he poured whisky into each glass, drank them both and returned all of it to the drawer. 'You have just made my day,

Sonny,' he said as they both laughed at the stunt. 'Welcome home!' he added.

Two weeks later, Sonny began training with Northern Star. A few of the players from his earlier time there had since moved on to other clubs or had retired, and among the younger element he sensed a wariness at his sudden presence – perhaps because of the club's low standing at the end of the previous season. The fans, though, had no such reservations and news of his return was broadly welcomed. He felt no irritation or anxiety that once again he had to start over; steadfastly he settled into his new role and calmly awaited the moment when his skills would be evident.

Sonny and Janice announced their wedding date, given them by Rev Rodgers the vicar of St. Hilda's church in Tanlow. Rev Rodgers, a friend of Janice's father – due in the main that they both played for Tanlow cricket club – extended warmth and kindness to the couple as he went through the order of service with them in his office at the vicarage one rainy night. Sonny asked Simmonds to be best man, he happily accepted and between them they put together Sonny's stag night – drinks in The Feathers, to be kept confidential. When the wedding invitations were sent out Sonny included his one-time foster parent Mrs Johnson on the list. The invitation offered that they would send a taxi to both collect and take her home whenever she felt ready, and for her to be accompanied by any companions that she wished.

In the interim months to their wedding, Sonny and Janice began a search for a home of their own. They found what they were looking for ten miles north of Leeds in the historically listed and tranquil village of Trough where old and new homes co-existed, and only residents or wanderers had cause to be there. The barely five-year old, detached property which captured their interest sat behind high timber gates and was built of smooth stone, the colour of pale straw, that easily caught the glow of natural light; with a level back garden that looked across to a grassland hillside they believed it the perfect family home.

Their subsequent offer of purchase was accepted, and they duly moved in. At that point Sonny had begun driving lessons. He was surprised to discover he had no natural aptitude for it and failed his first driving test. Janice told him he treated driving as though a game of football and saw any destination as an opposition goalmouth to be arrived at by whatever means possible. Even after he passed the test on his second attempt it was Janice who drove them wherever they went.

Sonny's stag night saw his friends gathered in The Feathers and he walked in to shake many an eager hand. Through in the lounge room he noticed old Justin, alerted by the commotion, half out of his chair to see what was going on – and felt bolstered that nothing in Cowton ever seemed to change. At some point in the evening Ferrets brother Colin came in and sat on his usual barstool, he showed little interest that the room was busier than normal and engaged with his mobile phone in routine manner. As Sonny left for his taxi home just before midnight, Colin turned to him and said, 'Knock one in for our kid, will you!'

'The next one's for him,' Sonny promised. He craned a forearm and formed the top of the letter F with his fingers. 'And that'll be to say it's his!'

The following Wednesday evening, in front of a cheering home crowd, Sonny kept his word to Colin.

Sonny and Janice were married at St Hilda's church one bright Saturday morning. His fame as a footballer ensured regional journalists and television camera crews were in attendance along with a large crowd of well-wishers, all gathered down a grass-sided lane beside the eighteenth-century church. The crowd applauded as the couple came out and, to the peel of a singular bell, passed beneath the wrought iron lynch-gate that was tied with ribbons – which, as dictated by custom, could only be cut by the newlyweds.

The reception, held at the cricket club, had Simmonds continue his duties as best man where he drew guffawed laughter with a skilful tale-telling speech. Throughout the day Janice radiated beauty – her mother, the glow of parental pride.

Standing on the veranda Mr Parker, a self-professed cigar aficionado, lit one of Enrique's cigars, given him by Sonny, and deemed it one of the best he'd ever smoked; Sonny considered how Enrique would have smiled at the compliment. The only person missing on the day was Mrs Johnson who due to personal mobility problems had to decline her invitation. She sent her love and best wishes in a message read out by Simmonds. As day matured into evening Sonny, at some point, danced carefree with Samantha on the crowded dance floor. 'I'll love you forever for that email,' he said.

'What email! Have I been hacked?' she said in mock shock as her hands played at windscreen wipers to loud music.

No more was said of it, and the function rolled on into the night.

On the football pitch Sonny found his skill button, and goals became almost expected of him; *This is who I am. This is what I do!* was his message to all. As his goal tally mounted, he believed himself driven by only few things, he wasn't about to fail Janice or Jaren – another truth was that once on the pitch he simply let loose a given talent. By the end of the season Janice was expecting their second child, and Sonny signed a five-year contract with Northern Star.

Annabel Renata Lopez was born one November night. Sonny and Mr Parker celebrated with beer at The Reindeer – and Mr Parker smoked the last of Enrique's cigars.

Printed in Dunstable, United Kingdom